"We?" Cherry jumped on the pronoun as Leslie had known she would. Meddling auntie. "Who's *we?*"

"Declan Zyler stopped by," Leslie answered, then quickly changed the subject. "So, what do you think of that beer? Is it any good?"

"Declan was over? And you lost track of time?" Orbra pounced before her partner in crime even had the chance. Her eyes were narrow with delight. "Well, well, well—"

"It was nothing like that," Leslie said with exasperation. "He just came over to check on something with the railing, and—"

"If Declan Zyler came over to my house, not only would we lose track of time, he wouldn't be leaving until the sun came up," Cherry said with a wicked grin. "At least if you're not interested in him, will you put in a good word for your cougarly aunt?"

"Is cougarly even a word?"

"Oh, so now we're the grammar police, are we?"

Other Titles by Colleen Gleason

THE GARDELLA VAMPIRE CHRONICLES
Victoria
The Rest Falls Away
Rises the Night
The Bleeding Dusk
When Twilight Burns
As Shadows Fade

Macey/Max Denton
Roaring Midnight
Raging Dawn
Roaring Shadows
Raging Winter
Roaring Dawn (2016)

THE DRACULIA VAMPIRE
Dark Rogue
Dark Saint
Dark Vixen

THE MEDIEVAL HERB GARDEN SERIES
Lavender Vows
Sanctuary of Roses
A Whisper of Rosemary
A Lily on the Heath

CONTEMPORARY GOTHIC ROMANCE
The Shop of Shades and Secrets
The Cards of Life and Death
The Gems of Vice and Greed

STOKER & HOLMES BOOKS
(for ages 12-adult)
The Clockwork Scarab
The Spiritglass Charade
The Chess Queen Enigma

THE MARINA ALEXANDER ADVENTURE NOVELS
(written as C. M. Gleason)
Siberian Treasure
Amazon Roulette

THE GEMS OF VICE AND GREED

COLLEEN GLEASON

AVID PRESS

PROLOGUE

L ESLIE VAN DORN HAD NEVER in her life done anything so impulsive and impetuous. By all rights—especially in light of what had happened in the last year—she should have been clammy and sick to her stomach as she signed the papers, transferring more than three-quarters of a million dollars out of her account.

Three-quarters of a million dollars.

What was I thinking?

But when the realtor handed Leslie the keys, she felt a rush of anticipation, freedom, and only a tiniest tingle of apprehension. After all, she still had a good chunk of money left from the sale of her managing shares of InterWorks. And if this new project of hers didn't work out, she knew she could find another job.

Not that she wanted to be back in the cutthroat corporate rat-race that was the world of technology, but if her dream didn't come to fruition, she'd just drag herself back up, dust herself off, and move on to Plan B. Whatever that was. If nothing else, the last two years proved she was both resilient and resourceful.

But as she looked down at the handful of old metal keys, Leslie could no more tamp down the surge of excitement and delight than she could turn out the sun, for Shenstone House—the turn-of-the-century mansion she'd been in love with since she was a teen—was now hers.

Located in tourist haven Sematauk, Michigan, the brick mansion sported turrets, dormers, a widow's walk, narrow winding staircases, and a wraparound porch—and it all belonged to Leslie van Dorn, the founder and former CEO of InterWorks Corp.

As she walked out of the realtor's office in Center City, Philadelphia—seven hundred miles away from the biggest impulse purchase she'd ever made—Leslie drew in a deep breath and expelled it slowly. Less than a year ago, she'd been a single, career-driven businesswoman, engineering the successful public offering of the technology company InterWorks…and unexpectedly pregnant.

She'd been seeing an equally career-focused man, Gideon Nath, with whom she had little more than a friends-with-benefits relationship and mutual agreement to escort each other to business functions, since neither of them had time for a real relationship. It was a convenient arrangement that suited them both.

But then Gideon had met Fiona Murphy and fallen in love… just around the time that Leslie found out she was nearly three months pregnant.

It had been a mess.

Gideon insisted Leslie should marry him, despite the fact that she didn't love him and he certainly didn't love her. She was stunned and off balance enough to agree—at least until she saw Gideon and Fiona together and realized she could never keep him from the woman he loved so deeply, the fun, energetic woman who perfectly softened his formal, reserved personality.

And so Leslie told Gideon the baby wasn't his. That she'd had a one-night fling on a business trip—that part was true, at least— and he was free to marry the woman he wanted without feeling as if he were walking away from a responsibility.

Whether she would have ever told him the truth, Leslie didn't know—and never would find out, for less than a month later, on October 15, she miscarried.

Even now, ten months after that awful day at the Bryn Mawr Hospital emergency room, a wave of grief washed over her at the memory. The baby had been a girl. She would have been named Gwendolyn, after Leslie's grandmother.

Maybe that was why Leslie decided to upend her life, give up—no, *change*—her career, and move back to Michigan. Back to the beautiful west side of the state where she'd spent so many summers with Grandma Gwen and Aunt Cherry. It felt right to start over, and to start over *there*.

Thanks to the IPO for InterWorks, she had the money and resources—though certainly not unlimited—to invest in something she'd often dreamed of doing: a bed and breakfast in the small, trendy tourist town of Sematauk, right on sparkling Lake Michigan. Located barely an hour south of Grand Rapids (the largest city on the "west coast" of Michigan), and three hours from Chicago, Sematauk was a tourist destination from May through September.

The fact that since she'd always coveted the old Shenstone House made her ownership even more exciting. She felt as if she would be coming full circle, returning to the town of her summer memories for a softer, quieter life.

Leslie hadn't seen the house in person for more than two decades, but she was a shrewd businesswoman and had done her due diligence before making the purchase—at a well-negotiated price. She knew exactly what she was getting into.

The place needed a lot of TLC, some renovations to keep its historical building designation, and some updating as well, but she was more than ready to dive in and give herself something new to focus on.

The fact that Shenstone House was supposedly haunted didn't bother her in the least.

ONE

LESLIE WAS HEADFIRST INSIDE AN ALCOVE in one of the bathrooms digging out old insulation and rotted drywall when something shifted and a bunch of *stuff* came tumbling down on her. Pieces of drywall, plaster, and insulation—fortunately, nothing really heavy, but it was a mess nonetheless.

Coughing and rubbing the back of her head, she backed out of the crawlspace where some old pipes had been laid to run water for an ancient bathroom. It was the only one that had never been fully modernized, probably because it was in the farthest corner of Shenstone House and accessed only by a narrow hallway that led to the back—likely servants' area—of the house. That was another reason the bath had never been updated. Whose servants needed hot running water, after all?

Drywall dust coated Leslie's shoulders, arms, and torso, and still hung in the air, waiting for a place to alight. She brushed ineffectively at the powder, coughed some more, and berated herself for not wearing eye protection. Her baseball cap had kept most of the dust from her face, and of course she'd been wearing gloves and jeans, but she still had some grittiness in her eyes.

It had been a very busy month since she'd arrived in Sematauk on the tenth of September and dug into her new life. She'd moved into her Aunt Cherry's guest room for the first week—just until she made certain the house was livable and the wiring was up to code. It was, and since then, she'd been living in a comfortable bedroom suite just off the kitchen, which was where the previous owner had lived.

It had taken working with contractors that first week, plus the help of her aunt and her aunt's best friend Orbra, to do a major update on the living suite (which included a luxurious bathroom, bedroom, and small office/sitting area): a hardwood floor, freshly painted walls, and new hardware and vanity in the bathroom. But that cozy little corner of Shenstone House, right off the kitchen, was now her little sanctuary amid the rest of the construction and renovation. Hopefully before spring, the rest of the house would be updated and ready to be lived in—or, more accurately, rented out as bed and breakfast rooms. Contractors had been coming and going erratically, but Leslie, who felt the need to be hands-on as well as keep herself physically busy, was doing a good portion of the demo and cleanup work herself.

She suddenly became aware of an irritated voice in the distance.

"Helloooo? Anyone here?"

She frowned and grabbed her cell phone from the table where she'd left it for safety, and saw five missed calls and two texts. *Oh crap.* It was the guy for the wrought iron on the stairs. She'd been waiting a week to get him in here. Who'd have thought a blacksmith would be so busy in this day and age?

"I'm here," she called back, then coughed again as she began to hurry from the back of the house, creating a cloud of drywall dust around her like Pigpen.

"Hello?" The voice was even less pleased now, and it sounded further away.

"Wait! Don't leave!" she shouted, pushing through the double maple doors that connected the kitchen and dining room. They swung back into place behind her with gusto and a pleasant squeak.

"Ms. van Dorn?" the man called back.

"Yes, sorry," she said, rushing into the hall that led from the parlor to the guest rooms. "I lost track of time. You must be Declan Zyler."

"Yep." He looked her over just as frankly as she was looking at him, though Leslie doubted he could see much beneath her coating of drywall and dust, baseball cap, and worn jeans.

How far I've come from the boardroom. She controlled a gleeful smile. *And thankful for it every day.*

But that thought went out of her mind as quickly as it came, for it was followed by the realization that Declan Zyler looked *exactly* like she'd pictured a blacksmith to look...back when she had time to read those historical romance novels about young ladies of the gentry who fell for the inappropriate groom, tutor, or—most titillating of all—the muscular, sweaty, lowborn blacksmith. Forget the dukes and earls...she liked the stories about star-crossed lovers from different "sides" of society.

Leslie just hadn't expected such a metalworker in the twenty-first century to look so...raw and wild. His hair was the color of mahogany—a dark, rich red that was nearly black—and he needed a shave, for gold and red stubble glittered over his chin and jaw. He had the build of her imagined blacksmith too, for he wore a white t-shirt, which clearly showed the muscles of his pecs, and an open red and blue plaid shirt with the sleeves rolled up. The flannel shirt obstructed the shape of his biceps, but his golden brown forearms—freckled, lightly scarred and burned, and very powerful looking—were bare.

Those were not the kind of muscles a guy got from working out at Gold's Gym.

"Well? You going to show me the stairway?" Zyler was looking at her as if she were a toddler. Or a damned mess, which, in this case, wasn't too far from the truth.

"Of course." She responded without flickering an eyelash. Working in a high-powered, fast-paced business world and interacting with her fair share of supposedly intimidating men (and women) had taught her how to turn on a dime, hide her feelings, and communicate clearly and effectively even when taken off guard.

So what if the man standing in her house was the most amazingly male creature she'd encountered in person in years? Leslie was cool and collected and businesslike as they came.

A lesser woman might have taken off her ball cap and yanked the fastener out of her ponytail, or brushed off her shirt—a dirty, baggy tee—or even apologized for her appearance. But Leslie didn't bother. He might look hot as sin and right out of her fantasies, but she wasn't in the market for a man at the moment. Not only that, she had absolutely nothing to prove to anyone… except maybe the bank that had given her the small business loan to help jump-start the inn.

"You probably saw it when you came in—it's the one leading to the second floor." She gestured back down the hall, the obvious way from which he'd come.

"Yep. But I didn't want to go poking around till I talked to you." From the tone of his voice, it was clear what he meant to say was *I didn't want to waste my time.*

They were in the foyer now, and both looked at the grand, sweeping staircase that started on the right side of the wide, shallow entrance hall and ended up sweeping left across the way in a balcony-like swoon. Two hallways spiked out from behind the balcony, leading to what would become guest rooms. In 1920s art deco style, the balustrade was a design of perfect curves, finial-topped semicircles, and twists and turns. It was very complicated and extremely elegant.

"Nice piece," he said, though Leslie could hear something more like reverence in his voice. "Some cast iron here in the ornamentals, but the rest of it's definitely wrought." He glanced up. "The difference being—"

"Cast iron is poured into molds and wrought iron is pounded into shape in a smithy," Leslie interrupted with a grin. "I did my research, Mr. Zyler."

His lips moved briefly; it might have been a smile, but possibly a grimace. The corners of his eyes crinkled a little too. "Can't tell you how many times I've been called to a place only to learn it's cast metal."

"My Aunt Cherry says you do a lot of restoration work."

"Cherry Wilder's your aunt?"

"Yes. Do you know her well?" Leslie didn't think he looked like a guy who'd spend a lot of time in a yoga studio, but then again…he'd have no problem balancing himself in Crow with those arms. She swallowed hard at the delightful mental image.

"Well enough. I just moved back a few weeks ago—I grew up here—and ever since I mentioned in passing last week that she reminded me of Helen Mirren, she's been on my case to come to one of her hot yoga classes."

Leslie laughed. Cherry was definitely a cougar on the prowl. "Well, she could be trying to get you into a belly-dance class, so be thankful for small favors."

His eyes crinkled and those lips moved again. Definitely getting closer to a smile. "Excellent point. And yes, most of what I do is restoration. To comply with historical society requirements, if the iron was originally wrought rather than cast, it's got to be replaced with same to keep the building's designation historical. Keeps me busier than I need to be, but busy enough." He stopped abruptly, leading her to believe he'd been about to say more.

"Which is why I called you," Leslie said. "Besides the fact that Orbra van Maak said I had to."

He exhaled a short laugh. "Ah. Orbra. I'll remember to thank her next time I see her. She's a piece of work too."

"I've been kind of scared of Orbra since I was ten, so yes, I agree."

Declan glanced at her with a sudden, full-blown look. "I get the impression you're not scared of many people, let alone a sixty-year-old woman who serves tea and crumpets."

For some reason, Leslie felt her cheeks grow warm. "Well, Orbra or a big spider—either will do the trick." Then she gestured to the stairway. "So, I could replace the whole thing with wood spindles, or even the iron ones you get at Home Depot or—" She stopped, because she was fairly certain those broad shoulders had actually winced. She hid a grin. Sensitive about his work, was he?

He'd returned to his examination. "I've done hundreds of projects, most of 'em for historical buildings, and I've never seen anything like this. The workmanship is unique—gorgeous, in fact—but this rust… Wrought iron doesn't just rust like this unless it's exposed to the elements for a significant amount of time. Cast iron would rust easier, like—see those pieces over there? The—excuse me, but cheap—fleur-de-lis sort of caps on the wall sconces? They're not rusting at all." He was frowning now, looking back and forth between the sconces and the spindles. "Was this place ever roofless? Flooded? Destroyed by a tornado? Windows broken?"

Leslie drew closer, her hands on her hips. "No. The building's been intact, as far as I know—it was even kept up after Alice ver Stahl moved into a nursing home five years ago. I tried to use a hard-wire brush to get rid of that stuff, but…it's weird. I don't think it's rust."

He was standing at eye level to the bottom of a stretch of the square-on-square railing, about eight stairs from the ground. Silently, he examined the coppery damage that seemed to be growing up from the bottom of the mooring spikes like rusty moss. He scraped at it with a finger, then leaned forward to sniff at it. Pulling away, he frowned, dug in his jeans, and pulled out a pocketknife.

"I don't know what it is. It's only on the bottom, too; not spread along the whole thing, as you'd expect rust to do," he muttered, using the tip of the blade to pick at the damage. "Hmm. Whatever it is, it's discoloring the metal…but I don't think it's from oxidation—the whole spindle would have the damage instead of just the bottom part. And it's just in this section of the railing. Strange."

He clicked his knife closed and slipped it into his jeans pocket. When he turned to look at Leslie, she was surprised at how green his eyes were. Wine bottle green.

"What do you think?" she asked. "Can you fix it?"

"Of course I can fix it. But it won't be cheap."

She sighed and crossed her arms over her shirt, releasing a soft puff of drywall dust. "I was afraid of that. But in order to keep my historical society designation, I've got to replace it accurately. When can you get me on the schedule to start?"

"Next week, probably."

"Probably? All right, then, that's sooner than I expected, to be honest. So why did it take over a week to get you out here to take a look at it?"

Declan gave her a forbidding look. "Had some things going on with my daughter. Was busy."

Leslie felt a surprising sort of deflation. His daughter. Which implied a wife too. Not that it mattered—she was too busy to be interested in a man. "I hope everything's okay," she said automatically.

"She's fifteen. What do you think?" he said wryly, then turned back to the matter at hand. "I want to know what's under there." He gestured to the thin base of the balustrade, the flat channel into which the stairway spindles were set. "Maybe there's damp under that skinny section there and that's causing the rust to work its way up from beneath."

"You said it wasn't rust," Leslie reminded him.

"Well, I don't know what the hell it is," he said, picking at it again with his thumbnail. "That's why I want to look under there."

She shrugged. "Fine by me. You've got to take it out anyway if you're going to restore it."

"You sure?"

"I'll help. I already tangled with some dastardly drywall anyway."

He eyed her for a moment, and she swore his lips twitched again. "Dastardly drywall?"

"It fell on me with no provocation whatsoever. I call that dastardly."

"I see." His eyes were crinkling at the corners, but for whatever reason, he didn't seem to want to let a full-blown smile erupt. He turned back to the railing. "Well, let's get to it."

Leslie didn't have to do much at first. She stepped out of the way as Declan removed the main column at the bottom of the stairway with a few well-placed thuds of a rubber mallet. Then it was short work to dismantle the handrail, separating it from the spindles, which positioned the organic, curvaceous design about three inches above the base.

While Declan carried the old pieces outside, Leslie began to work out some of the iron spikes from their moorings. They were set in a wooden track made from maple, which, she noted, definitely needed a new coat of varnish.

Several spikes came loose easily, and she moved a two-foot-wide section of railing away and leaned it against the wall. But when Leslie got to the area with the rust, they didn't want to budge. "Do you think they're cemented or glued in there?" she asked when Declan paused to watch her struggle with them.

"They would have been glued originally, but by now, it wouldn't be that strong. Let me try."

Leslie stepped aside. She had a moment of pure female appreciation as Declan stood in front of the railing and clamped his hands around one of the spikes, fist over fist, and pulled up.

Though the spike didn't budge, his muscles sure as hell did. She actually went a little dry in the mouth, watching the way his bare forearms rippled and his shoulders shifted as he tried in vain to wiggle the spikes free.

"What the hell?" he muttered, and the moment was over as he stepped back from the railing.

"I'm thinking cement," she said, bending over to look into the holes of the three spikes she'd already removed.

"That would be very unusual, but there's definitely something going on in there. Okay if I get a little more insistent with it?" he asked. "It might make a mess."

Leslie made a show of looking down at her powdery clothing and then around the foyer, which showed definite signs of being a work in progress. "I don't think that'll be a problem."

"I've got to grab a few tools from the truck. Be right back."

While Declan was outside, Leslie made her way back to where she'd left her cell phone and other tools. One of her life-altering changes when she'd left the corporate world was to no longer be a slave to her smartphone or computer, so she often made herself leave her phone in another room, or at least out of sight or reach. Another life improvement, as she called the list she'd created when she decided to leave corporate America, was to learn how to cook. She was getting pretty good at that, too. As for another one on the list—getting at least seven hours of sleep a night? That one was a piece of cake. She *loved* being able to sleep past six a.m.

Her abandoned phone had four texts that she needed to return (one was for a interview with a potential assistant-slash-teen-intern that sounded very promising), and by the time she was finished with that, she heard thuds from the foyer.

She returned just in time to see Declan prying up pieces of the maple base where the spikes had been positioned.

"Here we go," he muttered, and Leslie moved to help him as he pulled the stubborn section of wrought iron free. The whole base moved with it, and there was an eerie, groaning sound as the two of them dragged the rail from its moorings.

As it came free, the groan tapered off into an echo that didn't really belong to the sound of iron being wrested from wood. Leslie had the odd sensation that the entire house was shuddering, as if giving a reluctant release.

A chill skittered over her shoulders, and the scent of dust and must, and something else…something sharp and cold and unfamiliar…seeped into the air from the opening beneath the railing.

The hair lifting at the back of her neck, she glanced at Declan, feeling very strange about the fanciful thoughts that had overtaken her. He seemed oblivious to anything out of the ordinary, for he'd turned to set the section of wrought iron squares against the wall.

Now that part of it had been removed, Leslie could see how the rust—or whatever it was—had encroached not only onto the bottoms of the spikes, but inside the narrow, hollow base beneath the railing.

"Is it some sort of mold?" she asked, using a flathead screwdriver to poke and scrape at a portion of it.

Declan returned and looked down into the hollow of the railing's base. Pieces of insulation and other debris were stuffed inside, but moving some of it out of the way exposed the inside of the stairway wall. The coppery rust appeared to be all along the inside, and when Leslie looked at the underside of the maple channel into which the spikes had been thrust, there was more of the strange rust.

"It's more of a discoloration," he said, poking at it with his own tool. "It doesn't scrape off like mold or rust would."

Leslie stepped back and sighed. "I guess I'd better get someone in to look at it, and make sure." She crossed her arms and surveyed the damage—both literal and figurative. She could see her nest egg dwindling like a little puff of smoke.

Declan seemed to feel her pain. "Sorry about that. And I'll do my best to keep the costs down on the iron."

She smiled ruefully. "Ah, thanks, but I expect to be charged a fair price, Mr. Zyler. I knew what I was getting into when I started down this path—I mean, I suspected there would be surprises along the way. I just want everything to be done right."

"Right. I can appreciate that, but I also understand budgetary constraints. So let me know if you change your mind and want to just replace it all with the spindles from Home Depot." He swallowed hard. "I can't bring myself to do that personally, but I know someone who can." He managed a smile.

"Thanks. You'll really start on it right away?"

"Yes, tomorrow. I've got a few projects going, but I'll take this section with me and get working as soon as possible. And call me Declan. Or Dec. Mr. Zyler just makes me feel uptight." Now, there was a real smile.

"And I'm Leslie." She held out her hand for the shake that hadn't happened originally, and wasn't surprised when she felt a shock of awareness when their hands touched.

Somehow, Leslie suspected she'd make certain to find a way to use the blacksmith's skills at Shenstone House as much as possible.

Even if it cost a fortune.

TWO

"WELL, HAVE YOU SEEN the ghost yet?" asked Orbra van Maak unceremoniously as she approached Leslie's table. She was carrying a tray with a full tea service on it: two delicate china pots, two cups and saucers, a small plate with paper-thin lemon slices, a sugar bowl, and a tiny creamer pitcher. "You've been living there almost a month."

Leslie looked at Aunt Cherry, who sat with her at a small, round table in the corner. Cherry was rolling her eyes at her friend's demand as the Dutchwoman loomed expectantly over their table. The proprietor of Orbra's Tea House didn't seem to be in any hurry to set down the tray for her customers—at least until she got a response to her question.

"No," Leslie replied. "Not a sign. No slamming doors, no footsteps in the night, no fluttering curtains over a closed window…not even an inexplicable chill wafting through the air."

"You can put the tray down, Orbra," Cherry said, gesturing to the lace-covered table. Beneath the large doily was a blue floral cloth of cotton, and each place setting boasted a small hand-painted china plate, flatware of real silver, and a lace-trimmed cloth napkin. "I told you Leslie is too practical for the metaphysical to speak to her." She said this with a wink at her favorite niece, who shook her head in mock disgust as the tray clinked into place in front of her.

"If there's really a ghost at Shenstone House," Leslie said as Orbra poured vanilla oolong into her cup, "then why didn't Alice ver Stahl see him? Or her. Does anyone know whether this so-called ghost is supposed to be a man or woman?"

"Alice ver Stahl was half-deaf and had cataracts. She never went anywhere in that house but the kitchen and the bathroom before they brought her to the nursing home. What was it, five years ago? She wouldn't have seen or heard a ghost if it pulled out a chair for her at the table." Orbra turned to pouring a fragrant floral tea of a much lighter color into Cherry's cup.

"She was half-deaf and had cataracts and lived alone?" Leslie was horrified.

"Orbra's exaggerating, my dear. Mrs. ver Stahl had a perfectly fine hearing aid, and her cataracts had been removed years earlier," Cherry said, and sipped her jasmine green tea. She smiled, curling her fingers around the cup as if to warm them. "Mm. This is still my favorite, even though the caffeine wreaks havoc on my meditations."

"The way you drink it, brewed hardly more than a minute, there isn't any caffeine in there to speak of," Orbra replied. She stood with her hands on her hips, clearly unwilling to move on until she got more information from her best friend's niece.

Unlike other tea shops with a Victorian flair, Orbra's wasn't decorated in pink, cabbage flower prints, or with too much lace. There was some lace, but it was restricted to covering the dark blue tablecloths, and an occasional doily. The rest of the decor was mostly cornflower blue, yellow, and white. Though there were tiny flowers printed on the wallpaper and fresh Gerbera daisies, sweet peas, and alstroemeria stuck in vases on each table, the florals weren't overwhelming.

"I don't like to make the men feel uncomfortable. You know a lot of them won't come into a place that feels too much like a woman's bedroom—unless it *is* a woman's bedroom," Orbra had told Leslie with a grin. "So I try to keep it feminine without going overboard. Regina Underwhite helped me find some of the antiques, along with that silver tea service in the front window. But I did the rest of it myself. And business is all I can handle, believe you me."

However, today Leslie and Cherry were the only customers in the tea shop. As it was early October, summer was over and school was back in session, and it was just past the high season of fall colors. Thus, Sematauk was devoid of the lake-loving tourists that kept it buzzing and humming from late May through the end of September. This meant Orbra had plenty of time to sit and pepper Leslie with questions.

"Mary," the proprietress shouted toward the swinging doors that led to the kitchen, "bring out those scones, will you, hon? I'm going to pull up a chair myself."

But just as she was wrangling a heavy Victorian side chair to their table, the door opened and three elderly ladies came in on a swirl of leaves and chilly autumn air.

"I *told* you it was on this block," said the one who was clearly the oldest, and, it seemed, the loudest as well. She had thick iron-gray hair and a tall, sturdy build, and was practically shouting at one of her companions as she led them through the door.

The first elderly woman was carrying a walking stick, but didn't actually appear to need it for locomotion. "Hello, Orbry!" she crowed as soon as she saw the proprietress, but she stopped just inside the threshold to look around, taking in all the Victorian decor. "Nice flowers in here. Good thing Rose didn't come. She's allergic to all them flowers. Now, Pauline, you watch here so you don't trip on that little step—you know you're blind as a bat."

Smiling with pleasure, Orbra abandoned her friends in order to greet the newcomers. "Now you just stop your complaining, Helen Galliday," she said, "and sit yourself down. I'll fix you all up a cup of tea." She embraced the loud woman, then greeted the other two—each of whom she also knew. Leslie's eyes widened when she got a good look at the youngest and chicest of the three and immediately recognized her.

Huh. Well, what were the chances?

"We'll sit with them," Helen said, thrusting her walking stick toward Leslie and Cherry. "I ain't hardly seen Cherry since she was toddling around in a saggy diaper!"

She didn't wait for a response and barreled her way across the hardwood floor, her cane thumping with alacrity. For a woman who appeared to be past seventy, she was remarkably agile, and was seated in the chair Orbra had meant for herself before anyone could respond.

"Leslie, this is Helen Galliday—a friend of my mother's from way back. And this is Pauline Whitten," Orbra said, gesturing to the one at whom Helen had been shouting, "who also went to school here, and Iva… What's your married name now?" she said to the youngest of the trio—a woman of sixty-fiveish with round apple cheeks and neatly styled blue-white hair.

"Nath. Iva Nath." But Iva was reaching to shake Leslie's hand. "What a small world, isn't it? I believe you and my step-grandson Gideon were friends, back in Philadelphia? You were at my wedding with him, weren't you?"

"Yes, I certainly was at your lovely ceremony. And yes, Gideon and I were friends. We still are. I hope he and Fiona are doing well," Leslie replied sincerely. In the last year, she and Fiona had actually gotten to know each other quite well, and though Gideon's wife was a little airy-fairy for Leslie—with her palm reading and New Age-y personality—Fiona was a lovely person, quite funny, and charming as well. Definitely a nice balance to the stiff and formal Gideon.

Leslie didn't have one ounce of envy toward the woman who'd married Gideon, and that was the truth. In retrospect, she considered it a sort of gift that Gideon had fallen for Fiona; otherwise Leslie might have ended up married to a man she didn't really love. And she'd probably still be in the middle of the rat race of corporate America.

But who knew…in another scenario, she might even have carried the baby to full term.

At that thought, grief stabbed her deep and dampened her eyes. That, she amended her private thoughts, was her one regret.

"I knew you had moved to Michigan—to open a B&B, is that what I heard?" Iva said.

"Yes, and it's haunted—but Leslie hasn't seen or heard of the ghost yet. She's been here more than a month," Orbra informed them just as Mary appeared with a large tray of scones. "And nothing. Not one sign of the ghost. I don't think she's trying hard enough."

Besides blueberry and apple cinnamon scones, the newly arrived tray also held tiny white stoneware pots of clotted cream and jam, finger sandwiches with salmon salad or cucumbers sliced paper-thin, and profiteroles. There were small plates and tiny spoons, irregular lumps of sugar in a dish, a narrow bowl of fresh berries, and half-dollar-sized open-faced quiches.

"Your inn is haunted?" Iva said, and her eyes sparkled with interest.

"Sounds like a great way to scare off potential customers," grumbled Helen. She picked up one of the triangular sandwiches with fingers curved like talons. "We had a ghost back in Maine once—remember that, Pauline? In that old house that belonged to Belinda?"

"Yes, of course I remember," replied the third woman. She had perfectly manicured fingernails painted a shocking pink with a stripe of lime green down the side of each one. Plump and soft, Pauline Whitten seemed to be between Helen and Iva in age—likely just about the age of seventy. "It was only a few months ago, Helen, when that all happened with Diana and Ethan and—"

"Don't try an' tell me my memory's going," groused Helen, showering crumbs everywhere. "At least I can hear everything—which is better than you, when I have to repeat it all the time."

Hadn't Helen just accused her friend of being blind, not deaf? Not that Pauline Whitten seemed to exhibit either symptom. Leslie glanced at Cherry, and saw that she and Orbra were laughing silently together. Tears were streaming down Cherry's face.

"And the three of you ladies drove all the way from Philly?" Orbra said to Iva when she could speak clearly. "You have my condolences."

"It's really Hollis who's the saint. He drove us, the lovely man, and that's why I told him he could golf as much as he wanted while we're here. And if he could get tickets, he could go to that college football game—the big in-state rivalry, whatever it is. I told him the only thing he *has* to attend is the reunion." Iva's cheeks went slightly pink with pleasure at the mention of her husband, to whom she'd been married less than two years.

"Oh," Leslie said, reaching for a small blueberry scone. It was warm and practically crumbled in her fingers, chock-full of tiny wild blueberries. "You're here for the big class reunion on the nineteenth."

"That's right. There ain't enough of us left from each of the classes—we're all dead—so we bunched 'em all together into one big reunion," Helen informed her. "It's my fiftieth reunion, and Pauline's forty-fifth, and Iva's—what one is it?"

"Thirty-fifth."

"Right. Thirty-fifth." Helen paused, peering at Iva as if she didn't know whether to believe her or not. "I thought you were older than that. Aren't you—"

"You'll never guess who's staying in the Sunflower House," Iva exclaimed. She glanced at Leslie. "It's too bad your bed and breakfast isn't ready yet, because you could have been the one to host him."

"Who?" asked Cherry.

"It's a famous writer," Helen said in what was possibly supposed to be a low voice, but rang in Leslie's eardrums nevertheless. "Mildred didn't tell us his name—claims she was sworn to secrecy, the crotchety old bat—but we figured it out. She can take her mysterious winks and hints and—"

"Mildred is the owner of the Sunflower House," Orbra told Leslie in an aside before turning back to Iva. "I heard someone was coming to stay there in the off-season—some big celebrity who wanted privacy. I was hoping for Robert Redford myself. It used to be Paul Newman I hoped would show up, but then he died. And then James Garner, but he died too." She *tsked*, as if it were the poor actors' faults they'd passed on before chancing a visit to Sematauk.

"Who is it?" asked Leslie—more interested in keeping the topic away from her not-so-haunted house than who the celeb was…because she was still remembering that odd sort of groan and shudder she'd felt when the staircase railing was opened. Not that anything had happened otherwise, but it had only been yesterday.

How long did it take for ghosts to bestir themselves once awakened? Didn't they most often show themselves at night, anyway? After the so-called witching hour of midnight?

Leslie hadn't slept at home last night, as it turned out, for Cherry had made her share a bottle of wine and watch reruns of *30 Rock* till after midnight, and she ended up sleeping in her aunt's guest room. So this would be Leslie's first night in the house since the stairway had been opened, since she'd felt the house shudder and moan—and what sort of nonsense was she thinking?

Maybe she'd inhaled too much drywall dust or paint fumes. Leslie gave herself a mental shake and tuned back in to the conversation—still apparently about the identity of the mysterious celebrity staying at Sunflower House.

"It's the man who writes them big action books, Mildred said. She told me in confidence, hear? They make movies about 'em with Tom Cruise—is that the guy?" Helen peered at Pauline as if to read the answer in her bottle-bottom glasses. "The one who danced in his underwear?"

"That's Tom Cruise, yes. Action movies based on books, starring Tom Cruise. Jack Reacher?" Orbra asked.

"No, not that one. The other Jack," Helen grumbled, frowning. "The author, I mean. His character had a Greek name or maybe a Roman name…something like one of them musicians nowadays."

"At least, that's what Mildred was dropping hints about," Pauline said.

"Wait, are you talking about Jeremy Fischer?" Leslie said, a spark of interest sizzling through her. "He writes the Bruno Tablenture books?"

"Yes, that's him! Not Jack. Jeremy. He's done locked himself away in the tower room at Sunflower, going to be writing on his new book, Mildred said."

"Jeremy Fischer? For certain?" Even Aunt Cherry seemed impressed, and it took a lot to impress her. Or maybe she was just assessing her chances of getting to meet the man. "How do you know? He's such a recluse. He doesn't even do book signings."

"I told you, Mildred dropped a *lot* of hints for us. She even got a bunch of his books about Bluto, Brundo—whatever—those detective stories on her bookshelf in the sitting room. We're staying there too, you know," Helen added for Leslie's benefit. "Mildred just put them books out casual-like, but all of a sudden there were a bunch of them there. And they were signed. But I know it's him. He's telling everyone his name is *John* Fischer, though." She rolled her pale blue eyes.

"So tell me about this haunted house of yours," Iva said, turning back to Leslie.

The sudden change of topic caught her by surprise, but Leslie recovered immediately. "There's really nothing to tell. The house needs some updates—it's been empty on and off for the last thirty or so years. The last woman who lived there stayed on the main floor, so there's work that needs to be done on the second and third floors. I just had someone in yesterday about replacing a big wrought iron staircase." And, thank goodness, she'd just this morning hired a high school student as an intern to help her out after class and on the weekend with whatever needed to be done.

"Are you talking about that big, grand staircase in the foyer? It always reminded me of that stairway Rhett carried Scarlett up in *Gone with the Wind*," Iva said with a sigh. "I loved that movie."

"That's the one. Some of the spindles are missing, and other ones are rusted."

"Leslie needed a blacksmith and I told her to call Declan Zyler," Orbra said with a wink at her friend. "Cherry here can't wait to see him in action in that hot, dark smithy—all sweaty and muscular and—"

"And I figure if he's doing work for my niece, I have an excuse to—er—check up on it." Cherry grinned, looking very much like a naughty Helen Mirren with her spiky champagne hair and pink lipstick. "Leslie was on the front page of the paper today too—did you see it? Not because of the staircase, but because of her being famous and her plans to open a bed and breakfast. But you can see the missing section of railing behind her. Unfortunately, Declan wasn't in the picture. Did you get my extra copy, Orbra?"

"Of course. It's in the back. I'll get it later. What were you going to do if he had been in it? Hang it up in your office?"

"Maybe." Cherry's eyes danced mischievously, then she glanced at her watch. "Time to go. I've got a hot class and have to turn on the heaters."

"You've got hot flashes?" Helen demanded in her growly voice. "And you're going to turn on the heaters? That's about the dumbest thing—"

"No, she's got to teach a hot *class*," Orbra said. "Cherry's got a yoga studio, and one of the classes is done in a very hot room."

"I've always wanted to try doing those Yogi Berra things," said Helen, crumbs flying again. "I could probably put my foot behind my head, now that I got a new hip—"

"So about this ghost," Iva said, closing her soft, wrinkled hand over Leslie's as she shook with silent laughter. "Can I come over and walk through the house? I have a real sense for the otherworldly…maybe it will show itself to me." Her eyes danced with enthusiasm, and Leslie had a moment of relief that Fiona wasn't here too—for she and her grandmother-in-law were peas in a pod when it came to that sort of thing.

"Of course, feel free to stop by any time. I'll show you around—it sounds as if you've been in the house before."

"Yes, well, back when we were growing up—"

"What's this about the ghost?" demanded Helen. "Have you seen it, then, missy?"

"Don't shout," Pauline said, elbowing her companion. This was the first time she'd joined the conversation since the tray of scones and sandwiches had been delivered. She appeared to have sampled a bit of everything, if the remains on her dainty plate were any indication. "She's just sitting across the table from you. And you're talking about Shenstone House, aren't you?" She directed her question to Leslie.

Apparently, the conversation was going to center around the so-far-nonexistent ghost, despite efforts to the contrary. So Leslie decided she might as well dive in. "Who is supposedly haunting the place anyway?" she asked. "I don't know whether I'm supposed to be seeing a male or female ghost."

"Well, you do know the history of the house, don't you?" Pauline Whitten pulled herself upright and, gripping a teacup between two sets of fingertips, fixed her eyes on Leslie.

"A little of it. I know it was built at the turn of the century, and that in the twenties, a rival of Al Capone's used it for a hideaway from the cops in Chicago."

"I know about all that," interjected Helen. "My mama used to tell me stories about during Prohibition. Those damned gangsters used to come over here from Chicago across Lake Michigan to get away from the authorities. They'd bring their families and make like a vacation. Or their girls—you know the ones, the floozies with the short skirts and rolled garters. They even smoked cigarettes and drank *whiskey*."

"Oh, come now, Helen. You like your Maker's Mark just as much as anyone else I know," Pauline said.

"I do, but I ain't breaking the law drinking it!"

"Yes, there were hideaways all along the west coast of Michigan, all the way up to Traverse City," Pauline continued. "They probably used the Great Lakes to smuggle in booze too, from Canada. Didn't even have to go all the way to Detroit— could just go right over past Sault Ste. Marie and through Lake Huron to Ontario."

"The name of the bootlegging gangster who owned Shenstone House was Sal 'Red Eye' Marciano," Leslie continued. "And there's a rumor he hid a bunch of jewels here in the area."

"That's right!" Helen jabbed her talon-finger at the table at large. "We used to sneak around that house, trying to find the hidden gems. Place was empty as often as it was lived in, you know—probably got a curse on it, now't I think of it—and there was a time we sneaked inside too. Had a smoke, even. Never got caught, neither!"

"We never did either," said Pauline smugly.

Cherry and Orbra were laughing. "We sneaked in there too. But our generation was more interested in smoking pot and making out in the house than finding a cache of jewels."

Leslie looked around at the table in amazement. "Are you telling me you *all* were sneaking into Shenstone House?"

"Well, yes. An abandoned house, just far enough outside of town and in the woods to be secluded, but not so far away from everything so as to be scary…what do you think?" Cherry said.

"I never did," Iva said primly. Her friends looked at her with disbelieving eyes. "I didn't *sneak*. Tommy Bradberry had a key, and we used to go in there to make out."

"That's because the people who was living there when you were hot to trot traveled to Europe all the time," Helen said. Then she wheeled her eyes toward Leslie. "And you never sneaked inside yourself, missy? You had to be the only generation that didn't do that."

"I was only here for a few summers in my early teens. Besides, I think Mr. Mineera was living there at the time. He had big dogs."

"Ah, yes, that'll do it," Cherry replied.

"Look! There he is!" Helen fairly bolted out of her chair. "That has to be him!" She leveraged her walking stick to heave herself to her feet. "Right there on the corner! You shoulda been watching!" she screeched at Pauline, and almost lost her balance in the process. "We almost missed him. Not that you can see anything anyway—"

"Who? Where?"

"It's that Jeremy Fischer. See, the guy with the beard? It has to be him. He's with Mildred and— Hey! Why does Aaron Underwhite get to meet him?" Helen's nose was pressed to the tea shop window.

Leslie looked outside as well. Sure enough, standing on the street corner was a small cluster of people: a woman who was probably the innkeeper at Sunflower House, an attractive man of about forty with dark hair and a full beard and mustache, and an elegant couple in their late forties. The last were dressed in business suits and were shaking the man's hand.

"Aaron Underwhite's the mayor, Helen," Orbra said. "I suppose he's probably welcoming the celebrity to our town. He and Regina are always very gracious to anyone who visits."

This pulled Helen away from the window. "Aaron Underwhite is the mayor? And he's married to Regina Clemons? Didn't she used to go with Colter Bray? And now she's married to the Underwhite boy? I'm gobsmacked!"

Orbra appeared to share Helen's emotion. "How do you remember all of those people? They were at least twenty years younger than you—and you haven't lived here for fifty years."

Helen tapped her temple with a curved finger. "Perfect memory, right here. Never forget a face or nothing." She turned back to the view. "Now how the hell am I going to get me an invite to meet Jeremy Fischer?"

"You're staying in the same inn, Helen," Pauline said. "I'm sure you'll figure something out."

The gleam in the elderly woman's eye was enough to make Leslie shudder. She was suddenly relieved her own inn wasn't quite ready to open. She didn't think she could handle customers like Helen Galliday.

THREE

S TEPH? YOU HERE?" Declan called as he came in through the back door, clumping into the mudroom in his heavy work boots.

He was sweaty and smelled pretty ripe from spending three hours in the smithy working on Leslie van Dorn's stair railing. He hadn't planned to start working on it so soon—he hadn't been exaggerating when he said he had plenty of jobs—but she kept popping into his mind and he found it difficult not to think about her.

He wasn't exactly sure *why* she'd lodged there in his head. It wasn't like there'd been some great big sizzle of attraction between them. Sure, he saw how pretty she was under the ball cap and dust she wore, but as far as he was concerned there was a lot more to a woman than the way she looked. God help him, he'd learned that the hard way.

Whatever. He wasn't going to drop everything to get her job done, but he'd work on it when he had the urge to do so.

"Steph?" he called again, hesitating on the threshold. Normally, he'd strip everything off in the back hall of wherever he was living and leave it—wet, stinky, and smoky—until later, but living with a teenaged girl he hardly knew put a cramp in that style.

Dec still could hardly believe the phone call, six months ago, that had upended his entire life. One minute, he'd been enjoying the single life—working his ass off on various locations in Savannah or Atlanta and making a buttload of money, hanging with his buddies, dating occasionally…and the next minute, he was answering the phone to a girl—woman—he'd dated the summer between high school and college. The old Seger song "Night Moves" mashed up with Kid Rock's "All Summer Long" (both good old Michigan rockers) pretty much described the summer he spent hanging out with Cara Doucette.

He'd answered the call, recognizing that it was from back home in Sematauk—maybe his friend Jed had gotten a new number—and nearly fell out of his chair when the voice said, "Declan? This is Cara Doucette. A real blast from the past, huh? How are you? You got a minute?"

She'd spoken so quickly, spewing it all out in one breath, that it took him a second to catch up. "Hey, Cara. Nice to hear from you. Yeah, I've got a few minutes." He did his best to keep the question and wariness from his voice. From his and his buddies' experience, when an old flame looked you up—whether it be via social media or directly like this—it was because she was interested in one of two things: another hookup, or to show the guy how successful/happy she was without him.

Fortunately, she didn't beat around the bush. In fact, Dec had the feeling she was actually reading off something she'd written, for she launched right into a speech that yanked the rug of life out from under his booted feet.

"I have something to tell you. I should have told you back then, after we broke up, but I didn't. There were lots of reasons, and I'm sorry for it, I made a mistake. A big mistake. Except she's not a mistake at all. Oh, damn." Her voice dropped, implying she'd gone off script. "Dec, I'm just going to come right out and say this. That summer you and I were together—well, I got pregnant, had the baby, and you're the father."

He pulled the phone away to stare at it. A roaring sound filled his ears, and his insides surged and swirled into something worse than the morning after too many beers. His brain pretty much exploded into nothing…then crashed back into his skull with a whirlwind of emotions.

"Declan? Are you there? I know it's a shock, but…"

He hardly heard anything she said at first, and it took him a long time—a *long* time—to calm down enough to get the basic facts. He was the father of a fifteen-year-old girl named Stephanie. Cara had gotten married to her ex-boyfriend—the one she'd broken up with just before she and Declan got together; Dec had been her summer fling and rebound—and they'd raised Stephanie in Sematauk. She never told anyone except her husband that Stephanie wasn't his child.

"So…why tell me now?" he managed to say from between stiff lips. Somehow, he couldn't drag in a deep enough breath.

"Because she wants to meet you."

Something rushed through him—warmth and delight, followed abruptly by a stark, ice-cold chill. "Ohhh…kay," he managed to say. The questions swirling around in his head—he could figure out all the answers later…and dissect the emotions (shock, anger, confusion) as well. Now, he would take one step at a time.

And so he had. He'd met Stephanie—flown up to Michigan, spent a weekend with her that went surprisingly well—then flew back to Savannah, where he was working temporarily. He was both stoked and terrified that he had fathered this lovely young woman and didn't know a thing about her.

Over the next few months they got to know one another better—they talked on the phone, she visited him, he visited her, they emailed—and then over the summer he got the second unexpected phone call.

The one that really shuffled his life around.

"Dad." She was sniffling and crying into the phone, and he felt a shocking surge of protectiveness blast through him. "I n-need to ask you for something. A really big f-favor."

"What is it?" Terror, followed by a million questions. Was she in jail? Had she gotten knocked up? *Had Cara's husband done something to her?* "What's wrong, Steph?" He tried to keep the panic from his voice. Wasn't sure he succeeded.

"I just found out"—she was really sniffling, but clearly struggling to keep her voice steady—"that Dad—my other dad—

is being transferred to *New Hampshire*. And they want to move me to New Hampshire, and change schools right in the middle of high school." Her gulp was audible through the phone. "And I was wondering if there was any ch-chance you could— Well, you could come here and I could live with you." The last few words came out in a rush. "I know you move around a lot and you can do your work anywhere, otherwise I wouldn't ask, but I really don't want to move to New Hampshire." Her voice rose in a desperate wail that she was clearly still trying to keep under control.

And before he realized what he was saying, what it would mean, Declan heard the words come out of his mouth: "I think I could do that."

Yeah. Just like that.

Damn-ass marshmallow that he was, he couldn't stand to hear a woman cry.

So, a little more than two months ago, just before school started, Dec found himself setting up house with his fifteen-year-old daughter—a sophomore in high school. A completely foreign entity to his thirty-three-year-old bachelor self.

"Steph! You here?" he called again, really tempted to do the back-hall-stripping thing. Usually when Stephanie was home, it was evident due to some sort of noise—most often music or her voice on the phone or Skype. Or the running shower.

Feeling as if the coast was clear, he'd just pulled off his shirt (which, while it was still decent, made him feel a little uncomfortable around this teenager he didn't know that well, and *really* uncomfortable when her friends were around because he always had the sense they were whispering about him and gawking) and, with a glance through the half-open door that led into the kitchen, began to unfasten his belt.

"Hey, Dad!" The sounds of clomping feet from the depths of the house brought him up short.

Shit. He quickly refastened his belt and grabbed the sweaty mass of the shirt he'd discarded from the floor. He was still wearing a beater tee—which, hell, he might as well be shirtless the way it stuck to him—so he shrugged back into the sleeves of his flannel. Declan walked into the kitchen just in time to meet his daughter as she bounced in from the general area of her bedroom or the bathroom.

His daughter.

Declan still couldn't quite wrap his head around it. This young woman, this bright-eyed, smart, I-can-even-talk-to-adults fifteen-year-old was his offspring. He didn't remember himself at fifteen—or even seventeen or eighteen, or hell, even at *twenty*—being as mature, levelheaded, and *confident* as Stephanie was.

"Hey," he said nonchalantly. "How was school? What are you doing tonight? Have lots of homework?" Those were the three questions he'd come up with that seemed reasonable and logical for a parent to ask his child, and so far, she hadn't seemed to be bothered by them or feel as if they were an invasion of privacy.

Stephanie was at the counter, slamming jars of peanut butter and jelly onto the granite surface with no thought to the potential result of glass abruptly meeting stone. "I think I got a job," she said, yanking a loaf of bread out of the pantry.

She had long, dark blond hair, which she usually wore in a messy bun or spent hours either straightening or curling and letting it hang down past her shoulder blades. Today, it was long and straight, and she wore a loose, long-sleeved shirt and skinny jeans (not *skinny* skinny jeans; he'd learned the difference between the two when he'd taken her shopping for school—an event he wasn't sure she'd ever convince him to repeat).

"A job?" he repeated, eyeing the sandwich taking shape in front of her with interest. "Pass me those jars, will you?"

"Here," she said, passing him her just-made sandwich. "You can have this one. I'll make another."

For some reason, this made the back of his throat burn with emotion. "Thanks," he said gruffly. "Didn't mean to take the food out of your mouth."

She glanced at him over her shoulder, her eyes big and dark and brown. If Declan hadn't seen the results of the DNA test with his own eyes, he would never have believed she was his child. "It's no problem, Dad," she said. "I can make another one."

Damn, the sandwich tasted good. Particularly good. "So, a job, huh?" He tried not to sound as completely surprised as he was. She hadn't mentioned anything about getting a job. And she was only fifteen…

"Yeah." Now he could see a giddiness beneath her demeanor. "It's like a Gal Friday sort of position. I'll be working a couple hours after school each day, and then more on the weekend. She's really flexible, and I'll be able to do a lot of different things."

"She? After school *every* day? Don't you need a work permit? Aren't there child labor laws?"

"It's under-the-table money, Dad," she said, hands on hips, eyes rolling like a pro. "Like babysitting? I don't need a work permit for that. And if it begins to interfere with my school— which it won't—Leslie said I just had to tell her and we'd adjust as necessary. Did you know she used to be the CEO of InterWorks?" Stephanie's eyes were wide. "She's almost as famous as Marissa Mayer and Meg Whitman! She was even on the cover of *Fortune* magazine. And she's only thirty-four—I mean, I guess that's young for all that."

Declan's thoughts were galloping off in several different directions, and it took more than few chews and a swallow before he could rein them in. "Leslie? As in Leslie van Dorn? At Shenstone House?"

"Yes! And she hired me!" Stephanie was dancing around the kitchen, heedless of the goop of jelly that splattered off her knife and onto the hardwood floor. "Can you believe it?"

No. He actually couldn't believe it. And he wasn't exactly sure how he felt about it, for several reasons. "You didn't tell me you were going to get a job," he began. "And what exactly are you going to be doing for Ms. van Dorn—not Leslie," he said firmly. "She's Ms. van Dorn."

"She told me to call her Leslie." Some of the giddy light was fading from her eyes.

"She's your employer—supposedly—and you need to show her respect." Oh really? The kind of "respect" Declan had been known to show some of his employers? The little voice in his head reminded him smugly of the way *that* had turned out.

He batted the thoughts away and continued his lecture. "Ms. van Dorn it is—and you still haven't told me what you're going to be doing for her." Already he had visions of her using a table saw, or lifting heavy sheets of drywall, or covered with dust and mold and bits of insulation…

What on earth was this woman thinking? Stephanie wasn't equipped to work on that house. She was a high school girl, not a contractor! She was *a high school girl*, not some cheap laborer.

"Fine. *Ms. van Dorn*," Stephanie said flatly. "And what do you mean by supposedly?"

"It sounds very informal to me," he said, backing off a little in the face of her expression. His daily goal was: no tears and no shouting… "And vague. That's not really a good way to start a business relationship."

"She's going to pay me ten dollars an hour, and I'll be working from three to four thirty Monday through Thursday. Fridays I don't work because of pom, and then I work noon till four on Saturday. How is that vague?"

That actually sounded pretty reasonable. But Declan was the father here, and though the last thing he wanted was a confrontation with his daughter—no way, no how—he still had a responsibility he was taking seriously. "We'll see."

"We'll see? What does that mean?" Hands on the hips again. Now her eyes were flashing with fire.

"It means I need more information. Now, what sort of homework do you have tonight? And don't you have pom practice tonight anyway?"

Pom. He was still trying to wrap his head around the fact that his daughter was a cheerleader—but, as he'd learned the hard way, she *wasn't* a cheerleader, even though she wore a uniform that looked like that of a cheerleader, and had pompoms like a cheerleader, and stood on the sidelines at the football games and shouted and danced and did all the things cheerleaders did...

What the hell was she if she wasn't a cheerleader? Apparently there was some difference between cheerleaders and pom, though he sure as hell couldn't figure it out. All Declan wanted was to be certain she wasn't one of *those* cheerleaders who slept with half the football team like they'd done back when he was in high school.

He happened to know about that from personal experience.

"Yes, I have pom. That's why I was getting something to eat. But now I have to go." She looked darkly at the half-made sandwich in front of her, and Declan submerged a rush of guilt. He had taken her food.

"Uh," he said. "How about an apple?"

"It's fine." She spun and yanked open the pantry, rummaging around in there as he pulled the bread toward him and finished swiping peanut butter over it for her.

"Here. Can you eat it on the way? Am I driving you or is someone—"

"Brooklyn's picking me up. I told you that yesterday," she said, emerging with one of those really expensive granola bars in her hand and another in her mouth. They were hardly bigger than two of his fingers, cost more than two dollars each. And with only five or so in a box, he winced every time he saw her down two or three in a row. Apples and bananas, peanut butter and jelly, were a lot less expensive. And people said teenaged boys would cost an arm and a leg to feed them...

"Here," he said, offering her the sandwich.

"I'm fine. I've got these." She showed him two more granola bars and he sighed inwardly.

"All right. Well, we can talk more about this later," he said as she snagged up her backpack, water bottle, and six dollars worth of dark chocolate and dried cherry granola bars—which was hardly a nutritional meal for a growing girl.

"Whatever." The door banged behind her, leaving Declan holding the sandwich.

He sighed, then took a bite as he headed to the bathroom to shower. He figured he better put himself to rights before he went to have a chat with Leslie van Dorn, celebrity CEO.

FOUR

EVERY TIME LESLIE WALKED by the dismantled stair rail in the foyer, she was drawn to it. There was something about that slender, gaping channel that ran halfway up the side of the stairs that called to her. It needed to be cleaned up—all that insulation and dust lingering in that hole were releasing God knew what into the air; not to mention critters using it for nesting. Besides, she wanted to know what that mold or discoloration was from anyway.

Not that she didn't have a million other things to do—but thank goodness she'd found someone to help out with some of them. Stephanie Lillard had been eager, smart, and willing to jump in and help, and though Leslie had originally thought she might want to hire someone a little older, Stephanie had come highly recommended and Leslie decided to give her a shot.

It was into the evening before Leslie decided to tackle the project of the insides of the stair railing base. Between meetings all morning with contractors, then one with her bank, the late afternoon tea at Orbra's, and an extended appointment with an interior designer to work on new window treatments for the entire house (Leslie didn't even want to think about *that* bill), she'd hardly had a moment to spare, and she'd hardly been home.

"It's really not that important," she told herself as she donned heavy gloves and located the broom and vacuum cleaner. Declan Zyler was just going to put the railing back the way it was; who cared if there was dust or debris inside it?

But something compelled her to poke around in the long, narrow hole.

"There could be rodents nesting in there," she muttered to herself, and shined a flashlight down into the depths. The sun had nearly set, and the light in the front hall wasn't as bright as it would eventually be, because two of the sconces had to be rewired.

"I wish I could figure out what that rusty discoloration is." Oh, damn—she needed to get a mold expert out here to check it out to make sure it wasn't something she had to treat. "I knew I was forgetting something." She made another mental note to call tomorrow. "Maybe I'll send a sample off to one of the universities to see if they can identify it."

With her gloved hands, Leslie began to pull out debris from inside the railing base and tossed it onto a large tarp she'd spread on the foyer floor. As she removed a large piece of something that looked like pink insulation, she realized with a start that it wasn't insulation at all.

She withdrew the piece and held it up, frowning. It looked like a wide scarf, or—no, it was a lady's wrap. The large crystal button, the size of a half-dollar, would have held it together right in the center of her bosom, and the stole would have covered the woman's upper arms and torso like an off-the-shoulder dress. It was lined with white satin, and the exterior had been a lush rose-pink velvet. But now it was discolored in areas with rust. Or something else.

Weird location to put something like that. How in the world had it even gotten there in the first place? Leslie felt a shift in the air…something cool and eerie stirred, sending a chill skittering along her arms. She tossed the wrap aside—but not on the tarp—and gingerly looked back down into the hole. There was a definite lower temperature emanating from the darkness there, accompanied by the smell of age and…

Perfume?

She pulled back and sniffed the air. Yes, all at once there was the faint scent of something floral and musky in the air.

Leslie shivered a little and looked around. The windows were black, for the sun had set and she was still waiting for the curtains to be installed. The nearly leafless trees, pines, and thick bushes that in the daytime provided charming seclusion for the house now rose in dark shadows to ban more than a hint of streetlight and other illumination from the town below. The flashlight in her hand and the lamp that burned in the foyer reflected in the dark windows, and all at once she felt very alone. *Very* alone.

Silly.

This was the same house she'd slept in for weeks now, the same lovely, charming building she'd adored for decades, the same home that looked cheerful and welcoming during the day. The simple matter of the sun setting didn't change a thing.

But the opening of the stair rail did.

Leslie caught her breath. Again with the creepy thoughts from nowhere! But the hair on the backs of her arms was taut and raised, and she rubbed herself briskly through the sleeves of her shirt.

The house had sighed when they pulled away the railing, hadn't it? The entire place had sort of…exhaled. Shuddered. She hadn't imagined it, had she?

But how could a house exhale? It was silly.

She looked at the exposed opening, slender and unassuming as it appeared.

What else could be down in there?

At least it's too small for a body.

Leslie felt a wave of relief when she realized that and gave a short burst of nervous laughter. After all, Fiona had found a skeleton in the closet of her antiques shop back in Philadelphia. But Leslie was being ridiculous—how often did that sort of thing happen in real life? Never. Hardly ever. This house had been lived in for decades. Surely if there was anything to find, it would have been discovered long ago.

And about the cold chill…probably the base of the stairway butted up to the cellar below, and that was likely the source of the draft, coming up from down there.

Nevertheless, she felt slightly off balance as she beamed her light down into the narrow opening and began to use the broomstick to poke around in there because it was too deep for her arm to reach any further. Besides…she didn't know what she was going to find, did she?

Leslie dragged the handle along the bottom of the hole and felt it catch against something. Carefully, she slid it up along the side until she could remove the object. An evening glove, dirty and dingy, with three round gold buttons on it about the size of peas. It was stained with the familiar rusty discoloration that she wasn't certain was actually rust.

Well, at least it's consistent.

That chilly draft seemed to be a little stronger now, and Leslie just felt…strange. Like there was something in the air.

Maybe if I had a cat, it would sense the supernatural. Or better yet, it wouldn't *sense anything and I'd know for sure.*

Once again, she looked around, half expecting to see something…and at the same time, berating herself for being silly. Forcing her attention back to the project at hand, though part of her was actually considering aborting it, Leslie dragged the broomstick through the bottom again. This time, she heard a soft metallic sound as it brushed something against the wall.

Shining the light inside the hole once more, she peered down, one eye closed, and saw the way the light glinted off something shiny in the depths. Not silvery—so not a nail. But goldish.

She tried for several minutes to use the broom handle to fish out the object, but it was too stubborn and kept sliding off. A wire hanger, she decided, suddenly determined to discover what else was down inside there along with a glove and a wrap.

Leslie hadn't forgotten the legend about Red Eye Sal's supposedly hidden jewel cache, and though she didn't put much stock in rumors like that, she was curious. *What if?*

Suddenly a little more enthusiastic, she hurried off to find a hanger. She was halfway to the kitchen when there was a loud crash from the foyer. The sound made her heart catapult into her throat and her head go light before she realized it was probably the broomstick she'd hastily shoved against the wall, falling over.

Jumpy much, Les?

Nevertheless, her knees were still a little weak and her insides a bit tumultuous as she continued into the kitchen—which was probably why, when she saw the face at the door, she shrieked.

FIVE

DECLAN DIDN'T LEAVE HIS HOUSE until after seven, which made it almost dark. He'd showered and shaved, then he had a few voice mails to return (one was a weekly call from Cara, checking in on how things were going—he had to give her credit and gratitude: she'd turned out to be a great mother), and an order for fifty more iron rods to post online so he could make the cutoff for delivery this week.

He was just finishing when he received a text, this one from Steph.

U should come by and watch pom practice tonight.

Curious, and more than a little relieved she didn't seem to be mad at him anymore, he replied: *Any particular reason?*

Her reply, almost immediately: *Mrs. Danube is here.* Followed by three winky smileys and one with its tongue sticking out.

Declan laughed, and felt his cheeks flush a little even though no one was around. Emily Danube, the mother—the *divorced* mother—of one of the other girls on the pom team had managed to sit next to him during the last two football games, and she'd also invited herself in on the night she drove Steph home from practice. He'd ended up sharing a beer with her at the kitchen table while their daughters did something on the computer.

She thinks ur hawt.

Speaking of hot, his cheeks—really?—were getting there. Thank goodness no one was around. Honestly, it was too weird and creepy that his daughter—whom he really hardly knew—was trying to set him up. Wasn't that supposed to be weird for kids, to think of their parents hooking up with someone?

Not that Emily Danube was someone who'd send him running in the other direction. She might be a few years older than he—after all, he'd only been eighteen when Cara got pregnant—but she looked good. Though she was always well dressed and neat, she didn't have that brittle, try-too-hard aura that divorcees sometimes got once they became single again and began to focus on dating. From what he understood, she co-owned a spa and salon on the edge of town that offered everything from hair styling to massages to nails—and something called mud wraps. Not something that sounded appealing to him.

But the massages…most definitely. He wondered idly whether Emily Danube was a massage therapist, and the thought settled in his mind. *That would be…interesting.*

Well? Stephanie texted back.

Aren't you supposed to be practicing? How can you be climbing onto the top of a human pyramid if you're texting me?

The response was an angry smiley followed by three exclamation points, and Declan laughed again. It was an ongoing joke between them—for apparently, only cheerleaders climbed into human pyramids and did flips in the air; the pom squad danced and shimmied. Heaven forbid a dad should mistake one for the other.

See you when you get home, he replied, and tucked the phone into his pocket. He'd see Emily Danube soon enough—probably at the Homecoming game Friday night. Although if it rained like it was supposed to, he wondered if she'd even come and risk having her hair and makeup ruined.

Declan left the house, locking it behind him and wishing—not for the first time—they had a dog. He hadn't had a dog since he was a kid, and something about living back here in Sematauk made him want to have a soft-eyed canine that would always be happy to see him.

He'd been lucky getting this particular bungalow on one of the main streets just outside the touristy area of the town. It had a second, detached garage, which the previous owners had used to store their two boats: a sailboat and a speedboat. This meant the outbuilding was perfectly suited for him to set up his forge. The exterior of both buildings had dark red wood shingles, big black shutters, and a white picket fence that surrounded the tree-studded lot. Stephanie had loved it—called it a doll house, to his dismay—and wanted to replace the shutters with white ones that had cutout hearts on them to match the cutout one on the swinging gate.

Declan had firmly declined. But he had allowed her to choose the color for the living room walls (thankfully, a reasonably easy to live with light blue) and the curtains for the kitchen (not quite as easy, due to the colorful *owls* splashed all over them). Their only real battle had been over the shared bathroom, which she'd wanted to do in Mickey Mouse (black, white, and red—with Mouse accents) and he'd been happy with just the black and white. They'd compromised—no Mickey tissue holder, shower curtain, or toilet cover, but a Mickey toothbrush stand. And one picture of the Mouse.

"Be thankful I didn't want the Little Mermaid," she'd told him cheekily.

She was a great kid. She really was. How the hell more lucky could he be?

He frowned as he began to walk briskly down the street. He still had to deal with this Leslie van Dorn hiring Stephanie problem. The thing that burned his ass the most was the fact that she'd done so without even mentioning it to him yesterday. She was a seasoned businesswoman. She should know better. Hell, she'd even been on the cover of *Fortune* magazine (yes, Declan had looked her up after Stephanie mentioned it).

In fact, there was a lot of information about Leslie van Dorn on the Internet, including several articles about the initial public offering for her company InterWorks, press releases about the company's successes, and even a few photographs of her at various Philadelphia events. In some she was with a handsome, dark-haired man named H. Gideon Nath III—an attorney who was clearly a personal friend, not a business associate.

Nath sounded like a real tool, Declan sneered mentally, with his ever-present initial H, and the pretentious "the Third" designation following his name. He probably wore monogrammed boxers with all three initials and a big III on them to hide his unimpressive cock. He and Leslie were well suited to each other: the celebrity CEO and the slick, Armani-suited lawyer.

In those pictures, the sleek, perfect Leslie van Dorn sure as hell didn't look much like the disheveled, dust-covered woman he'd met yesterday, wearing a ball cap and baggy clothes. True, he'd seen the cool determination in her eyes under the casual jokes and conversation, and he hadn't been lying when he mentioned she didn't look like she scared easily, but she was a far cry from the hotshot exec ("Twenty-five Women Ready to Shake Up Their Fields" was the name of one *Fortune* article in which she'd been featured) he'd seen online.

But unkempt as she'd been, van Dorn sure as hell knew what she was doing, hiring people. And that made him even more irritated with the situation. Why did she think she needed a fifteen-year-old girl to work for her? And why would she be hiring her without talking to her parents?

He had a bad feeling about it. A very bad feeling. He didn't want Stephanie to be taken advantage of. He had visions of her slaving away doing all sorts of menial labor—clearing out moldy debris (without a face mask), climbing on a tall, rickety ladder to reach the ceiling in the foyer in order to scrub the plaster design around the chandelier, carting asbestos-ridden insulation to the Dumpster out front—while Ms. van Dorn sat in her office and filed her nails and did press interviews via Skype or those fancy star-shaped conference-call phones.

The more he thought about it, the more irritated he became. He'd just spent the better part of his day working on iron spindles for her main staircase, trying to do it as quickly and inexpensively as possible (that was before he realized he was dealing with a woman who'd made a couple million in a public offering). And now she wanted to take advantage of his daughter as well?

These thoughts fueled his stride as he made his way down three blocks past the main drag—by Orbra's Tea House, The Balanced Chakra Yoga Studio, and numerous clothing stores, jewelry shops, and restaurants. He sniffed longingly when he passed Trib's, the best restaurant in town, with killer pizza and a beer list that went on for five pages.

The brisk air and energetic stride eased some of his annoyance with Leslie van Dorn's high-handed employment move. By the time Dec had walked past all the shops and up the hill of Shenstone House's residential street, the sun was down and the only light, though generous enough, was an occasional passing car and the streetlights along the way. But the drive leading up the hill to the house was dark, and as it was shrouded by thick trees and bushes—almost a forest there, really—he was walking more by faith than by sight, guided only by the faint glow through the windows ahead of him.

He knew better than to go to the front door; by the time he'd finished with their meeting yesterday, he'd realized Leslie lived in the back of the house by the large, sunny kitchen while the rest of it was being worked on—so that was where he headed. It occurred to him at that point that, first, he probably should have called (who knew if she was even home), and then, as he came up and around the bend that opened into a large, flat parking area, that there was the same dark blue Mercedes that'd been there yesterday. So she was probably at home.

A figure moved inside the kitchen—Leslie—and he went directly to the door. He was just about to raise his hand to knock when she screamed.

He didn't really think; he just lunged for the door and yanked on it. It swung open just as she came toward him, her hand over her chest as if she was attempting to prevent a heart attack.

"Oh my God, you scared the *crap* out of me!" she said in a high-pitched voice. "All of a sudden you were there—why didn't you come to the front door?"

"I'm sorry," he said automatically. "I saw you here, and—Well, I was about to knock. I wasn't just looking in."

"Right. It's all right. Come in." She was wearing gloves and had her shiny black hair hanging loose. But this time, she wasn't coated with dust, and she was wearing a snug t-shirt and bottoms that Declan had recently learned were called yoga pants. And, he noticed via his natural sweep of a glance, her feet were bare and decorated with grape-colored toenails. "It's just so dark and lonely up here, and something fell down in the front room, so it made a loud noise that startled me—and then I looked up and there was a face in my window."

Leslie laughed, and Declan got the impression she was more than happy he was there to defuse whatever had given her the willies a moment ago.

"I should have called," he said, looking around the kitchen.

It was his first good look at it; he'd had a glimpse yesterday when he was looking around for Leslie. He was impressed by the size and homeyness of the place. Clearly, it had been recently remodeled, for the appliances were sleek and modern, and the island in the center was covered with a thick slab of bronze and black granite, and yet the overall feel of the space was warm and inviting.

"Well, calling's generally a good idea. I might not even have been home—I wasn't all last night. In fact, I'm supposed to meet Aunt Cherry for dinner in a bit," she said as she glanced at the wall clock above the stove. "But I've got time. Have a seat."

Declan obeyed, selecting one of the mismatched (purposely, he was sure) chairs at the battered wooden table. It was thick and solid, and probably over a hundred years old—an eclectic touch in a granite and stainless steel kitchen. The scars gave the table character, and the vase of fresh flowers and dried autumn cuttings sitting in the center of it let him know Leslie might be in the middle of a renovation, but she was still enjoying her new home. On the table was yesterday's local newspaper.

"You're on the front page," he said, picking it up. The large photo just above the fold was of Leslie—without the ball cap and looking almost CEOish—standing in front of the dismantled stairway. She was holding swatches of fabric and an antique light fixture.

"Yes, you just missed being in the photo yourself," she said. "They did a nice job on the article."

"I guess you're used to dealing with the press." He set the paper down.

She smiled slightly. "A hometown lifestyle reporter is a lot easier on the nerves than a room full of AP journalists, I'll admit. Especially ones from the financial papers. They'd wait to catch us after the board meetings, and it could really be brutal—especially as we got closer to the public offering. Give me a hometown newspaper over the *Wall Street Journal* any day."

Yes, they certainly came from different worlds. Declan's mood soured a trifle. Boardrooms, press conferences, executive meetings, private jets…Leslie van Dorn was way out of her league here in touristy little Sematauk, hiring teenaged girls and flannel-garbed blacksmiths to do her bidding. He wondered how long she'd last before she got bored and decided to head back to her uptight lawyer in Philadelphia. H. Gideon Nath. The Third.

"So, did you need to see something in the foyer?" Leslie said, jolting him out of his thoughts. Her unspoken question was, *What are you doing here?*

"Uh…no. I'm here for a different reason."

Leslie lifted one eyebrow, and he recognized wariness filtering into her expression. Her body language shifted: she eased back a little, and her eyes narrowed with subtle suspicion.

What, did she think he was going to attack her or something?

Although…he was here, showing up without calling, well past business hours. He supposed he could cut her a break. A very tiny one.

"I understand you've hired my daughter. I'd like to know exactly what you're planning to have her do, and I have to tell you, I'm not very happy about the situation. I'm her father—she's a minor—and I didn't know anything about it."

Her reaction was one of pure bewilderment and astonishment. "Excuse me, but I have no idea what you're referring to." The CEO had spoken.

"Stephanie Lillard is my daughter. You hired her, didn't you?"

"Oh!" Leslie's eyes widened and comprehension washed over her face. "She's your daughter? I had no idea— She didn't— You obviously have different last names. And I did speak to her… mother." Her voice trailed off at the end of the sentence, as if she realized things might not be as simple as she'd thought. "I'm guessing there's a divorce situation or something going on here, and that's why you weren't aware."

Declan controlled his irritation—now more with Stephanie and her mother and less with the woman in front of him— and replied. "Something like that. Steph's mother lives in New Hampshire, and I'm the parent *here*. So *I* should have been the one involved in this from the beginning."

"I can understand your frustration; had I known, I certainly would have spoken with you yesterday. Stephanie simply didn't mention that you were her father."

"Obviously." Declan couldn't control a grimace, nor could he ignore a little twinge that stabbed him in the belly. A guy moves halfway across the country to live with his daughter so she doesn't have to change schools, and she can't even remember to keep him in the loop. For having been a father less than six months, it sure as hell hurt more than he'd thought it would.

"I'm really sorry. And clearly you have questions about the situation—which I'm happy to answer. She is, I realize, quite young. But I was very impressed with her and I wanted to give her the chance to try it out." Leslie rose from the table. "Would you like something to drink while we talk? Coffee, wine, soda? I might even have a beer. Oh, and I have some tea Orbra gave me as well. Her special autumn blend. She's going to be sampling it at the game tomorrow night."

"Just water. Thanks." Declan was having a bit of a time trying to release the prick of hurt that still lodged beneath his heart. But it wasn't Leslie van Dorn's fault, and he sure as hell wasn't going to say anything to Steph about it.

"Again, I'm sorry about the confusion. With your different last names…I had no idea Stephanie was your daughter. But you had some questions—and rightly so. What can I tell you to ease your mind?"

Declan realized he was no longer speaking to a busy, stressed homeowner client—now he was faced with Leslie van Dorn, CEO and millionaire. The tone of her voice, the expression on her face: both had gone completely businesslike and impersonal. Appropriate, but a little unsettling for some reason. He liked her better when she was using words like *dastardly* to describe a piece of drywall.

Not that he liked her—or needed to like her—any more than he normally liked a client. Which was to say, no more than necessary.

His contrary brain immediately reminded him of Bethany Hamberg again—a thought that he shoved away with the force of a sledgehammer on an anvil. "Well, to start," he said, fumbling for this thoughts, "Steph mentioned her working hours—an hour and a half each day after school—"

"Except Thursdays, and Fridays if there's a home football game," Leslie clarified as she set two tall glasses of water, both with lemon wedges, in front of them.

"Right. She mentioned that. And then four hours on Saturday afternoon. But I'd like to know exactly what she's going to be doing during those work times."

"Of course. I envision her as a sort of assistant, Jill-of-all-trades for now. Initially, I intend to have her handling social media accounts for the business—her first few tasks will be setting up Twitter, Facebook, Instagram, and whatever other social media sites that make sense. I figured a teenaged girl would be more than familiar with how to do that. Additionally, we have a basic website that's already been created, and she'll be doing simple updates to it as necessary while we're going through the remodel process. I'll have videos and photos of before and after, and on some of the restoration processes—in fact, your work on the stairway was one of the topics I'd intended to highlight. I'd like Stephanie to edit and post the pictures and videos on the site and on social media as a way to generate interest in the B&B before it even opens. There will also be some market research involved too, as well as listing some of the old items left here on eBay or other auction sites."

Declan was beginning to feel slightly foolish. "So, administrative work is what you hired her for?"

"Why, yes. You didn't think…" Her eyes suddenly lit with humor. "I see. You had a completely different scenario in mind, didn't you? I assure you, Mr. Zyler, I want experts like yourself doing the work on this house—not a fifteen-year-old girl. That's not to say I wouldn't hire a bunch of teens—boys, but girls too if they were interested—to haul away debris and help with some of the demo, but that wasn't why I hired your daughter."

"I admit, I was pretty mad on the way here, figuring you were taking advantage of a young, star-struck girl. My apologies."

"Star-struck?" Leslie seemed genuinely perplexed.

He shrugged and sipped his water. "You were on the cover of *Fortune* magazine. You're almost as famous as Marissa Mayer, she told me." His lips quirked in a smile. "We don't get many celebrities here in Sematauk."

Her own mouth turned up at the corners, and she gave a short laugh. "Well, I'm flattered. But the days of boardrooms, shareholders, and press conferences are long over for me. And apology accepted. I'm sure if I were in your shoes, with a daughter to protect, I would have been similarly concerned and upset." The smile faded from her expression, and Declan had the impression she'd just thought of something sad.

There was silence for a moment as she drank from her water, and Declan tried to figure out how he could finagle staying here a little longer now that their business was done—and then he was surprised at himself for that very crystal-clear thought.

But he realized, suddenly and surprisingly, that he didn't want to leave. Maybe because he didn't want to walk back through town and stop for something to eat alone, or, worse, try and find something to make for dinner at home. Or maybe because he liked the feel of this house, the homey comfort of this astonishingly large kitchen with its sleek appliances, fancy urban lighting, and chop-block wooden table. Or maybe he simply wanted the company. *Her* company.

"Is there anything else I can tell you that would alleviate your concerns?" she asked, sounding once again like a cool, impersonal businesswoman. "I hope you'll give your permission and allow Stephanie to keep the job, Mr. Zyler. She was very excited, and to be honest—it would be a great experience for her. Working with a celebrity and all."

Declan looked up sharply and was relieved to find her eyes sparkling with humor and her mouth curving again. She was quite a gorgeous woman, he realized with a start—especially in person. Much more attractive than when she'd appeared perfect and well groomed in the photos he'd seen online. And even more lovely now that she wasn't covered in dust.

Her hair was down and smooth except for a soft curl at the ends hanging in a sleek, inky swath around her shoulders. She'd tucked one side of it behind an ear, and a diamond the size of his pinky nail (surely it wasn't real, was it?) glinted on her earlobe. There might even be some mascara or eyeshadow or whatever that was called—the stuff around her blue eyes that made them look larger and darker.

Perhaps that was why he wasn't in any hurry to leave.

"Yes, Stephanie can work for you. Thank you for alleviating my concerns. And—it's Declan. Not Mr. Zyler, all right?"

"All right." She stood abruptly. "I know it's too soon to ask you how things are going with the railing, but—"

"I was actually working on it today."

"You were? Already?" The surprise and delight on her face washed away the crispness of Ms. van Dorn, celebrity CEO, and replaced it with a softer, more approachable version of herself. "I didn't think you'd be able to get to it so quickly."

"Well, I had some spare time this afternoon," he lied, suddenly feeling sensitive about how he'd pushed aside two other projects to work on this one—just so he'd have an excuse to see her again soon? Nah, that was silly. He wasn't about to make the same mistake he'd made with Bethany Hamberg—getting involved with a client only to be discarded when the job was finished.

"It's a beautiful piece," he continued, "and I was looking forward to working on it. So I started tinkering around when I had some extra time. Drew a few sketches so I could finalize a rubric." *Don't read anything into it*, he told her *and* himself. "It'll still be a few weeks before it's done."

"Well, I'm glad you started on it already. I'll try to be patient, but—it's just that it's such an important part of the house. The staircase is the first thing you see when you come in. I want it to be right." Then she sobered. "After working with the wrought iron, do you have any further ideas about what that discoloration might be? I have to have a mold expert come out and sample it, but…"

He shook his head. "No. But it's not rust. That much has become clear, as it doesn't seem to be able to be removed."

"Can I show you something?" Leslie gestured in the general direction of the front room.

"Sure."

He followed her out into the foyer and saw the tarp on the floor, with a small bit of debris on it. A broom lay nearby.

"I was cleaning out the opening beneath the railing," she told him, picking up an old piece of something pink. "And look what I found inside."

He accepted it, and it took him a moment to realize what it was. "It's like a mink stole—but it's pink. It was down *inside* there?"

"Yes. Isn't that a strange place for something like that to be hidden? Look how pretty its big crystal button is—I'm sure it's not made of real diamonds, but it's very elegant. And there was an evening glove in there too." She showed him an elbow-length white glove with gold buttons that had seen better days. It was dirty, moldy, and…

"It's got that same discoloration on it."

Leslie nodded. "I'm going to try and wash it off. It's on the velvet wrap too. But what I don't understand is how it got inside there."

Declan walked over to take a closer look at the situation. "So it was tucked inside this hole. Someone either had to dismantle the stair railing in order to put it down there, or they had to open up the side of it—the outside of the side of the stairs—and put it there."

"I was thinking the same thing. But either way—why? What a hassle that would be. Why not just...I don't know, burn it? Throw it away? Put it in the attic if they wanted to get rid of it?"

"Hell if I know. How old do you think they are? Any ideas? Maybe that will help answer the question."

"There aren't any tags on either of them, so that doesn't help. The fabric of the wrap, though...it seems like it could be pretty old. It's real velvet, I think—not a polyester blend. So it could be from the early part of last century. And with it not having a tag, that might also be an indication—I don't know if they were regularly putting tags on clothing until at least the twenties."

"There's a vintage clothes store in town—you could have them look at it. Gilda Herring's the owner. She's a little intense, but she knows her stuff." He handed it back. "I mean, if you really want to find out."

"Well, I think I do. It's just so strange—such a strange place. It's not as if it were a closet... Wait. What if it *was* a closet, that place under the stairs? That would explain it."

Declan peered down into the hole again, shining the flashlight she'd obviously been using. "It's only that narrow space, Leslie. It doesn't appear to be attached to a larger space like a closet. Besides, at this height of the stair rail, it's much too low to be a closet. It's only a few inches off the ground up to two feet. Not really closet space."

"True. But it could be a hidey-hole sort of thing. Not a full-fledged closet. But you're right." She smiled up at him, a little bit of bashfulness in her expression. "I don't know why it's bothering me so much, but it is. I guess I'm a Nancy Drew at heart."

"Well, the only way to know for sure would be to take a closer look at the wall here, on the outside of the stairs. Looks like the wallpaper is pretty old—been here a long time. If it was put over it to cover up a closet—or hidey-hole door," he added with a sudden grin at her, "it was a while ago."

"Right. Well." She stepped back. "Thanks for your help and thoughts on this. I'll— Oh, wait. There was something else down there. I was just getting a hanger to try and fish it out when you arrived—"

"You mean when I scared the shit out of you?" he said dryly.

"Yes. Guess I'm going to get some motion-detector lights out there in the back so you don't do that again." She grinned, holding his eyes for just long enough that he felt a definite sizzle of attraction. Then she pointed to the hole again. "It looked like something metal down there. At least the space isn't big enough to hold a skeleton." Leslie laughed, but there was a tinge of nervousness in her chuckle.

"Want me to try?" he asked.

"Your arms are longer," she replied.

"That they are."

"But a little more…muscular," she added, and her voice dropped slightly on the last syllables. "Maybe you won't fit."

Was he imagining it, or had her cheeks turned a little pinker?

"Only one way to find out," he said cheerily.

Declan wasn't an ass—he knew (and appreciated) that women noticed the way he looked, the way his occupation had caused his arms and shoulders to develop into smooth, sleek muscles. He'd made certain he had the legs and an ass to match by biking and running as well. That was part of the reason he was more than a little uncomfortable with Stephanie's girlfriends being around when he was shirtless—or even in a tight tee. It just didn't feel right when they gawked at him.

But Leslie van Dorn was a grown woman, and he didn't mind it at all that her eyes seemed to linger on his arms. Not that he only wanted to be appreciated for his muscles. But it wasn't a bad way to start.

He turned his thoughts from this unexpected path and focused them on the opening. Shining the flashlight down inside, he didn't see much of anything but debris and shadows.

"Maybe it would be easier to look behind the wallpaper, just to see if there's an old door or cubbyhole," Leslie said. "It's going to be a big project—there's no need for you to waste your time. I'm sure you have other things to do."

Declan paused. Here was the opportunity to excuse himself, escape, grab a bite to eat, meet up with Brad for an IPA…think about—maybe even work on—the other project that awaited him back home. Instead of doing the logical thing, he heard himself saying, "I don't really have much else going on. I don't mind helping, and I'm a little curious too. But didn't you say you had to meet your aunt for dinner?"

Way to go. Now he was giving her the chance to escape. A good idea, that, to be fair.

"Oh, right. Well, I could invite her up here—she'd probably bring pizza if I asked—and if she knew the guy who thinks she looks like Helen Mirren was in residence, I have a feeling she'd be here in a flash."

He'd turned to look at the wallpapered area just below the empty section of the balustrade. The triangular shape of the wall angled down to its lowest height of six inches, studded at the end by the now-missing post.

"It's all one piece of wallpaper," Leslie said, standing very close and shining her flashlight over the area, following its path with her hand as if to feel for a seam beneath. With her nearly brushing his shoulder with hers, he could smell some essence emanating from her…something very pleasant that had his hormones springing to attention.

"Lord, I can't wait to get rid of these huge cabbage roses," she added, clearly referring to the fussy hand-sized white and blue flowers splashed over a dark pink background. "I know it's historically accurate, but yuck."

"This area is too small to be anything like a cubby. But maybe here…" he said, and rapped his knuckles against the wall at an area that was two feet tall.

They both paused, because his knocking had sounded hollow. Neither spoke as he rapped in random spots along the wall, both toward the bottom of the stairs and toward the top.

"It only sounds hollow here," he said, pausing at the section that was barely hip-high on him.

"Too small and short for a closet. And it's a little higher up the stairs than the rusty discoloration. But…" She stepped back, and he saw that her blue eyes were sparkling. "I want to see what's behind there."

Her enthusiasm was infectious—or maybe it was just her. "Well, let's take a look. You said you wanted to get rid of the wallpaper…"

"Yes. It's got to go anyway. Might as well start it tonight." She produced a utility knife. Crouching in front of the wall, she made a wide slice down the center of the area, then began to pick at the open edge of the wallpaper.

She didn't really need his help, it became clear, so Declan stood there and watched the *Fortune* magazine cover girl as she tore off a big swath of paper and tossed it behind her to rest, curling, on the tarp. Her glossy black hair shifted, slid, and glinted in the light, and the back of her snug t-shirt rode up a little in the back as she crouched there, exposing an elliptical section of skin the color of champagne.

Declan found his attention fixated on that teasing glimpse of skin, wondering if it was as soft and sweet as it appeared. If it had notes of melon and peach, or cinnamon and ginger when one pressed one's lips and tongue to it. He swallowed and tried to regroup, reining in the sudden fanciful path of his thoughts. But then he noticed how the yoga pants hugged her ass—a heart-shaped one that was nicely outlined due to the squatting position in which she crouched.

"Whoa." She almost fell backward onto said ass, barely catching herself with a well-placed palm behind her. "Look at this!"

Jolted from his thoughts, Declan crouched smoothly, his shoulder bumping hers as he looked where she was pointing, down at the base of the wall. He felt a spike of interest that didn't have anything to do with Leslie van Dorn this time. "Whoa is right."

He reached out to trace a finger over the exposed section of wall, where there was a seam in the wood that had been camouflaged by the wallpaper and a thick layer of plaster beneath.

It was a rectangular shape, near the floor, not big enough for anything but maybe a pair of boots—completely innocent looking until you gave a closer look at the hardwood floor beneath your feet.

"There's something strange here," he muttered, shouldering his way closer. "The seam of the wood's off—like it's been replaced—and see the way this piece of wall doesn't quite fit against the floor like the rest of it..."

"I'll get some tools." Leslie scrambled to her feet, leaving more space for him to poke and pry.

Declan rapped on the floor near the rectangular shape. Hollow. He rapped to the left and then to the right, near the base of the stairs. A duller noise, less hollow sounding. It could be anything. He'd seen hundreds of old houses, patched together, slapped into a semblance of shape, then their cosmetic changes hidden beneath superficial facades of wallpaper and paint...but this felt different.

This seemed like something more than just a patched piece of drywall.

Leslie was back, her grape-painted toenails appearing next to his cross-legged thigh. She had small feet, white, and they were pretty, as feet went. Nice arch. Her toes were straight and slender—

"Do you want this?"

She was dangling a small crowbar in front of him, and he took it without looking up. "It's going to make a mess," he warned, but didn't hesitate—she clearly knew what the results would be.

Leslie stood behind him, close enough that he could almost feel her shins brushing against the base of his back as he set the crowbar into place and pried.

The rectangular piece of drywall pulled loose at the floor, and he felt a rush of air escaping at the opening. Declan put the tool aside and pulled up on the bottom of the patch, prizing it away to reveal a dark space.

"Oh my God," Leslie said from above him, her knees bumping the side of his arm. Her voice was high and excited. "It's a hidden stairway!"

SIX

LESLIE COULD HARDLY CONTAIN her delight, and she was on her knees, practically pushing Declan out of the way before he could even look through the opening.

"I can't believe it," she exclaimed. "You buy an old house, and you always dream about finding hidden stairways and tunnels and lost rooms, but when it actually happens…"

"You do?" he asked, amusement in his voice.

Leslie, crouched next to him and balancing on the balls of her feet, looked over and found his face very close to hers. For a moment, her thoughts hitched as she became aware of his warmth and the pleasant scent of him, then went on full steam ahead. "Yes, you do—if you grew up reading Nancy Drew and Lois Duncan and the Chronicles of Narnia! I mean, I always wanted to find a wardrobe that led to a secret world."

"Apparently I missed out on all the fun." His voice was wry and tinged with humor, and he graciously moved out of the way so she could get a better look, steadying her by the arm when she nearly lost her balance in her eagerness. "I wasn't much of a reader."

"No wonder the wall patch was so small and low to the ground—it's just the top of a spiral staircase, right beneath the main stairway!" She shined her light down inside a hole the size of a trapdoor. The iron-railed steps curled down into the darkness like a strand of DNA. "Do you think it's safe? I want to go down there."

"Not afraid of what you might find?" he asked in that same amused voice. "There might be spiders."

"I'm sure there'll be spiders." She hesitated, warring with herself. It was one thing to encounter spiders in the light, where she could see and avoid them…but it would be a totally different ballgame to be climbing down a stairway in the dark and potentially walking into spider-laden cobwebs. Or having the arachnids lowering themselves onto her head or shoulders—

"Want me to check the stairs first and make sure they're sturdy enough?"

Leslie fairly sang out with relief. "Yes, but don't look at anything," she told him, scooting back. "I want to see it for myself."

"Kinda hard to test out the steps all the way down without looking around," he muttered, but she saw his mouth continuing to twitch in a barely restrained smile. "I'll do my best to *feel* my way down, and hope I don't miss a step."

"Well, of course you can look—but don't tell me anything." Leslie peered around his shoulder as he carefully stepped down into the opening, using the edge of the hole they'd revealed to help lever himself in. "And get rid of any spiders in the way."

"So mice and rats and snakes are okay?" he asked with a teasing challenge. "How about bats?"

"It's only spiders and Orbra that scare me," she reminded him with a grin. "I can handle anything else." Even ghosts.

Leslie waited, watching impatiently as he took his time testing his weight on the steps and then slowly, very slowly, made his way down. Just before his head disappeared through the hole, he looked up and their eyes met.

"I have to admit, this *is* pretty cool," he said, then ducked below before she could react to the heat dancing in his eyes.

So he was having fun too. Leslie smiled. *If I'd stayed in Philly, this would never have happened to me.*

At that moment, she decided to add "Discover hidden treasures and secret rooms" to her life-improvement list.

"Well?" she called down, shining her light after him. The top of his dark head was just out of her reach, moving slowly down in a tight spiral. His broad shoulders fit—but just barely—within the width of the tight stairwell, which, from her angle, appeared to be closed on two sides.

"I'm on the ground. Oh my God! You won't believe this!"

"What?" Leslie nearly threw herself down the stairs, then she realized he was looking up at her from the bottom, laughing. "You're teasing me." She was grinning now too, and began to ease her feet through the opening.

"I'm trying not to look around too much, so hurry down. I got rid of all the spider webs, so it should be clear sailing." He came back up a few steps. "Here, let me help you." His hand closed around her ankle, then stopped. "Put some shoes on, Leslie. Who knows what's down here."

"Ugh." She pulled back. "You're right. Hold on."

She moved away quickly and slipped on her Dansko clogs, then was back at the hole and easing her feet through it, holding on to the edge just as he had. Once again, Declan's hand gripped her ankle, this time helping her to blindly find the step below. His fingers were warm and strong on her skin, and Leslie felt that same physical awareness as yesterday when they shook hands for the first time.

He had his cell phone out and its flashlight on, and she was holding the real flash as she made her way down the stairs.

"I'm pretty sure it was a speakeasy," he said as she reached the bottom.

As she descended, her eyes had grown progressively wider, and her excitement spread from a small flutter to a full-blown stomach of butterflies.

"Wow. It's like they were interrupted or something." Leslie stepped onto the ground, Declan steadying her as she gawked at the space spread out before them. "And never came back."

"Maybe it was the announcement that the votes had passed, and Prohibition was ending."

"Or maybe it was a raid, and they all got carted off to jail."

"Nice and optimistic, aren't we?" he muttered, but loudly enough for her to hear.

Their lights didn't illuminate the area all that well, but Leslie could see the makings of what looked like a lounge and bar. Sofas and club chairs, torn up and frayed by the rodents—which had been disturbed and were now scurrying around in the shadows—were arranged in a large U-shape. Two low tables sat in the center, covered with drinking glasses, bottles, and a large crystal decanter. Some of the vessels were broken or lying vertically, others still upright but filled only with dust and dirt. On one wall was a counter with cupboards below it and glasses on shelves above. Corks, bottles, a corkscrew, even small pieces of cloth that looked like napkins were strewn all over the counter.

Leslie turned in a slow circle, shining the beam of light around to illuminate the walls. Two sides were paneled with heavy, solid wood—maple, she thought with delight—and the other two walls appeared to be drywall or plaster, and wallpapered. A huge painting with a gilt frame at least six inches thick hung on the largest expanse of wall, as if to be the focal point. It depicted a young woman of twenty or so, with boyishly short blond hair and large brown eyes. She wore feathers in her hair, jutting from a jewel-encrusted headband that cut across her forehead, a fur scarf the length of a boa, and a shift-like dress that appeared to be sewn with more gems: diamonds, sapphires, and pale blue gems that were probably topazes or aquamarines.

Aside from the jewels on her clothing, the blond woman also wore a heavy necklace that covered her throat and the upper part of her chest with an array of sapphires, including an apricot-sized one that settled just above the beginning of her cleavage. It had been cut in the shape of a six-pointed star. The woman's dangling earrings were also star-shaped gems—sapphires as well.

"That's amazing." Declan was also staring at the painting. "It must weigh two hundred pounds."

"I wonder if that's Red Eye Sal's wife or his mistress," Leslie said, picking her way across the room carefully to avoid scuttling rodents, their droppings, or any other unsavory items. "Or someone else's. She's wearing clothes from the right era. I wonder if those are the jewels from the so-called hidden cache."

"A hidden jewel cache? Oh, here's another one." Declan aimed his phone light at a second portrait.

This one was much smaller and of a different beautiful woman holding a small, fluffy brown dog on her similarly glittering lap. She was older than the other subject, perhaps in her late thirties or early forties. She too dripped with gemstones—these were rubies and garnets of all shades of crimson and rose. And like those in the other painting, star-shaped stones were featured on her necklace, bracelet, and a brooch pinned to her gown.

"This is unbelievable," Leslie murmured, staring at the paintings, then once again turning in a slow circle around the space. She couldn't contain her grin. "I'll need to get some more lights down here, clean it up a bit… What a great conversation piece this'll be for the inn. I'll have to create a more accessible way to get down here, of course…maybe there's an escape route or exit that'll be easier to use."

Declan had begun to ascend the stairs, and he paused halfway up. "There's no connection to the section under the stair railing." His voice was muffled, and she heard him rapping on the wall and ceiling. "It's completely separate, as far as I can tell."

Leslie had almost forgotten about the reason they'd actually found this secret entrance. She peered up past him, unable to see much. "The implication being that whoever hid the wrap and glove in the base of the railing didn't know about this place?"

"Or weren't trying to hide it down here, anyway, whether they knew of it or not. You coming up, or are you going to stay down and bask for a while?" His voice was teasing again.

"I'm coming up for now."

Leslie followed him up the stairs, and once at the top watched as he set the piece of wall back in place. "So the mice don't come up exploring."

The sound of Van Morrison's tune "Brown Eyed Girl" suddenly filled the air, and Declan clapped a hand to his pocket.

"My daughter's ringtone," he said with a layer of exasperation as he fished out the singing phone. "I thought it was fine with a normal ring, but— Hey, Steph, what's up? Everything okay? I thought you had a ride home tonight—" He listened, then nodded and said, "Right. Sure, give me about fifteen minutes... Well, no, I'm not at home. I have to go back and pick up the car... I'm at Le— Ms. van Dorn's... Yes, we did talk about the job...no, I— Look, Steph, we can discuss this later." His voice became firmer, and Leslie was almost certain his cheeks had gone a little red. "Do you want me to come pick you up or not? All right, great. Yes, tell Mrs. Danube I appreciate her driving you tomorrow. Yes—*Stephanie*," he said from between clenched teeth. His cheeks flushed darker and he turned slightly away from Leslie. "Yes, I'm sure I'll have the chance to thank her myself too. See you in a bit."

He shoved the phone back in his pocket. "Teenaged girls. I'll never understand them." His voice was easy, but that flush remained and Leslie fought to hide her smile.

"Thanks again for your help, Declan."

"My pleasure. I'll be interested in seeing the speakeasy once you have better lighting down there." He paused for a moment, then offered her his hand in a sort of awkward farewell. "I'll be in touch."

"Thanks."

Leslie closed the door behind him just as her cell phone pinged. It was a text from Aunt Cherry, wondering where she was. Leslie gasped when she saw the time—she was twenty minutes late and she'd never texted to change plans—and quickly replied that she was on her way.

Five minutes later (Leslie prided herself on being someone who could put herself together at a moment's notice), she was driving down the dark, curving drive. Her headlights cut into the heavy growth on either side, and it occurred to her that it was going to be hell getting out of here in the winter when there were heavy snowfalls...which there always were, due to lake effect snow.

"Going to have to hire a good snow-removal service," she said aloud. Yet another thing to add to her—

An odd movement among the trees brought her up short, and Leslie slammed on the brakes. Her tires ground sharply on the stony drive and she jerked a little behind the seatbelt. What was that?

Her heart thudded and she peered into the darkness, but the trees and brush were too thick, growing halfway over the opening so that they almost made a canopy and cutting out the moon and stars above. She could hardly make out anything but dark shapes among more dark shapes.

Leslie frowned, watching for a long while, then finally began to make her way down the hill. Whatever she'd seen could just as easily have been a deer as anything else. A shifting of a sapling, even. A dog. A person.

Then she let out a sigh of relief. It was probably Declan. He said he'd walked. It was a lot more of a direct route, cutting through the woods rather than going down the curving driveway. Maybe he'd gotten another phone call and didn't leave right away.

Or maybe it had just been an animal. There were lots of deer around here. Most likely of all, it had been a trick of the eye—for she'd seen the movement in her peripheral vision.

Leslie put the thought out of her mind. She had news—big news—to share with Aunt Cherry, and she couldn't wait.

SEVEN

THE BEST EATERY IN TOWN was called Trib's, and it was packed with locals on this Thursday night. Delicious smells along with the sound of live acoustic guitar, underscored by conversation, burst through the door as soon as Leslie opened it.

Though Trib's was considered a pub, its ambience was about as far from the quintessential English public house as Sematauk was from Philadelphia. Inside, the walls were exposed brick behind artfully "torn" wallpapered plasterboard, the ceiling was high, and it was lined with industrial pipes and tiny hanging crystal lights. The art was loud, colorful, and exclusively Andy Warhol.

Leslie found Aunt Cherry—along with Orbra, Iva Nath, and her distinguished husband Hollis—sitting at a round table beneath a four-foot-square print of Warhol's tomato soup can piece. There were several empty chairs at the table, and for a moment, Leslie feared they were to be joined by Helen Galliday, her peremptory cane, and her beleaguered companion Pauline Whitten.

Her apprehension must have been written on her face, for Cherry laughed and pointed to an empty seat. "Don't worry—the old bat Helen eats at five and goes to bed early. She won't be here, and neither will Pauline. Sit! We've been waiting to order till you got here."

"I'm so sorry! We lost track of time, and—" Leslie clamped her lips together and picked up the menu to scrutinize its extensive beer list. "Are there any good IPAs on here?"

"We?" Cherry jumped on the pronoun as Leslie had known she would. Meddling auntie. "Who's *we*?"

Damn. "Declan Zyler stopped by. So, what do you think of this beer Soft Parade? Is it any good?"

"Declan was over? And you lost track of time?" Orbra pounced before her partner in crime even had the chance. Her eyes were narrow with delight. "Well, well, well—"

"It was nothing like that," Leslie said with exasperation. "He just came over to check on something with the railing, and—"

"If Declan Zyler came over to my house, not only would we lose track of time, he wouldn't be leaving until the sun came up," Cherry said with a wicked grin. "At least if you're not interested in him, will you put in a good word for your cougarly aunt?"

"Is cougarly even a word?"

"Oh, so now we're the grammar police, are we?"

"Oh, Leslie's interested in Declan, all right," Orbra interjected. "Look at her cheeks! They're turning pink."

Leslie rolled her eyes. "That pink you see is nothing more than shame over my aunt's desperate ways." Geesh. She hadn't felt this awkward about her relationship with a man—or lack thereof—since high school.

Determined to put space between herself and her aunt's highly charged interest, she turned to greet the older man sitting two seats away from her. Though he was at least seventy, he had a full head of pure white hair and was dressed in a suit and tie despite the informal place and occasion. "Mr. Nath, it's so nice to see you again, and don't mind my aunt. She's…different. Too many failed yoga headstands, I suspect. Her arms just gave out, and *clunk*—onto her head. How's Gideon doing?"

"Working too much, as usual," replied the senior H. Gideon Nath, shaking his own head. "But less than he used to, at least."

"That's good for you, Hollis, because otherwise you wouldn't have the opportunity to travel with me as much as you do," Iva, who was sitting between her husband and Leslie, reminded him. She patted his hand with hers, a large yellow diamond catching the light.

He smiled at her, and, not for the first time, Leslie was struck by the adoration in his eyes. The two had each found their soul mate—if one believed in such a thing—at a late age, and it was beautiful. She hoped they'd have many years together.

"Well, as long as you don't drag me to one of those fun shay conventions again—"

"It's *feng shui*, as you very well know, Hollis." Iva shook her head, but there was affection in her expression as well. She turned to Leslie. "I do hope you're going to let me come and check out your house. I'm certain I'll be able to sense whether it's haunted. The trick will be to keep Helen from wanting to tag along—any ghost that's worth its salt will remain tucked away in its grave while she's there."

Leslie was saved from having to reply by the arrival of the waiter—who turned out to be none other than Trib himself. The proprietor was tall and slender, pushing fifty, and had a bleached buzzcut that was just long enough on top to be rakish. He wore a yellow flowered bow tie, sleek eyeglasses that probably cost four figures, and a turquoise polka dot shirt. He looked as if he'd just stepped off a page of *Vogue* or *The Advocate*.

"So at last I get to actually meet the new owner of Shenstone House," he said with a subtle pout. "I saw the article in the paper today, and am *desperate* to stop by and see what you've done to the inside. Is this your first time here at Trib's?"

"Not at all. But usually you're busy when I've come in," Leslie told him. "A pleasure to finally meet you. I have to say, you've got the best pizza I've ever had. The Wise Guy—the one with sausage…oh my God, it's amazing. And there's something about the sauce…I think you must have laced it with crack or something."

"That's right, sweetie," Trib said with a pleased nod, as if the compliment was nothing more than his due. "I'm glad you're back. And with these two ruffians." He winked broadly at Cherry and Orbra, who were only half listening, as they had their heads together. "What can I get you all?"

They'd just finished placing their order when the door swept open and two men came in.

"Oh no. Helen's going to have a fit," Orbra muttered to Iva and Cherry. "We'll never hear the end of it."

"Why? What's— Oh, is that the writer?" Leslie was only able to get a glance at the newcomers without rudely craning her head to look.

"Hell, for all we know he made his escape from her at the inn and that's why he's here," Cherry said with a husky laugh.

"Is that the mayor with him?" asked Iva, peering through her reading glasses, which she seemed to have forgotten she was wearing. She had turned in her chair, but this left her facing her husband so it wasn't as obvious she was gawking.

But no one needed to reply, for the two men had been seen by Trib and he beckoned them over. "There's no room at the inn but here at this table." He looked around the crowded restaurant with satisfaction. "And it's not even high season. Mayor Underwhite, you don't mind sitting here with these lovely ladies—and a very special gentleman, I might add," he said with a warm look that was—probably for the best—lost on Hollis Nath.

"I'd never say no to sitting at a table with such lovely companions," said Aaron Underwhite. "I hope you don't mind, Jer—John. There doesn't seem to be anywhere else to sit."

"Not at all." The writer directed a smile at the table in general as they chose two of the three open seats. "John Fischer," he said, shaking everyone's hand in turn just before taking his seat.

Until now, Leslie had no idea what the author Jeremy Fischer looked like—his photo didn't appear on any of his book covers, or even on his website. She guessed it was because of privacy, rather than because of his looks—for the good-looking man who sat down across from her had no reason to be shy in that area. He had soft gray eyes, a broad jaw, and a slender nose. His thick coffee-colored hair was worn short and brushed forward on top, as if to hide a receding hairline. It was threaded with gray, especially at the sideburns, and sported a bit of curl at the ends. His beard and mustache were neatly trimmed, and rather than looking like an unkempt vagabond, he simply looked collegiate. The round glasses perched on his nose gave him an air of absentmindedness and studiousness—as if he were mentally focused on whatever book he might be writing, despite sitting in a crowded restaurant.

"John's in town working on a project," said Underwhite with a barely concealed sense of pride. "He needed a quiet place to hole himself up."

Jeremy—or John, as he was calling himself—made no comment. Instead, he gave a brief smile then turned to pore over the menu, leaving his companions to wonder about his "project" and whether the rumors were true.

"Where's Regina?" asked Orbra. "Should we pull up a chair for her too?"

"She'll be here in a few," replied the mayor. He was about the same age as Fischer and Trib, and he had very short hair that was thinning on top. Underwhite wore a smartly cut, very expensive suit that seemed like overkill in a small town like Sematauk, especially after business hours. He was short and stocky, with ruddy cheeks and soft hands, and exuded an underlying air of importance laced with gregariousness.

As soon as he ordered a beer, Underwhite turned his attention to Leslie. He flashed perfect white teeth and said, "Pleasure to finally meet you, young lady. Sorry I haven't been by to give you an official welcome—been very busy with all the big Fall Colors tours. Want to keep those seniors and lovebirds coming back every fall, so I have to be as visible as possible. Very pleased to hear things are coming along so well at Shenstone House. Nice article in the *Gazette* yesterday—Brad Beatty always does a good job."

Young lady? Leslie hadn't been called "young lady" since she was just out of college. She was barely twenty years younger than the mayor, if that, and she'd dealt with men his age and older for years in the corporate world. She was just about to make a cool retort that might have included the words "older man" when Cherry moved next to her, and there was an instant, sharp pain in her ankle.

"Oh, did I kick you?" her aunt asked innocently—but there was a flash of warning in her eyes. *Be nice.*

Whatever. "Brad spent a lot of time at the house, looking at all the things I've been having done," Leslie replied briskly. "He took a lot of photos too; said he was going to write an article and submit it to *Midwest Living,* as well as the Grand Rapids and Chicago papers. Some sort of pre-publicity press."

"That's excellent news," Underwhite said with a smile. "Beatty knows what he's doing when it comes to publicity—look at what he's done with B-Cubed."

"B-Cubed?"

"Brad Beatty Brews—B-Cubed Beer. His IPA is our most popular local beer, and it's made right here in Sematauk. Anything that helps a local business, like yours or his, helps Sematauk—and vice versa."

It was on the tip of Leslie's tongue to tell Cherry and Orbra that she and Declan had discovered a hidden speakeasy when a waiter arrived with their beer—including one of B-Cubed's.

Conversation turned, not so accidentally, to books—with Cherry and Orbra doing their best to draw John Fischer into conversation about his suspected contemporaries.

Cherry started it by mentioning that she'd just picked up the latest J. D. Robb from the library. Orbra latched on, and was off and running.

"T. J. Mack is one of my favorites, of course, being as the author's pretty close to being a Sematauk native," she said, looking around the table—but pitching her words to make certain Fischer could hear. "I have all the Sargent Blue books on my shelf. They're just so funny, but they're suspenseful, too—grab you by the throat and don't let go the minute you start reading. I also love the Jack Reachers, and those other ones by Harlan Coben—but the Bruno Tablenture books—those are definite auto-buys for me. In *print.*"

Wow. Orbra was really buttering up Fischer if she was buying his books in print. Or at least claiming to. Leslie hid a smile as she glanced at the writer. To her surprise, he caught her gaze with his. Humor flashed therein as he winked, then tilted his head to sip from his B-Cubed longneck.

"So guess what I found," Leslie said in a low voice to Cherry as the books conversation trundled to a halt. "Or, I should say, *we* found, today."

"What?" Her aunt, more slender and toned at sixty than most women were at thirty, had settled in her seat and was eyeing John Fischer speculatively from across the table. "He might be able to keep up with me," she muttered. "And I've never minded a guy with a beard. Not at all. William Reckless had a very sexy one." She sighed with what sounded like regret. "Too bad he ran off to the monks in Tibet."

Leslie shook her head. Cherry had never been married, but she'd had her share of boyfriends over the years—and a wide variety of them. Since she'd grown up during the days of Woodstock, free love, and communes, it was to be expected she'd known men with beards and long hair. "And you've never dated a novelist, have you?" she asked in an undertone. "A guitar player—two of them, right? A chef, a baseball player, a poli-sci professor—and God knows who else."

Cherry grinned and ran a hand through her short, sassy-looking hair. "I've done a poet and a self-help author, so I think it's about time I tried out a fiction writer, don't you? Unless you're interested—and he does seem to be checking you out. Although, if you are, then you have to back off on Declan. No fair for you to be hoarding all the foxy men."

Leslie's eyes widened and her cheeks warmed. "Keep your voice down," she muttered, looking around to make sure no one had heard. "And don't you want to hear what I found?"

"Oh, right. Do tell! Orbry, lean in—Leslie's got news."

But before she could begin to tell her tale, a smartly dressed woman approached the table.

"Ah, Regina's here," said Underwhite, standing to greet his wife—at least, Leslie assumed Regina was his wife.

If she was, the two made an unusual couple—at least visually. Though they both seemed to be the same age, Mrs. Underwhite was much more slender than he—just as toned and fit as Cherry, but taller. Almost six feet, Leslie guessed, which put her five or six inches above her husband. She dressed as expensively as he did, however, in a tailored shift of Kelly green trimmed with black embroidery at the hem and ends of its long sleeves. Her hair was an unnatural blue-black without a hint of gray, and she looked as if she'd just left the salon.

As it turned out, she had. "So sorry I'm late," she said, glancing around the table. "Emily was running behind, and I was her last cut tonight. But I don't trust my hair to anyone else, you know." She turned to Leslie. "Emily Danube, at the Beau Monde Salon—best stylist and colorist in the county, if you're looking for someone. Worth waiting for, even if she's running late. You're Leslie van Dorn, aren't you? The new owner at Shenstone? I'm so sorry we haven't met before now—but better late than never. Regina Underwhite." She smiled pleasantly, her teeth as perfect as her husband's, which caused Leslie to wonder if they'd used the same orthodontist.

"Pleasure to meet you," she said, shaking Regina's offered hand. "Thanks for the recommendation—I do need to find a new salon and stylist now that I've moved to the area, so I'll give them a call."

"Emily books up months in advance, but if you tell them I sent you, I'm sure they'll fit you in. She always keeps a bit of padding for emergencies." Regina looked around the table and laughed lightly. "Well, now that we've got that settled—I'm sorry I'm late, darling," she said again. This time, she leaned toward her husband, who'd risen to pull out her chair, and gave him a warm kiss on the lips.

He smiled, moving a hand affectionately across her shoulder, then sat back down next to her. "We waited for you to order. I hope you're hungry."

"How sweet of you. Thank you, Aaron. I was hoping to have some news for you about the salon's expansion plans, but all Emily Danube wanted to talk about was Declan Zyler."

"Declan Zyler? What about?" Orbra demanded, flickering a glance across the table, and all of a sudden, Leslie felt a sudden sense of disquiet…and, strangely, it grew into a sense of disappointment at Regina's next words.

"Oh yes, she was going on and on about how she'd been going to the football games with him to watch their daughters on the pom squad, and how he had her over the other night for a beer. The man is nice enough, I suppose, but he doesn't really do a thing for me," Regina said, sliding a sidewise look at her husband and smiling.

He beamed and patted her hand. "You're a brains over brawn kind of woman, I know."

"Well, he sure as hell does a thing for me," Trib said as he placed a new beer in front of Fischer, and another in front of Underwhite. "Too bad I'm almost twenty years too old for him."

"Not to mention the fact that he goes the other way," Orbra said dryly.

Trib sighed. "A man can dream, can't he? I keep trying to think of excuses to stop by and see him working at that forge of his." He looked up and around the restaurant. "Been thinking about adding some wrought iron accents to the place, you know. Lots of 'em."

They all laughed, and Cherry said, "You let us know how that works out, Trib."

Regina looked up. "Hello, Trib. I'll have my usual, if you don't mind." Then she spoke to the table at large. "I suppose you've all been discussing business before I got here? Or plans for the class reunion?" She turned back to Leslie, who was beginning to wonder if she'd ever be able to tell Cherry about the speakeasy. "Aaron is the mayor, but of course he ropes me in to a lot of special projects." Her eyes danced, indicating that she didn't mind it one bit. "I have an interior design practice, but I'm very involved in anything related to the town or special events here. Including the big, multiyear reunion."

"No, no, we weren't actually talking business at all, Reggie," Underwhite said. "You didn't miss a thing."

"Would you all like to order, now that Madam Underwhite is here?" Trib asked, nudging her playfully from behind.

The consensus was for the pizza with the "crack" sauce, and they ordered a vegetarian one for Cherry and Regina, and another two with a variety of toppings, and then, finally, Leslie was able to tell her story.

"There's a hidden room in the cellar." She was mainly speaking to her aunt and Orbra, but the others could hear as well. "I think it was a speakeasy."

"A speakeasy?" Iva fairly squealed. She looked as if she were about to erupt from her chair and run to Shenstone House to see for herself. "Where? How big was it? Was there anything in it?"

The Underwhites and Trib were listening too. (Hollis Nath had left the table to take a phone call.)

Leslie was only too happy to fill in the details about where the entrance was and what she and Declan had found when they pulled off the patched-up piece of plasterboard. "There are bottles and glasses all over the place, and the furniture is in bad shape. But there are two oil paintings that are absolutely stunning—each of a woman wearing amazing jewelry. Though they're portraits, the gemstones are really the focus of the picture, and as soon as I saw them, I couldn't help but wonder whether they were paintings of the missing legendary jewels of Red Eye Sal. If they even exist."

"Oh, they exist all right," Trib said. He'd pulled up a chair and spun it around, straddling it so he could rest his hands on the top of its back. "Well, at least one piece does—or did." Regina, Underwhite, and Trib exchanged glances. "No one's sure about whether there was a whole cache of jewels like the legend says, or just the one necklace."

"What did the jewels look like?" asked Orbra just as a waiter delivered two of the three pizzas they'd ordered. "The ones in the paintings, I mean."

"One was all sapphires. It was as if the woman was wearing a collar just dripping with them—of all different shades of blue, too, so some might have been blue topazes. They covered the top of her chest like this." Leslie used her hands to demonstrate. "And she had matching earrings and a bracelet. It was a ridiculous number of gemstones, all set in silver—or maybe platinum. And at the bottom of the necklace, the part hanging the lowest, was—"

"A star-shaped stone," Cherry said. Her eyes were sparkling, just like the sapphires. "Those are definitely Red Eye Sal's missing jewels. The star is the giveaway."

"That's right. The jewelry was all made by the same designer—supposedly a woman whom Red Eye Sal loved but couldn't have because she was married to another man. Apparently the fact that he himself was married wasn't a factor," Aaron Underwhite said dryly. "But the jeweler—I forget her name?" He looked at his wife.

"Margarita, wasn't it?"

"Yes, that was it. Margarita's trademark was having the gemstones cut into a star shape—or she set them so closely and perfectly that they looked like one stone, as if a single jewel had been cut into a star."

"Either way, each piece she designed always had a six-pointed star with a sort of fat center on it. Very distinctive," Trib said. "You said one set in the paintings was sapphires…so the other painting was of the gold topazes?"

"No…it was garnets and rubies. What do you mean *the* gold topazes? It sounds as if you know about these jewels," said Leslie.

"Well, we all know about the topazes, that's for sure," Cherry said. "But I don't know if anyone ever believed there was anything else in the so-called jewelry cache of Red Eye Sal other than the topazes, and maybe some pearls."

"I feel as if I'm missing half of some story that you all know. Would someone please fill me in?" Leslie asked, reaching for a piece of pizza. It was covered with fresh tomatoes, torn basil, plots of house-made mozzarella, and roasted peppers—and it smelled divine.

The others looked at each other, and Mayor Underwhite was the one who spoke. "Since I probably know as much as anyone about it," he said, sliding his own piece of pizza onto his plate. He served Regina as well, then settled back in his seat, preparing to tell a story.

"The topazes were—are—the only pieces of this so-called collection that anyone ever remembers seeing. That's why most everyone believes it was nothing more than a legend that Red Eye Sal had other pieces in his cache. There was a set of earrings—both star-shaped and gold—and a necklace, though it was much less grand than the one you described, Leslie. And there were some pearls, with mother of pearl star shapes as well—which is probably what launched the idea of the legend, even though no one that I know of has ever seen any others. But two sets of jewelry, both with stars...you can see where the romantic idea came from." He paused as if to collect his thoughts, using a knife and fork to cut a generous piece from the point of his pizza. "And, if those paintings you say you saw are accurate, then it seems as if it might not just be a legend after all."

"The topazes and pearls were owned by the van Gerste family, who I think were distant relatives of Sal," Regina said. "Or somehow had a connection; I'm not sure, because they never owned Shenstone House. We knew their daughter, Kristen." Her voice had become sober. "We were in the same year at school."

"Is she the one who... Oh, I'd forgotten about that," Iva said in an almost whisper. "That was...what...1985? Just a year after I moved to Philadelphia."

Trib was nodding. "Yes. 1985. The year we graduated." He glanced at Leslie. "Kristen was in our class. She was a beautiful young woman, with dark hair and amber-colored eyes. Smart, too—not valedictorian smart; that was Aaron here—but she had a respectable grade point. Very popular with her classmates—pretty much all of us liked her. Homecoming queen, cheerleader, class president—you know the drill." He paused, seeming to collect his thoughts.

"Kristen got permission from her parents to wear the Red Eye Sal topazes to our senior prom," Regina said. "It was a big deal—her parents were wealthy, and she always had nice clothes and expensive shoes, but the fact that she was going to wear these heirloom jewels to the prom was a really big deal." Her voice trailed off. "I knew Kristen quite well. We weren't absolute BFFs or anything like that, but we were in the same group of friends. I played basketball and ran track, she played tennis and was a cheerleader. And we lived near each other—Kristen, Aaron, Trib, and I. Though the van Gerstes' house—and Aaron's too—was a lot larger and fancier than mine or Trib's." She smiled fondly at her husband.

"Kristen was dating the captain of the football team," Aaron said, taking up the story. "Marcus Levin. That's only relevant because of how the night played out. Prom night, I mean."

"The night she was wearing the topazes," Leslie said.

"Right. Kristen was a trendsetter," Trib said. "So when she got permission to wear the jewels, she decided to go all the way and do a vintage look. Vintage clothing was just becoming the thing in the eighties, and she found this gorgeous beaded flapper dress at an antiques market. I still remember it…she looked like an angel in that sparkling gown. It was pearlescent, iridescent, all shimmery gold and pink and peach…" He sighed, his eyes going dreamy and faraway.

"Anyway," Underwhite said, drawing the conversation back to him, "she wore the dress and topazes to the prom, with Marcus Levin as her date. But they had a huge blowout fight near the end of the night—it was a complete spectacle, right in the middle of the dance floor.

"They were playing 'Waiting for a Girl Like You'—I'll never forget it: that song was the theme for the prom, and the queen and king had just been crowned. They were supposed to dance together first, then the rest of their court was to join in, couple by couple—and it all went to hell," Regina said. "No one was dancing, Kristen was screaming awful things at Marcus while he stood there laughing at her, and then she left. Walked out, crying, and left the prom, all by herself.

"The high school isn't far from our neighborhood—only two miles or so. You can see it from Shenstone House, actually. It's just beyond the woods that butts up to the bottom of your hill and goes along Faraday Street. Oh, and Kristen's family never owned Shenstone," Underwhite added for Leslie's benefit, "which is another reason people didn't believe there are jewels belonging to Red Eye Sal hidden there."

"I tried to go with Kristen, to talk to her," Regina said quietly. "But she didn't want anyone around, and my date…well, he encouraged me to let her leave by herself if that was what she wanted. I did make him take me home then, and we looked for her on the way to give her a ride, but we didn't see her. No one did." When Leslie glanced at Underwhite, Regina said, "Oh, it wasn't Aaron who talked me out of going after her. It wasn't until later that I realized what a great guy he was."

"A damned sight nicer than Colter Bray," Underwhite commented, shaking his head. "I would have sent you after Kristen if you'd been my date." He looked at Leslie, giving a wry smile. "I didn't have a chance with the likes of Regina van Arndt when we were in school. I was an acne-faced nerd, and that was long before nerds and geeks were made cool by *The Big Bang Theory*." He laughed, and Regina laughed with him and patted his hand.

"Anyway, that big fight broke up the dance," Trib said. "The blowout between the most popular and well-liked girl in the school and her asshole of a boyfriend. No one liked Marcus Levin unless he was on the football field. Or running by in shorts," he muttered. "And no one really knew what the fight was about."

"So Kristen left the dance by herself, wearing the topazes, upset and angry and crying…and she was never seen alive again," Underwhite said, finishing off the story.

Leslie, who'd been expecting an unpleasant end to the story, frowned. "Did they determine what happened?"

After a moment, Regina spoke. "Late the next day, they found her body in the woods not far from the main road between the school and town. The topazes were gone."

"They think it was a robbery, plain and simple," said Underwhite. "She was still fully clothed and had died from a broken neck. There was evidence of a blow to the back of the head, too—we all followed the story, of course; I remember it like it was yesterday." He reached over and covered Regina's hand with his own. "We all liked Kristen. It was so awful."

"So they never caught anyone?" Leslie asked.

"No. And the topazes never showed up anywhere either—they must have been removed from their settings and sold separately, or are hidden away in someone's safe," said Trib.

After a few moments of everyone quietly eating, Orbra spoke. "So now that you've found those paintings, there is evidence that there actually were other jewels in Red Eye Sal's collection."

"I wonder if they're hidden in that secret room," Iva said just as her husband slid back into his chair next to her. He murmured an apology, and dove into the pizza. "Or if there are other secret rooms in the house! I really do need to come over and look, Leslie. Will you be home tomorrow? Can I come by?"

"I'll be there all day—except I think I'm being dragged—er, taken to—the football game at the high school tomorrow night." Leslie grinned at Cherry.

"What's this about secret rooms?" Hollis asked, then sighed with satisfaction as he enjoyed his pizza. "Hardly ever get to eat like this at home."

"Only two pieces, darling," Iva reminded him. "You know what the doctor said about your cholesterol."

"Right." Hollis rolled his eyes at her. "Where is this secret room you found, Leslie?"

"It's under the main stairway in the foyer. Probably the people coming to the speakeasy would walk right in the front door and then head below through the secret doorway. You have to kind of duck your head and climb down—it's not much more than a hole in the floor that leads to a spiral staircase."

"Did you have to take the staircase apart to get to it? How did you even know to do that?" Underwhite asked.

"No, Declan just pulled away a section of the wall at about the midsection of the stairs."

"Oooh…what was Declan doing at your house?" asked Trib with a wicked smile.

"He's restoring the wrought iron stairway—the one in the front foyer."

"That's a big job," Regina said, looking at Leslie with raised brows. "And an expensive one. I hope you don't need him to replace the whole thing—surely it would be thousands of dollars. Remember when I was working with Bayley Brothers on the remodel at Kendall Street, darling? We had wrought iron work done there, but that was before Declan Zyler moved back to town. It was very pricey."

"Yes, but the railing is old, and of course Leslie doesn't want to take the chance anyone could get injured," Cherry said.

"And in order to keep my historical home designation, it has to be restored in the original manner. So, yes, it will be expensive. Maybe I'll find the missing jewels and that will pay for it," Leslie said with a chuckle.

As the others joined in, John Fischer spoke up: "Well, I for one would like to see this secret room. If you're giving tours to others"—he nodded toward Iva—"can you count me in? Sounds like a great idea for a book." He gave Leslie a subtle wink—as if everyone at the table hadn't figured out he was a writer—and selected another slice of pizza.

"Sure. Why don't you come over at eleven tomorrow morning? Anyone else?" she asked, half laughing as she looked around the table.

"I'd love to, sweetie, but I'll be here mixing up my crack pizza sauce. With its five secret ingredients," said Trib with a wicked smile. "For sure another time."

The Underwhites demurred, as well as Orbra ("Lunchtime's busy, you know"), and Cherry groused that she had to teach a Pilates class at noon.

"You can come over tonight and look," Leslie suggested to her aunt. "It's only nine o'clock."

"Not tonight—remember, you said you'd help me move those display cabinets at the studio?" Cherry said. "Or now that you found an exciting secret room, maybe you don't have time for your auntie anymore." She pretended to pout.

"Right. Sorry. I forgot you turn into a pumpkin at nine."

"If you got up at four thirty so you could teach yoga at six you wouldn't make fun," Cherry told her.

"I have no idea why you need an hour and a half to get ready in the morning," Leslie said. Ever since she'd left the corporate world, she'd happily slept in till at least seven and spent less than a half-hour showering, dressing, and doing her hair—a great improvement over the ninety minutes she used to take to do her hair and makeup, and dress in pressed suits and Italian pumps every morning.

She was never going back to that world.

"We'll be over tomorrow at eleven," said Iva, standing as her husband tossed a couple of twenties onto the table. "But speaking of tunring into pumpkins…I'm about there myself. Good night, all."

The dinner party broke up rapidly after that, and Leslie walked with Cherry out the door of Trib and across the almost deserted main street, down the block, then around the corner to her second-floor yoga studio. It took a little less than an hour to move the display cabinets that held books, tees, yoga pants, and fitness accessories—and for her to fill in a few more details about the speakeasy *and* Declan Zyler.

"I wouldn't let what Reggie said about Emily Danube stop you," Cherry said as she locked up the studio.

"What are you talking about?"

"You know what I'm talking about. Stop playing dumb, sweet pea. I'm your favorite aunt and you're my favorite niece—"

"I'm your only niece—"

"And that's beside the point. Only a straight man or a lesbian wouldn't see the point in getting to know a guy like Dec Zyler a little—well, a *lot*—better. So unless you find out otherwise, assume there's absolutely nothing going on with him and Emily Danube."

"Right, auntie. Whatever you say." Leslie popped a kiss onto Cherry's cheek then headed off to her car.

She had to admit, she'd taken her time rearranging the cabinets and chatting with her aunt. She suddenly found she wasn't all that eager to return to a large, dark, empty house alone.

For the first time since moving in, Leslie was fully aware of how isolated Shenstone was, up on its low hill, surrounded by a generous, forested area. Even though the town was less than a mile away, the house felt farther away from everything because it was higher up and shrouded in woodlands.

And now that she'd learned about Kristen van Gerste—hadn't her body been found in the same wooded area? Farther away, closer to the highway, but still…

"That was thirty years ago," Leslie told herself out loud as she turned down her street.

And then there was the movement in the brush she'd seen—or thought she'd seen—just before she left tonight, while she was navigating down the S-curved drive.

"Don't be an idiot," she lectured herself as she nosed her Mercedes into the driveway. It was probably a deer. Or a dog. Or a figment of her imagination.

Who wouldn't be on edge after having the bejesus scared out of her by Declan Zyler showing up at her window?

Leslie didn't see anything out of place as the car crunched up the drive (going to have to get it paved before winter, she thought), and her high-beam headlamps spread a large and comforting semicircle as she turned into the parking area.

The lights were on inside, just as she'd left them, and her house looked as inviting and homey as usual. Feeling relieved, and rather foolish for her apprehension, she climbed out of the car, keys jangling in her hand.

But Leslie had just reached the back door when, from the corner of her eye, she caught a movement at the edge of the woods. She spun around, heart in her throat, just as the bushes shook and trembled.

Something was there.

EIGHT

LESLIE STIFLED A SHRIEK just as the largest cat she'd ever seen bolted out of the bushes and tore across the yard. She had only a glimpse of a taffy-colored, bushy-furred feline, and then it was gone. Back into the darkness, leaving the bushes shuddering in its wake and Leslie weak-kneed with her heart thudding.

"Well," she said when her lungs started working again. "Well, that was fun."

She stood there for a moment, wondering what had caused the cat to burst from the woods at top speed, then dart back into the night. Had something been chasing it?

The night was still. Not even a breeze to ruffle through the leaves or stir her hair. The warm glow of lamplight spilled from the kitchen window, and Leslie let herself in at last.

She gave one last look out into the night, wondering if the cat had been a stray (she hadn't seen a collar when it streaked past her), then closed the door.

Inside the kitchen, where the new-grout and -paint smell still lingered and the appliances gleamed, she made a pot of camomile tea (Orbra would approve) and sat down with her laptop to research Red Eye Sal and his lost jewels. Tomorrow she'd take photos of the paintings, and see if she could determine who the artist had been.

By eleven, she had found several interesting sites and articles, and was also yawning. It had been a long day and tomorrow would be just as busy. Leslie already regretted agreeing to break up her morning by giving a tour of the speakeasy room to Iva and John Fischer, but she'd committed, and that was the plan. Hopefully they wouldn't stay long.

And then tomorrow night was the high school football game. Leslie couldn't even remember how she'd been wrangled into going—oh, right. It was Homecoming, and Orbra's Tea House was one of the sponsors. They were going to be giving away samples of hot cinnamon spice tea to the attendees. Leslie hadn't graduated from the local high school, but she knew it was going to be the event of the week. She wondered if Helen Galliday would go and thwack her way through the rows of bleachers with her cane.

Just as Leslie was climbing into bed, she remembered she hadn't told Cherry and Orbra about the pink velvet stole and glove she'd found in the stair railing. She'd show Iva in the morning, and maybe one of the ladies would have an idea about the origin of those pieces of clothing, and why they'd been stuffed inside the stairway.

So many things to do…so many things to think about…the least of which was launching her new bed and breakfast business…

She must have slept, for all at once, Leslie was suddenly *aware*. Her eyes flew open wide and her heart thudded with the shock of an abrupt awakening. There'd been a noise…a loud, tumbling, rolling sound.

Inside the house.

She sat up, listening hard. Silence.

Her hands were clammy. She felt utterly out of sorts, having been snatched from the depths of deep sleep. It was two a.m., according to her clock.

"Maybe something fell over in the front room," she told herself, happy to break the silence with her own voice—though she didn't speak very loudly. It was probably something just like the broom that had fallen earlier tonight and caused her to get all wigged out.

But that hadn't sounded like a broom. It was heavier. And it thudded and clattered and clumped, as if it were rolling across the floor.

Could part of the stair railing have come loose and tumbled to the ground?

Leslie forced herself to climb out of bed, reaching for her cell phone and the pepper spray she kept handy. Just in case. Armed with both, sliding into her clogs (she felt less vulnerable without bare feet), she crept out of her bedroom and through the office attached to the kitchen.

Wearing a t-shirt and boxer shorts, she walked soundlessly across the kitchen and into the hallway that led to the foyer. It was chilly—really quite cold—out here. Did the furnace need repair now too?

Or maybe it was just fear and nerves that caused goose pimples to erupt everywhere on her, and the tip of her nose and fingers to go icy.

Still gripping her phone in one hand, the pepper spray in the other, she made her way down the hall. She could see a glimpse of the foyer ahead, dark and shadowy without any hint of light other than the faintest glow from a small, low nightlight she'd plugged in at the juncture of hall and foyer.

Just before she reached the front entrance, Leslie paused. Listened, then caught her breath. In the distance, she heard a sound…soft and melodious. *Music?*

From where? Now her breath was coming in short, quick puffs…and she was so cold it felt as if she were encased in a block of ice.

The music was louder now, more discernible. It seemed to be coming from the foyer. Heart ramming so sharply she felt it jolting her whole ribcage, Leslie swallowed hard. Then she stepped forward and peered around the corner to look into the high-ceilinged entry hall.

Nothing seemed to have been disturbed. But the music was definitely coming from…*upstairs?* Her breath catching, Leslie looked up at the wide, swooping curve that ended above and across the room in a balcony overlooking the foyer.

There was something there.

Something…light. Glowing. Shimmering.

Her heart was lodged fully in her throat by now; Leslie couldn't have screamed if she'd wanted to. The music was louder now…it sounded familiar…soft and subtle and haunting.

Leslie fumbled with her phone and turned on the flashlight to beam it up toward the glow at the top of the stairs. Not that the wimpy illumination from her phone projected very far. And whatever it was up there, it wasn't moving. It was just…standing there. A shapeless column, shimmering softly in a pale, pearly glow.

Now that she had some light, Leslie could see how cold the room was: her breath was visible. It wasn't just fear that made her shiver and tremble. The temperature had dropped, suddenly and sharply, and Leslie—confronted by this glowing image—realized she was either looking at a supernatural phenomenon, or someone was playing an elaborate trick on her.

"Who's there?" she called, still gripping the pepper spray. She couldn't make herself move any closer to the steps, however. "Show yourself!"

At her words, the column—that glowing image—seemed to shift and move…and then all at once, it was coming toward her, down the stairs, rapidly and loudly.

Leslie couldn't control herself; she shrieked and stumbled backward, catching herself with her hands on the ground as the sounds of thudding, rolling, tumbling filled her ears, filled the entire foyer. Underscored by the familiar music, the noise echoed in the space until the nebulous entity reached the bottom of the stairs and swooped around the space…then disappeared.

Everything was still.

The music stopped.

The glow was gone.

Even her breath no longer created fog, for the temperature rocketed back to normal.

But lingering in the stillness was the faint scent of a woman's perfume.

A sweet, floral scent that Leslie didn't wear.

Declan pulled up the driveway of Shenstone House at eight o'clock the morning after he'd scared the crap out of Leslie van Dorn.

He hoped he wasn't too early, but his day started pretty much with dawn, getting Stephanie out the door for school before seven, then downing his first cup of coffee, reading the news, and doing administrative work online.

He suspected a go-getter like Ms. van Dorn would be up early as well, but still, maybe he should call first. Just in case she was still in bed. Or in the shower. Or better yet, just getting out of the shower—

Declan surprised himself with a sudden smile.

Maybe he wouldn't call.

Maybe he'd take his chances.

Well, now—that was an unexpected train of thought. He scratched his newly shaven chin thoughtfully then figured, what the hell? If he got the chance to see the hot celebrity CEO in a towel—or even her nightshirt—it wouldn't be the worst way to start the day.

He climbed out of his truck and walked across the parking area, pausing briefly to consider whether he should go to the front door or the kitchen. There was a rustling in the bushes, and he turned to see a huge cat—thirteen, maybe fourteen pounds—prowling out from the tall, brown grass like a miniature lioness.

The cat paused when he saw Declan, then went about his business—which seemed to be exploring around the trash cans. Looking for food, probably—

"Oh, no," Declan said when he got a better look at the creature. There were missing patches of hair, and his tail was bent. The top third dangled like a forlorn flag, and he was limping.

"You poor thing. What happened to you?" He crouched and called softly, "Here, kitty. Come here, kitty."

The cat paused its exploration of the tightly closed trash cans to consider his offer. Declan called a few more times and made crooning noises while the feline's pair of amber eyes watched him mistrustfully. When he made the mistake of inching toward the cat, however, the tabby had enough and bolted away from the trashcans, darting through a hole under the wraparound porch.

"Damn," he muttered, and made his way over to peer through the broken latticework around the base of the porch. He had his head under the edge and was shining his phone flashlight into the darkness when the kitchen door flew open with a sudden and loud swish.

He jolted upright, banging his head as the cat darted even further into the darkness. Declan eased out from under the porch, the back of his skull throbbing and cobwebs clinging to his hair and shoulders.

"What are you doing?" Leslie van Dorn was dressed in neither a nightshirt nor a towel, and she did not appear pleased to see him. In fact, even though she was in a sweatshirt and—were those boxer shorts?—she looked even less composed than she had the first day he met her, when she was decorated with drywall dust and cobwebs.

"Why are you creeping around my house again?" she demanded before he had a chance to reply. She sounded halfway between suspicious and hysterical.

Definitely not the Leslie van Dorn he'd come to know, however briefly.

Wary, Declan stood, brushing off his jeans. "There was a cat. I was trying to get it to come to me, but it got spooked and ran under the porch. It looks like it's pretty hurt."

The tight look on her face eased. "Was it taffy colored? A big one? I saw it last night—it scared the crap out of me when it came dashing out of the woods from nowhere."

He was about to open his mouth to say something stupid ("A little high-strung, are we?" or "Maybe you scare more easily than I realized") and thought better of it, especially when he noticed her bare legs beneath blue and green plaid boxers. They were very nice legs. Long and shapely and— "Uh, it's still under the porch… I don't suppose you want to try and lure it out? I think it needs a vet."

She looked at him appraisingly. "So now you're a cat rescuer too." Her expression had softened even more, and Declan almost wanted to squirm under her gaze.

"Too?" he asked lightly.

But she didn't reply; instead, she went back into the house, presumably to get something for which a cat would leave its sanctuary.

Moments later she returned with an open can of tuna and set it on the ground near the trash cans at his suggestion.

"Even if it comes out, we might not be able to catch him," she said. "At least the first time."

"Right. Well, it's up to you if you want to feed a stray. I just wanted him to see a vet. His tail's half whacked off and he's got patches missing from his fur...and even though he ran away like a bat outta hell, he seemed to have a limp when he was walking more slowly."

Leslie's expression had returned to normal, and she was watching the hole under the porch with a sad expression. "I don't mind feeding him. I wouldn't mind having a cat around," she said, almost to herself. Then she looked up. "Maybe if we go inside he'll come out."

Declan was very fine with that idea. Moments later, he was sitting at the big, scarred kitchen table while she made him a cup of coffee. "Is everything all right?" he asked carefully. "You seemed a little...tense when you came outside."

When she didn't reply and merely set his coffee down, perhaps with a little louder a thump than necessary, he feared he'd stepped in it. Declan wasn't certain what was going on with himself, but he knew he didn't want to piss her off. And not because he was afraid of losing a client...but because he—well, she had great legs and she smelled good...she was smart, and a little funny, and he'd thought about her quite a bit last night after he'd left Shenstone House.

A lot more than he'd thought about petite, bubbly Emily Danube after she'd sat at his kitchen table and had a beer with him last week, in fact.

Leslie still hadn't spoken by the time she sat down across from him, accompanied by a plate of washed grapes and bite-sized quiches that he recognized from Orbra's Tea House. (Not that he was in the habit of taking high tea or anything. He suppressed a shudder at the thought of being among all the lace and flowers and delicate china for any length of time, pinky extended while lifting a teacup…)

Declan, for whom the silence was becoming ominous, opened his mouth to speak, but stopped immediately when she looked at him. She had very large, very intense blue eyes and they were framed with thick black lashes. Instead of being angry or suspicious or even irritated, the expression therein was one of hesitation. Confusion. Maybe even a hint of worry.

"Something happened last night," she said finally. "And after, I—I didn't get much sleep, so I was a little grumpy when I heard you drive up, and then you didn't knock, and the next thing I knew, you were climbing under my porch…" The last bit came out more quickly and smoothly than the beginning, and Declan had the distinct impression she'd changed course from what she'd intended to say.

"I can see why you might have wondered what was going on. But I assure you, if I'd had the intention of creeping around your house, I wouldn't have driven up in broad daylight, parked my car in full view of your kitchen, and then dove under your porch."

"Right. I know that." The tense look was leaching back into her face. "I'm sorry I reacted so strongly."

"What happened last night that made you so tense that you reacted so strongly?" Something prickled at the back of his neck. Had someone tried to break in? Attack her? He forced himself to wait for her to speak, but his fingers curled into a fist beneath the table.

Leslie lifted her mug to drink something that didn't smell like coffee. It had an unfamiliar cinnamon-y, spicy aroma. She looked away, out the window, into the distance. "You're going to think I'm crazy."

Okay, so not an attack or a break-in... "*Going* to think?" he teased. "That assumes I don't already."

He was relieved when she gave a short laugh. "Right. I can only imagine what you think of me."

"I actually think quite a lot of you," he said before he realized the words were even forming. Then he froze, his eyes widening as she looked up in surprise. "It's true," he added to hide the surprise at his voice's betrayal. "You've accomplished a lot in your life." Now that just sounded lame. Like he was introducing her at the chamber of commerce or writing her obituary or something. Damn.

"Thanks." Her cheeks appeared a little pinker than they had been a moment ago.

"So are you going to tell me what's going to make me think you're crazy?"

She drew in a deep breath and pulled herself back from where she'd had her arms and elbows on the table as she leaned forward. Settling back in her chair, she looked right at him and said, "I'm pretty sure I saw a ghost last night."

"All right," he said after the briefest of pauses. "Tell me what you saw."

She looked at him with suspicion. "You don't believe me."

"You haven't told me anything yet, so I can't decide whether I believe you or not." He put down his coffee. "Are you in the habit of seeing ghosts?"

"No."

"Have you ever seen one before?"

"No."

"Do you believe in ghosts?"

"Y-yes...well, maybe...well, probably. Oh, hell, yes, I guess I do."

He controlled a grin. "Then if you say you saw one last night, I tend to think you did. I have no reason not to believe you."

The suspicion was still in her eyes, but her shoulders—which had drawn up closer to her ears—eased back down. "I was asleep, and something woke me up at about two o'clock. It was a loud noise, coming from the foyer. Like something had fallen down— down the stairs or from the ceiling to the floor. I got up and went out there to look, and I saw…something…glowing. Standing. At the far end of the balcony, at the top of the stairs. And the room was really cold. Unusually, oddly cold. And I heard music."

Declan was very careful to keep his expression blank, not to betray any of his thoughts while she spoke. "Go on."

"I had brought my pepper spray and my phone— Hey, I never thought of that—I wonder what would have happened if I'd sprayed it with pepper spray?" she said, her brows drawing together. "Anyway, I shined my phone's flashlight toward it. I was still on the ground, just coming out from the hall, and I called out to it—I figured either someone was playing a big joke, or the ghost had finally made its appearance."

"The ghost?"

"Cherry and Orbra claim the place is haunted, that people have been saying it for years." She shrugged. "I've been living here a month and haven't seen a sign of anything paranormal—until last night."

"So what happened after you shouted out at it?"

"It—came at me. Down the stairs, and I heard that same noise that had woken me up—as if it were running or tumbling down the stairs. It was loud, really loud, and there was music too…and then it disappeared. And afterward, everything was quiet, and I smelled a lady's perfume in the air. It's not the kind I wear. And…"

"And after that?"

"After that, nothing else happened. Everything was quiet for the rest of the night. But I didn't sleep much at all."

"I can understand why." Declan lifted his coffee to sip, aware that she was watching him without trying to appear anxious.

"You think I'm nuts, don't you?"

"Not at all. Look, I've worked in a lot of old houses like this— on a lot of different locations that have…well, histories. I've had my share of strange experiences. Doors slamming when no one's there. Creaking floors. Unexplained sounds. Even sudden changes in temperature, like you experienced." He spread his hands. "I have an open mind, and I'm curious."

Leslie's eyes suddenly turned very soft and warm. She glanced down at her tea as if to hide the expression. "Thank you for saying that, Declan."

Well, sure. Anytime, babe if it makes you look at me like that. "Mm…have you had a good look around this morning, since all this happened?"

She shook her head. "I finally fell asleep just before dawn, and I think you woke me when you drove up the driveway. So, no, I haven't ventured out there yet to see if…to check around."

"Want to take a look together?"

Leslie nodded. "I'm not really afraid of ghosts. I don't think. I just—it was such a shock. And then it came at me. As long as it doesn't hurt anyone…" She shrugged again, but her eyes were still a little wide. "Do you mind waiting while I put some clothes on? Have a mini quiche. Make another cup of coffee, if you like. I'll be right back."

"What're you drinking? It smells good."

"It's chai tea with milk and a little maple syrup for sweetener. There are cups for that too, for the little coffee maker. Help yourself."

Declan did as she suggested, wandering around the kitchen with his milky chai tea (not bad at all). Nice tile work on the backsplash. Some of the accent tiles looked like they were custom made, too, and they didn't look too modern.

An interesting array of cookbooks—French, vegetarian, wild game, Thai, vegan baking (how was that even possible? didn't vegans forgo eggs?) and more. There were glass-fronted cabinets with mix-and-match blue and white dishes, and a real fireplace on one wall. He noticed a calendar depicting lush English gardens hanging next to the landline on a small built-in desk with a Mac desktop. He paused when he saw that October 15, next

Wednesday, was marked by a small red heart with a "G" written inside it.

Declan suddenly felt grumbly and annoyed. Who the hell was G? What was up with the heart?

"All right." Leslie swept through the door off the kitchen, and Declan caught a glimpse inside the office beyond. "All ready."

She had brushed her hair (it was smooth and shiny now) and the scent of minty toothpaste wafted from her. Leslie was now wearing jeans that did great things for her ass, and a light blue "Smitten with the Mitten" t-shirt that displayed the outline of Michigan on it, as well as the shape of her curves beneath it.

Almost as good as a towel, he decided as he followed her down the hall from the kitchen to the foyer.

Then he redirected his thoughts and imagined how she would have crept along the same route last night. How many people—men or women—would have investigated something like that while alone in the house, rather than turning tail and bolting? And how many people would have spent the rest of the night in the house after being confronted by what Leslie had seen—or thought she'd seen?

His estimation of her clicked up another few notches…then clunked back down when he remembered the G-filled heart on her calendar.

Leslie walked boldly into the foyer, turning on the lamps to give as much illumination as possible—which was to say, not as much as there would be once she finished with the new lighting she'd told him about yesterday.

Declan looked around and didn't see anything obviously amiss. The patch of drywall he'd set back in place to close off the stairway to the speakeasy was still intact, and nothing else seemed to be disturbed. The tarp on which they'd piled some of the debris from the dismantled stair railing was still lying on the floor, shuffled up into a pile in the corner. The broom and dustpan remained from last night as well.

Leslie seemed to agree with his assessment that nothing had been moved, for she made no comment after walking a circle around the entrance hall. She started up the stairway, shining a flashlight on the steps. The beam skimmed back and forth over each stair as she made her way to the top.

"The—uh—ghost was about here," she said when she got to the far end of the sweep of stairs, on the opposite side of the high-ceilinged room. "I don't see anything…" She crouched to look more closely as Declan came up to join her.

He wasn't certain what to look for, and this was the first time he'd been upstairs. The balcony was like one side of an H, bisected by a single hallway that ended in a T-intersection at the back end of the house. He saw several doors that surely led to what would become guest rooms, and one door at the end of the corridor. The floor was hardwood, probably oak, that desperately needed to be sanded, buffed, and stained. In general, the upstairs smelled like fresh plaster and paint instead of old house.

As if reading his mind, Leslie looked up with a wry smile. "Things are moving along slowly but surely up here. I'll have eight guest rooms in all, five with private baths and two other bathrooms for use. I've had all the wiring updated and windows replaced, and the drywall crew is coming tomorrow to finish patching before the paint crew comes on Monday…and that's just the beginning." She shook her head, then flapped a hand. "I don't see anything out of place up here. There's no dust because so many of us have been in and out, so it's hard to tell whether what was here was something corporeal or not." She turned off her flashlight. "Eventually, these floors will be redone…but for now, I'm concentrating on the guest rooms."

He automatically offered her a hand and helped lever her to her feet. "Considering what you've done in the kitchen, I have no doubt it's all going to look great. And I can't believe you've got a crew coming on a Saturday. What did you have to do to get them to agree to that?"

She laughed. "It wasn't that difficult—it's a big job here, and the contractor is all about keeping me happy."

So what does *it take to keep you happy?* Declan was becoming more and more interested in giving it a shot. "Should we check in each of the rooms—just in case?"

"Good idea. Though I'm not sure what I'm looking for."

"Me either. But we should be thorough."

It took less than ten minutes to check each of the future guest rooms and bathrooms, and once again, Leslie seemed satisfied that nothing was out of place.

"So…" she said as they descended to the main floor. "If there was anyone here pulling a trick on me, there's no sign of it. I really think it was a ghost, Declan."

He looked at her as she paused on the last step. This put her just slightly below his eye level, with those dark blue irises close enough for him to see the flecks of black in them. She was looking at him intently—almost as if she wanted him to believe her—but his thoughts scattered when he realized how close she was standing, how good she smelled—all minty and lush and female—and that it had been quite a long time since he'd kissed a woman. And then there was the memory of that ass in those jeans…

"I…" he began, forcing himself to step back both literally and figuratively. His fingers had gone a little shaky, dammit. "A ghost," he reminded himself as he moved away from the stairs, ostensibly to check the stability of what was left of the railing. "Well…" He collected his thoughts rapidly. "I guess you'll have to wait and see if it comes back tonight." He glanced over as she stepped onto the floor.

It was on the tip of his tongue to suggest that he could come by later tonight and hang around to see if the specter showed up again, but the daddy gene he hadn't realized he owned until a few months ago shut that idea down immediately. He wasn't comfortable leaving Stephanie home alone overnight. And even if he did, he wasn't certain how he'd explain that he was going to spend the night at her boss's house.

Teens could definitely be a complication.

"Right." Leslie seemed pragmatic as she set the flashlight down on a small table in the foyer. "And if she doesn't reappear…well, maybe I could chalk it up to a— *No,* it wasn't a dream. I don't care how crazy it sounds; it was not a dream. I was wide awake. I was freezing and I heard the music, and I felt the hardwood floor under my feet." Then her eyes narrowed as she glared at him. "I've never sleep-walked in my life, so don't even think about that."

"I wasn't!" He grinned at the fierce expression on her face. She was all kinds of cute when she was determined. "So, do you want to go back down there?" He gestured to the patch of wall covering the hidden stairway.

"I do, but I can't right now." She picked up the cell phone she'd left on the foyer table and checked the time. "The tile guy is going to be here in fifteen minutes, and then I have a conference call, and after that I've got to make decisions on window treatments so I can get the order placed with the decorator before John Fischer and Iva get here—"

"John Fischer and Iva?"

Leslie looked distracted. "He's a writer...I think. You know, Jeremy Fischer? It's him, but he's undercover. And Iva Nath—an acquaintance of mine from Philly—wants to see if she can sense a ghostly presence here. I'm almost afraid to tell her about last night."

"Why?" he asked, though he recognized the name Nath as belonging to Leslie's uptight lawyer escort. His stomach sank a little.

"Because I don't think I'll be able to get her to leave after she hears that I saw a ghost." Leslie laughed. "She's a little intense."

Nath. How did H. Gideon fit into the picture with this Iva? And this John Fischer, maybe Jeremy Fischer, guy? Declan wanted to ask, but he realized it would make him sound like he cared too much—or was being too nosy. But all of her other visitors were "the tile guy," "the decorator," "a conference call"—none of them had a name.

At least it wasn't G-with-a-heart...except...oh, damn. G. *Gideon.*

Gideon Nath.

Declan's great mood soured, but he kept his voice even. "I can come back and remove that drywall in front of the hidden door if you want—what time is Iva coming by?" If he was there he might be able to casually find out what the deal was with the Naths… Good grief. Was he actually considering rearranging his day in order to do that?

"She's coming at eleven, and thank you, Declan, but that's not necessary. I know how busy you are. Didn't you just get a big new project?" she added with a big grin.

Right. He got the message on that loud and clear: get back to work, O menial laborer of mine. Just like Bethany Hamberg, once she'd gotten what she wanted from him. His mood soured. "That's right," he said. "I'll just get going now."

Leslie seemed to notice his change of mood, for she looked at him funny, but then her phone rang. "Ugh, sorry, but I have to take this—it's the plumber I've been trying to reach for two days now." With an abashed smile, she answered the phone, leaving Declan to show himself out.

To give her credit, Leslie did walk with him back to the kitchen and gave a little wave as he walked through the door. She even followed him out into the yard and looked over when he gestured to the empty tuna can.

"See you later, Declan," she called, covering the phone.

Right. Maybe he'd check in on that massage thing at Beau Monde Salon. He could work out a few kinks—both physically and mentally.

NINE

OH, LOOK —Orbra's Tea House is giving out free tea samples!" Emily Danube smiled up at Declan as they pushed their way through the crowd of teenagers and parents toward the bleachers.

The high school football stadium was packed everywhere—in the seats, walkways, and concessions and rest room lines. It was Homecoming, after all, and because of the upcoming multiyear reunion, there was an unusual number of people at the game, at least according to Emily.

"We'll be lucky if we can get a seat in the bleachers close enough to see the girls," she'd told him when they met up in the parking lot.

It hadn't been planned for them to meet up, at least on Declan's part, but he didn't mind that they had. After all, he was going to be sitting alone anyway, because Brad Beatty—who he'd normally hang out with—would be up in the press box covering the game for the paper. Dec hadn't been in town long enough to get to know many other people besides a few of Steph's friends' parents.

"It sure got cold overnight," Emily said as they pushed their way through the masses of people to reach the temporary gazebo Orbra had set up for her sponsorship. "Normally I'd go for hot chocolate, but tea has fewer calories—and it smells delicious." She smiled up at him, the tip of her nose red with cold and her breath making soft little puffs in the chilly air.

"That's Michigan for you," Declan agreed. "One day it's seventy degrees, and the next it's forty. Part of the Lake Michigan effect." He was glad he'd worn a hat and had gloves; it was going to get really chilly once the sun went down.

"Tea samples!" called Orbra from behind her table. There was a flurry of activity inside the small square space, which was enclosed by a U-shape of tables and covered by a temporary awning. Four people worked busily, filling paper cups from the tall silver canisters on a table in the back. "Get your tea samples!"

"Mmm. This smells good," said Emily, taking a small cup. The scents of cinnamon and orange wafted through the air.

"It's my own special blend. It's got whole star anise in it. Perfect for autumn," Orbra said.

"Hi there, Declan," said Cherry with a particularly smoldering grin. "You ready to come in and try some hot yoga? Anytime you want, young man, you just let me know—I do private lessons too!"

"I'll keep that in mind." He laughed, enjoying the meaningless flirtation—though Emily looked back and forth between him and Cherry as if she was scandalized.

He accepted the steaming tea she offered him just as a woman he realized was Leslie turned around from where she'd been digging out a new sleeve of plastic-wrapped cups from a large box.

"Stop bothering Declan, auntie," she said. She met his gaze for just a sec as she handed the man next to him a cup of tea, and Declan was aware of a sudden jolt of heat that had nothing to do with the cup he was holding. Her eyes looked very blue, partly because she was wearing a thick hat knitted of cobalt and cream with a big puffball on the top. She looked adorable with the tip of her nose red and her hands in bulky fingerless mittens, and Declan forgot all about Gideon-with-a-heart and the fact that he was merely a laborer in her eyes.

"Declan gets sweaty enough in his smithy, Aunt Cherry—he doesn't need your hot yoga too!"

Whoa. He blinked, then hid his surprise by taking a big slurp of tea. *Too hot.* Damn. He nearly scalded the inside of his mouth, and managed to hide the fact behind a nervous smile. What did one say to something like that? Was that comment meant to be as flirtatious as it sounded…or was it just meant to be a rebuke for Cherry?

Not only did he not know, but clearly Emily, who was still looking back and forth between him and the tea ladies, did. "We'd better get some seats before the marching band comes out, Declan, or we'll be standing all night. See you later, Orbra. Thanks for the tea! It's wonderful." She took him by the arm and tugged him away.

Before Declan realized it, he'd been replaced at the front of the tea line by other eager customers and was back to navigating through the crowd with Emily alongside him. He couldn't believe how many people were here for a high school football game. It was a mob scene. Wall-to-wall people. He didn't ever remember it being like this when he was in high school…though, come to think of it, he'd been on the field playing tight end, so he wouldn't ever have experienced the crowds—except what he saw in the stands.

Shortly after he and Emily managed to find two seats in the bleachers—really, it was so packed it was more like one and a half seats—she asked casually, "Who was that with Cherry and Orbra back there?"

Warning bells jangled in his mind. This was not a good sign— this subtle possessiveness, the taking of his arm and directing him away, this questioning—no matter how casual. She was a nice woman, Emily, and great looking, and their daughters were friends…but they hadn't even been on a date. Or kissed.

And, well…there was Leslie.

Who may or may not be seeing a hotshot lawyer named Gideon from Philadelphia.

And who was his *employer*, he reminded himself. Well, a client, really.

Who was mostly interested in him getting some work done for her—

Not that kind of work, he told his hormones when they leaped to attention at the double entendre.

"That's Cherry's niece, Leslie van Dorn. She bought Shenstone House."

"Oh, right. I saw the article in the paper the other day." Emily sounded less than enthused. "She doesn't look anything like the photo that was in the article."

He had no idea what she meant by that, so didn't comment. "I'm restoring the wrought iron stairway for her in the front foyer," Declan said, then realized maybe he should have just changed the subject. Because now he felt Emily stiffen a little next to him, and then move a little closer. Even though they were already thigh to thigh on the hard bleacher seat.

"I'd love to come over and see you working sometime," she said, looking up at him with a very warm smile. She was wearing a warm hat, too, with a big POM MOM stitched on the front of it in silver glitter. Her cloudlike blond hair sprang in soft, perfect curls from beneath the hat. Little pompom earrings dangled from her ears, and her lips were expertly colored in with a subtle shade of pink. She—or maybe it was her coat and scarf—smelled like some very nice expensive perfume.

"Sure," he heard himself saying before he could stop himself. "Come by anytime. I'm usually in the smithy from noon till four or so, depending how things are going."

"Great. How about I come by on Monday? The salon is closed on Mondays, and then I could cook you dinner after. I make a mean lasagna. The girls can do their homework together."

"That might work," he said cautiously. "I'll have to see what's on my schedule that evening. You know how it is with teenagers— they always have things going on they don't tell you about, then spring it on you at the last minute." *Please have something going on, Steph. Anything.*

It wasn't that he didn't like Emily. It was just that…whatever twinge of interest he might have had before meeting Leslie van Dorn had somehow fizzled out. And now he felt like crap, because clearly Emily was *very* interested, and thought he was too.

Had he given her that impression?

Hell, how was a guy to know where the line was between being friendly and being *interested*? Dammit.

Their daughters carpooled, so of course he was friendly and hospitable to the woman who drove his daughter around. He wasn't an idiot. Somehow, suddenly becoming the father of a teenaged girl had made even his personal life more complicated. And for all he knew, Stephanie might have helped exacerbate the situation by encouraging her.

Emily was about to say something else when the sounds of the marching band reached their ears, and everyone bolted to their feet to welcome the musicians—who were followed by the cheerleaders and pom squad. The football team was introduced to the roar of the crowd, the national anthem was sung, and then the home team kicked off to their visitors.

After that, Declan made certain to be very interested in the game (which was easy, because it was a good game against a nearby rival school), and to talk to everyone around them instead of limiting his conversation to Emily. He exchanged knowledgeable comments and some lamentations over bad plays with a few parents of both genders, all of whom were rabid football fans and not just there to watch the marching band, cheerleaders, or pom dancers.

The game clock showed ten seconds left in the first half, and the home team had possession. The ball was hiked and the quarterback caught it just as the clock ran out.

"Halftime!" squealed Emily, grabbing Declan's arm just as everyone else in the stands surged to their feet to watch the Sematauk quarterback complete a beautiful pass to one of his running backs in the end zone.

"Touchdown!" shouted the announcer as Declan and the other football fans went crazy, high-fiving at the last-minute score. "And Sematauk's up by ten at the half."

"Halftime!" exclaimed Emily again. "We get to watch our girls!"

Declan was still talking with the guy on the other side of him about that perfect touchdown pass when the squad came out onto the field with their shiny pompoms and long, slender legs.

"Here they are!" said Emily. "Watch, Dec!"

He *was* watching, but apparently he wasn't allowed to talk at the same time—at least, according to Pom Parent Code. Some unrecognizable rap song blared from the speakers, distorted and half-muted at the same time, as the girls shimmied and kicked in time.

"That's my daughter there, in the front row," he said apologetically to the man next to him. "The tallest blond with the highest ponytail." It was hard to differentiate between the girls, but that was the best way.

"Stephanie Lillard's your daughter?" The man next to him smiled and offered a hand. "I'm Greg Hammady."

"Hammady? You'd be—uh—Paul's father, right? Nice to meet you. I'm Declan Zyler. I guess I would probably have met you tomorrow night anyway. I understand I'm to be at your house for pictures for the Homecoming Dance at six o'clock, right?"

"I think so. Nancy, the photos are at six tomorrow night, right?" Greg turned to the woman next to him, obviously his wife and clearly the keeper of the family calendar. "This is Stephanie's father, Declan."

"Great to meet you," she said, offering a mittened hand. "Yes, we'll feed the group—I guess there are five couples going—and then we'll do pictures at six. Then off to the dance by seven."

"Oh, you'll be there too?" Emily asked, looking up at Declan. He could already see the invitation forming on her lips, and he swiftly turned back to the Hammadys.

"Thanks so much for hosting everyone," he said. "It's a lot different than when I was a teen."

"Watch them, Dec!" Emily gave him a gentle nudge from the other side. "This is my favorite part."

As soon as the pom squad finished their routine, Declan excused himself to go up to the press box and say hi to Brad. Somehow, he managed to get away without Emily insisting on going with him. As he jogged up the bleachers, taking two steps at a time as he dodged the people who were descending, he couldn't help but feel a little guilty about blowing her off.

He knew what it was like to be blown off. To think there was something going on, but really there wasn't.

Although he hadn't really done anything to make Emily Danube think they were together…unlike Bethany, who'd teased and flirted and made herself very available to him until he finally succumbed and went to bed with her in between sessions working on the wrought iron railing of her Antebellum gazebo.

He'd done some very fine work there, at her charming Charleston home—both on the railing and in the bedroom. Even now, he couldn't contain the ghost of a smile. Fine work indeed. But Bethany hadn't been interested in anything more than a fling, and once she was finished flinging, Declan had been relegated to nothing more than laborer status.

He'd learned his lesson, no doubt about it. New rule: no sleeping with the client. Made things a helluva lot easier when it came time to collect his check and move on to the next project.

Which was why it wasn't the greatest of ideas to be noticing Leslie van Dorn's bluer-than-blue eyes, the way her jeans cupped such a nice ass, and how she softened the minute he mentioned the stray cat and its broken tail. Not to mention the way she got all businesslike and frosty when she was explaining about hiring his daughter. An interesting woman, to say the least.

"Yo, Dec!" Brad was glad to see him.

"How goes it, bud? Hey, any chance I can watch the rest of the game up here?" Declan asked. "You've got one hell of a view going for you."

And there weren't any clingy pom moms either.

—⁂—

Leslie was so busy serving free tea samples she completely missed the halftime show—which included pom squad, marching band (playing a bunch of eighties songs that had been re-popularized by *Glee*), and Mayor Underwhite announcing the Homecoming court.

Fortunately, things settled down once the game started again, and she was able to take a break, leaning a hip against one of Orbra's tables as she tried out a sample of the tea herself. She'd been working so hard that she'd taken off her down vest and handwarmers after a while, but now that she wasn't moving as much, Leslie pulled the vest back on.

"You're going to have to get moving on things," Cherry said to her as she picked up her own cup of tea. "Or you're going to miss the boat."

"What are you talking about?" Leslie was genuinely confused.

"With Declan. That was Emily Danube with him when he came up to the table—didn't you see her? The tiny blond with the big boobs?" Cherry calling anyone tiny was rather amusing, for she was only five foot two (not to mention platinum blond) herself. "She practically dragged him away—did you see that?"

Leslie shrugged. "Well, it sounds like they're seeing each other. I'm not going to step on anyone's toes, you know. Remember, I'm new in town and I've got a business to start up. No sense in pissing off another business owner."

Nevertheless, she had to admit a twinge of disappointment at having her suspicions confirmed. She had noticed the pretty woman standing next to Declan, but that was only after she'd met his eyes and felt a delicious sizzle of connection there. Her lady parts still tingled at the memory.

And besides, he hadn't really seemed *with* Emily. He was just standing next to her; there was a subtle difference. But maybe Cherry had seen something Leslie missed.

"So, how did it go today?" Orbra edged over and inserted herself into the conversation. Like Leslie and Cherry, she was wearing a warm sweater, gloves, and a hat. But she also sported a frilly pink and white apron emblazoned with *Orbra's Tea House: The Hot Pot Spot*. "Did Iva come over this morning? Did she sense any ghosts? Did you show her the speakeasy?"

"She claimed she felt a definite chill in the air, and some sort of presence," Leslie replied, her tone very neutral. She wasn't about to raise a brow at anyone who claimed they sensed a supernatural presence—not after what she'd seen last night. "But that was it."

Nor was she ready to tell anyone else about the ghostly figure she'd seen. She was almost regretting having confessed it to Declan, even though he'd been so chill about it.

"Did John Fischer come today too?" Cherry asked in a sly tone. "If you lose your chance with Declan, you can always go for him."

"I thoughtyou were interested in being a cougar to the young novelist," Leslie retorted. What was up with her aunt interfering in her love life? "I'm not going to stand in your way. He is very nice, and not bad looking. Go for it, auntie."

"And—he's *famous*. And *rich*. And he probably knows Tom Cruise," Orbra said.

As Leslie was pretty much over Tom Cruise, and she had had her own brush with being famous—not to mention somewhat rich—none of these reasons made John Fischer particularly appealing to her. However, she didn't deny he was charming and pleasant, and when he'd showed up today at Shenstone House, she noticed his beard had been trimmed into something less bushy and wild. He'd looked less like a mountain man and more like a college professor, even though he'd been wearing a plaid flannel shirt and jeans.

Though he didn't have the muscular build Declan had, John Fischer was tall and lanky—without an ounce of fat on him. She wondered how he managed that if he was a writer and spent all day on the computer.

In fact, she thought he'd been about to ask her out when Iva interrupted and changed the subject, giddy with her exploration of the speakeasy. Not that Leslie could blame her.

"Did you ask him about his books?" Orbra demanded. "Did you find out what he's working on next? I'm dying to know whether Bruno Tablenture is going to find out who set him up to die in the last book."

Leslie shook her head, laughing. "No, we didn't talk about his books at all. Are you sure he's really Jeremy Fischer? It seems like he'd at least drop a few hints."

"You know how writers are. All reclusive and secretive," Orbra told her. "Anyway, maybe if you get to know him well enough—hint, hint—you could sneak a peek and see if he has any notes in his bedroom."

"Geez, Orbra." Leslie was appalled. "I hardly know the man and you've already got me in his *bedroom*?"

"Well, if you aren't going to jump in the sack with that massive piece of hotness Declan Zyler, you might as well go for Jeremy Fischer." The tea hostess grinned as Leslie rolled her eyes and turned away.

"You two need to find something else to occupy your time besides my love life. I'm not really interested in getting involved with anyone right now," Leslie said—even though it wasn't quite true. If the right guy came along, she'd get involved.

Now that she had a life, she was ready for a partner to share it.

The problem was, she wasn't sure if she'd know the right guy even if he showed up on her doorstep with flowers and a puppy. She hadn't had a long-term relationship since college; every man she'd date since had been more a convenience than offering a real soul-deep connection.

She wanted what Fiona and Gideon had. And what Iva and Hollis had.

Not just a friends-with-benefits situation, or a hot, sexy fling.

Though a hot, sexy fling might be a nice short-term distraction. Especially if it were with someone like Declan Zyler.

"Leslie?"

She looked up to find Orbra and Cherry laughing at her. Surely they had no idea what she'd been thinking about...did they?

"Don't think I don't remember you reading—and rereading—that old historical romance novel about the blacksmith and the lady of the manor," Cherry said with a wicked glint in her eyes. "I remember that summer you stayed with me after you graduated college—you must've read it three times. What was it called?"

"*Forbidden Love's Caress*," Leslie admitted. "The cover was pretty dog-eared, and no, I don't still have it. But I haven't had much time to read in the last few years—except…well, right after…everything." Her mood settled into something more sober.

"Nothing wrong with a good novel to take your mind off the crap of the world," Orbra said briskly. "Maybe you'll find time to read more again now that you're not flying all over the world and running a corporation."

"It's on my life-improvement list: read more light, fun, sexy novels," Leslie said with a sassy grin.

But Cherry was looking serious. "The fifteenth is Wednesday, isn't it, Les? Do you want to come over so you don't have to be alone? I can get Nolo to take over my classes that night."

Leslie shook her head. "No, that's all right, Aunt Cherry—but thanks. I think I'd just rather be alone." She smiled at the concern on her aunt's face. "I'll be fine. And if I change my mind and want company, I'll put on my yoga clothes and show up at the studio."

"Wouldn't be a bad idea, you know. Stretch out some of those muscles, take your mind off things, even meditate a little. Then we could grab something to eat after."

"I'll keep that in mind," Leslie said.

After that, things started to get a little busier again as the third quarter wound down and people left the stands for more concessions.

By the end of the game, they were out of tea and only had one sleeve of paper cups left. It wasn't until they were loading up Orbra's van that they realized there was no room for both Leslie and Cherry to ride with her.

"I forgot I made two trips," said Orbra, hands on her hips and very displeased at her lack of planning. "But even though we're out of cups, there's not an extra seat—"

"It's fine," Leslie said, waving her off with a smile. "I can walk home. It's only around the corner and up the hill. And it's a nice night."

"Are you sure?" Cherry looked guilty. "We can squeeze in the front passenger seat together. I've got a small butt."

"No, really, it's fine. I don't mind the walk at all. And honestly, I could use some peace and quiet. I love you both, but do you realize—you never stop talking?" She laughed, and the two older ladies looked at each other in mock dismay.

"Promise you'll call when you get home."

"Yada, yada," Leslie said, tugging her hat down over her ears. "See you later."

She hadn't been exaggerating—Shenstone House was only a little more than a mile from the school. But it wasn't until she started on her way, cutting across an expanse of grass toward the road that curved around the rear of the school's property, that Leslie thought of Kristen van Gerste and her ill-fated walk home from her senior prom.

They said her body had been found in the woods—presumably the woods that covered the hillock and area around Shenstone House, butting up against the edge of the high school's sprawling property. The same woods in which Leslie had seen…or thought she'd seen…something move last night.

For some reason, this made her shiver as she walked along the edge of the road, mittened hands tucked in the pockets of her vest. Though the night was clear, and the air was chilly, she found it invigorating.

Behind her, she could hear the sounds of celebration for the home team's victory: shouts, horns honking, music blaring. The noises made her feel less alone, and the illumination from streetlights made large pools of pale yellow light that accompanied her on the way.

Still, there was no one else around on this gravel road, as she headed in the opposite direction to most of the others from the game. Occasionally, a car would drive by without slowing, and she actually found that comforting.

Leslie wondered if this was the exact route Kristen had taken that night, or if she'd cut across yards and lawns toward her house.

Had cars passed her as they did to Leslie? And had Kristen still been wearing her heels, or had she taken them off by now? Was it cold? Was her hair up, or straggling down the back of her neck and over her shoulders? Was she crying or angry or both?

Leslie felt the hair at the back of her neck lifting and prickling as she trudged along, thinking about the eighteen-year-old girl who'd died…all for a necklace of topazes.

A pair of headlights cut like white light through the yellow glow of the streetlights, and Leslie automatically edged to the road's shoulder.

But instead of maintaining its speed, the car—no, it was a van or truck—slowed down, its tires crunching and grinding on the gravel as it came up closer. She moved into the grass, and waited for the vehicle to pick up speed again and pass by safely, but it didn't.

A little frisson of warning had her heart skipping a beat as the truck pulled up right next to her. As she glanced over, the window rolled down.

"Need a ride?"

TEN

WHEN HE WAS SEVERAL YARDS AWAY, driving along the dirt road, Declan spotted Leslie's cobalt-blue vest and the blue and cream hat with its jaunty ball on top.

Thanks to Cherry and Orbra—who had driven past him and Emily as they were walking through the parking lot—he'd not only been sent off in the right direction, but he'd had an excuse not to join Emily and a few other parents for a post-game drink at Trib's.

"Do you mind driving Leslie home?" Cherry had asked. "We didn't have room for her in the van and so she decided to walk." Her eyes glittered with undisguised mischief.

"Not a problem," Declan replied, trying not to sound relieved.

Emily hadn't been too happy about it, and tried to suggest they ride together. "We could drop her off and then meet everyone at Trib's," she said. "It's easier to find parking downtown with only one car."

"That's all right—I'm not sure I'm up for going out tonight," Declan had said, then ducked quickly into his car before Emily could discuss it further.

Damn, he thought as he pulled out of the parking lot. Was he being a jerk, or was it pure self-preservation?

He contemplated those questions with cold objectivity and thought he was allowed to decide whether he wanted to go out or not—even if others had different expectations of him. Then he firmly put the thoughts out of his mind, and a funny spike of anticipation jolted through him as he pulled up next to Leslie.

From the way she half turned yet kept walking, he could tell he'd spooked her—oh hell; that made it twice in one day—when he rolled down the car window.

"Need a ride?"

As soon as he spoke and she recognized him, she stopped and smiled. "Depends who's offering."

"Get in da car, lady," he said in a mock gangster voice. "If you know what's good for you."

"That sounds more like a promise than a threat," she said, climbing in.

Even in the dimness of the car's interior light, he could see the red tip of her nose and the sparkle in her blue eyes. Declan almost reached over and kissed her right then, but held back at the last minute.

"Good game, huh?" he asked casually, tightening his hands on the steering wheel.

"I didn't see much of it. It was pretty crazy inside the tea tent. But from the sounds of it, we did well."

"I was up in the press box for most of the second half—my buddy Brad Beatty covered the game for the paper."

"Wow. He sure gets around. He did the article on me and Shenstone House, and I hear he's also a brewer?"

"That'd be right. Journalist turned entrepreneur. Great guy. The Grand Rapids news station was there too—the sports anchor is an alum. Marcus Levin—used to play football here, I guess. So I might even be on the late night news."

"I'll make sure to watch for you." Her voice was…well, there might have been a hint of flirtation in it.

He glanced over at her and caught a good look at her profile. She was smiling. And such a nice, elegant nose she had. Plus that hat…there was something about the way it looked on her that made him want to cuddle her close in front of a fire. Maybe because it made her seem less like a slick businesswoman and more like a person who would be deadly in a snowball fight.

And maybe one who'd even roll around in the snow afterward. And then have to strip off all the wet clothes when they came inside—

"It was nice of you to give me a ride home. I didn't mind walking, but—"

"Your aunt told me they'd abandoned you, so I thought I'd do the neighborly thing and give you a lift."

"Oh. Thanks."

All of a sudden, she sounded more prim and cool and less warm and friendly. What the hell had he said?

Declan mentally shook his head as he turned onto the tree-shrouded drive that led up the hill to Shenstone House. He just didn't understand women. Half the time he didn't recognize the signals until it was too late, and then when he thought he was reading them right, everything changed. "See any more sign of that cat?"

Leslie made a short, sudden noise. "Oh. I thought you were going to say 'ghost.'" She glanced at him. "I haven't seen either. I hope the cat's all right. It looked pretty bad."

He couldn't help a smile. "Got any more tuna?"

She smiled back just as he pulled up to the back door of the house. Her car was sitting there off to the side, and a generous pool of light spilled into the parking area due to a motion detector.

"Yes, I bought several more cans today, and some cat food too." She shrugged, looking a little embarrassed about her soft heart. "I figure I'll see if I can lure him closer to the house, and maybe he'll become comfortable enough that I can capture him."

He turned off the engine, wondering if that was enough of a hint for her to ask him inside.

All at once, he realized how much he wanted to be invited in. But…he wasn't quite certain how to make it happen.

"Thanks a lot for the ride," she said. And the way her voice trailed off made it sound as if she'd been about to say something else, but changed her mind.

Leslie fumbled for her seatbelt. Declan heard the metallic click as it came loose, and it sounded so sharp and final he was certain he was losing his chance.

But then Fate intervened.

Just as Leslie bent toward the floor for her bag, she stopped short. "Ouch," she said, then reached up with both hands at the far side of her seat's headrest. "Oh, I'm caught."

She was trying to free herself, but her hair had somehow (thank you, Fate) gotten wrapped around the little plastic knob at the top of her seat that acted as a guide for the seatbelt.

"Let me help," Declan said, and leaned toward her.

She was tangled quite well. As he worked to free the thick, shiny lock of hair, feeling his way more than actually able to see what he was doing, Declan discovered her hair was silky and soft, and chilly from the cool night air. And it smelled like Leslie, all mingled with the scent of crisp autumn night that still clung to her from her walk.

He was very close to her—closer than he'd ever been—and her nearness made his big fingers clumsy and his heart race. Her mouth was inches from his cheek, his arm brushed against the front of her down vest—and beneath that was a bulky sweater, and beneath *that,* he was acutely aware, were the curves of her breasts.

"Thanks," she said when her hair was finally emancipated. Her voice sounded lower than usual, and he swore she sounded a little breathy.

"My pleasure," he said, allowing his fingers to smooth along the recently freed lock of hair to the end.

And then before he could think too much about it, his hand slid around the side of her throat to cup the back of her head, and he used his other hand to leverage himself against the car's console so he could get close enough to kiss her. And then he moved in.

To his great pleasure, she didn't resist, didn't even hesitate. Instead, she turned in her seat—the better to face him—and met his mouth with hers.

Her cold nose bumped his cheek, but the warmth from her lips and the slick heat of her tongue sent a jolt of pleasure through him. He sighed in the back of his throat and eased in closer, kissing her more deeply and thoroughly as he drew in her smell, her taste, the warmth of the attraction sizzling between them.

Leslie's hand settled on his thigh as she came forward to meet his deep kiss and demanding mouth, and a shock of desire surged through him. *Yes*, he thought. *Oh, damned* yes.

After a heady moment of sleek tangling of tongues and sliding of lips, she pulled back a little suddenly, muttering, "Wait…aren't you and Emily Dan—"

"No," he said firmly, and pulled her back to him, covering her mouth once more. She softened, and made a soft little sound that made him smile with pleasure against her lips. So he worked a little harder to taste and touch and stroke, closer and slower and with deliberation. He wanted more sounds like that, and other ones…louder, more urgent ones.

At some point, he eased back to catch his breath, to look at her and remind himself how beautiful she was and how lucky he was to be here with her taste on his lips and his hands warm from her body. She opened her eyes, and though the light was dim—and, damn, the windows were a little fogged up!—he caught her gaze in the near-dark and felt another stab of want.

She was a little out of breath too, and he could make out her lips: they were full and moist, parted in a way that looked sexy as hell, and her hat…that adorable hat was askew, ready to slip off the back of her head.

He wanted to invite himself inside, wanted to get back at it—and more—but he hesitated. That little voice in the back of his mind reminded him: *She's the client.*

But he told it to shut the hell up and instead reached out to fix her hat. "Can't remember the last time I made out in a car," he said in a voice much lower than usual.

"It's not very comfortable," she said, with a little smile. "I've got some…some tea inside. And I bought some beer. Would you like to come in?"

Yes. Oh yes indeed. Yes, I would like to come in and try this again, without a damn console or stick shift between us—except for mine—and maybe with fewer clothes. A lot fewer clothes. And no bucket seats. A couch would work…a bed, even better…

But "Yes" was all he said—and then fairly bolted from the car. She'd mentioned *tea* (tea?) and a beer—not a nightcap, not just a dangling, suggestive invite inside…but, nevertheless, a reason for him to come in. A generic reason. Not a winky-wink, "do you want to come inside and finish this up" invitation.

What did that mean? He shifted inconspicuously to adjust his erection to a more comfortable position as Leslie came around from her side of the vehicle.

By the time she got the keys out and let them into the house, Declan's brain—and hormones—had descended from "this is *ah-mazing*: curves, heat, wet, sweet—let's do it!" to a more controlled but no less interested state.

Thus, when the next thing he knew, she was backing him up against the kitchen island and moving right on in, he froze for just a sec. But when Leslie slid right up against him, and the edge of the granite bumped him in the low back, and he was suddenly accosted by soft woman and the interesting scent of chilly autumn air, Declan had no reservations.

He bent to meet her lips and went back into that hot, slick world of sensuality and intensity. But the granite edge bothered him, and the fact that she wasn't damned close enough was even worse…so he caught her by the waist and in one smooth move, turned, lifted, and settled that pretty ass right onto the counter.

And that worked just fine. She laughed a little against his mouth, but her hands were on his shoulders and her fingers tickled his hair, and things were getting even hotter and heavier and more intense when all of a sudden she gasped and tore away.

"Oh my God!" she cried, shoving at him and sliding off the counter in one frantic movement. "Declan!"

He spun, albeit a little slowly because, damn, he'd been *into* her—into the moment, the taste, the heat, the touch…and that was when he saw it: the mess.

Down the hall, beyond the kitchen, and everywhere in between: objects strewn about, chairs on their sides, books on the floor…

Someone—or some*thing*—had been there.

And was very angry.

ELEVEN

LESLIE STUMBLED AWAY from Declan, staring in shock at the disaster that sprawled before her. Every last vestige of pleasure and arousal evaporated as she realized *someone had been here.*

"Declan," she said again, starting down the hallway toward the main foyer. There was not the same upheaval here in the kitchen, but somehow she knew there was more…and it had to be in the front by the staircase and the newly exposed speakeasy room.

To her unabashed relief, he was there, right with her, taking her by the arm as she made her way with staggering, frozen movements. And then she noticed he was pushing past her, gently easing her back as he moved in front of her, and Leslie realized with a nauseating shock that he was worried the someone was still here.

The feminist side of her was annoyed that he pressed ahead, but the shocked and, yes, frightened side was kind of okay with it. So she grabbed his bicep (registering how incredible it was) with both hands and walked next to him just as they came around into the foyer.

It wasn't quite as bad as she'd feared. A sidelight window had been smashed, presumably so the miscreant could reach in to unlock the door. The tarp had been tossed aside, and the demolition debris on it scattered on the floor. The drywall cover to the speakeasy was tossed aside, and had cracked and crumbled at the edges. The table she'd put near the front door was upended, the neat stacks of paint cans toppled, the contents of her toolbox strewn all over the floor.

But nothing significant was destroyed, except—she moaned when she saw it—the brand-new light fixture that had just arrived had been smashed by a randomly flung tool.

"No," she cried, suddenly angry instead of dumbfounded. She'd waited four weeks for that damned piece to ship. "My new sconce!"

Declan had taken her hand, cupping his long, strong fingers around it as he scanned the foyer. She felt the tension in his grip and what was probably anger emanating from him as well.

"I'm going to check upstairs," he said in a low voice.

"I'm coming too," she informed him.

They began to climb the steps and learned that even one of the stairs had been destroyed, shifted out of place, and Leslie nearly fell on her face when she stepped on its loose edge and her foot slipped off. Fortunately, Declan's steady hand kept her from more than a sharp bump when she landed on her shin.

"What the hell," she muttered, getting angrier and angrier. "Vandals? Thieves?"

"Or someone looking for something," he said, still quiet. She felt rather than saw his eyes tracking sharply from side to side, up then down and around, and noticed that he seemed to be straining to listen.

Good idea. *Stop complaining*, she told herself. *Listen. Look around. Pay attention.*

It wasn't the ghost, was it?

The thought struck her like an icy dart. Surely not…surely… not.

Unsettled, she nevertheless pulled her hand from Declan's when they got to the top of the stairs. With a meaningful nod, she indicated for him to go down one hall while she checked the other.

It was to his credit that he didn't suggest they stick together. Apparently, the sight of her holding her cell phone firmly in her hand, its flashlight on but the device itself acting as a makeshift weapon, was enough to clue him in that she wasn't a weak, cowering female. Even though her insides were churning and her knees were a little unsteady.

If it had been the ghost…what did that mean?

If it had been a real flesh and blood mortal…what did *that* mean?

Leslie saw no sign of life as she poked quietly into each room, just as she'd done yesterday when she and Declan had searched for signs of the ghost being a human prank.

"This is getting to be a habit," she muttered when they met up on the balcony.

His lips moved in a wry smile. "It's sure as hell not a habit I'd like to continue. Although…" His eyes narrowed as they settled speculatively on her, and Leslie felt a sudden warm shiver at the expression therein.

She could almost imagine the rest of his unspoken sentence: *Although I can think of another habit I'd like to continue.*

Turning to go back down the stairs, she was both appreciative and a little put off that he hadn't said what they were both thinking. It wasn't the right time to be pursuing such a topic—after all, her house had just been broken into. But she wouldn't have minded hearing it put into words from him, even at such an inappropriate time.

Oh boy. Am I starting to fall for the guy?

"I'm going to check the speakeasy," she announced briskly. "I doubt anyone's still here."

"I tend to agree, but be careful just in case." He was right behind her—and that was where he stayed as she avoided the broken step, curved around at the bottom of the stairs, then ducked and maneuvered her way down the spiral into the speakeasy.

It seemed much darker than before—maybe because it was night and there was little extra light to filter down from the opening above, as during the day. Regardless, Leslie's little cell phone flashlight didn't do a great job of illuminating every corner of the room, but once joined by his, their lights commingled readily and delved into most of the dark corners.

"They—he or she or whoever—were down here," Leslie said unnecessarily. For even though the room had previously showed signs of disarray, it was obvious things had been disturbed here. "The big painting is crooked—oh, and the other one is gone!"

Her voice cracked with shock and anger, but almost immediately eased. "Oh, it's on the floor. They took it down?"

"Looking for a hidden cache or a safe, I bet," Declan said.

"The jewels," she said. "It has to be." She looked at him, allowing the irritation and apprehension to show in her eyes. "That's what comes from articles being splashed all over the paper, I guess. All the treasure hunters come out of the woodwork like—like *spiders*."

Suddenly weary—for what did this mean going forward? more break-ins?—she climbed back up the spiral stairs. Was this only the beginning of treasure hunters? Would every bit of marketing or publicity she did for the bed and breakfast bring out more of the gem seekers?

"Leslie." Declan took her arm as soon as he emerged from the hidden doorway. "You need to report this. And...I don't know if you should stay here alone tonight."

She forced a grin, suddenly fighting the desire to surge into his arms. She really could use a hug—and that was not a usual condition for Leslie van Dorn, badass CEO. "Is that your idea of a good pickup line?"

His smile was a little tight, as if he too were just as worried. But he winked and tucked a piece of hair behind her ear. Even his touch sent a comforting shiver over her shoulders, and his finger strayed along the sensitive skin of her throat. "I wish. Don't forget, I have an impressionable teenage girl at home. I have to set an example."

Leslie felt a tiny twinge of something. Not disappointment, but more like admiration for a man who was willing to put his daughter ahead of his own hormones. "Right. It might be a little hard to explain if you didn't come home tonight. 'Yes, Stephanie, I'm sleeping at your boss's house tonight.'"

He smiled, but it was different this time. Warmer. "If I had it my way, it would be more like 'I'm sleeping *with* your boss tonight,'" he said. He held her eyes with his, the black-flecked green of his irises bold and filled with truth.

To her surprise, Leslie felt her cheeks heat and a flush rise over her chest. "Well, you certainly don't beat around the bush, do you?" she murmured, then gave him a quick, saucy look before turning away.

Reality. Back to reality.

"I'll call the police," she said, looking down at her phone. But before she dialed, she stopped, exhaled, and looked up at him.

He was watching her with a look that made the bottom of her belly drop down low and sharp and deliciously…then it was gone. But the heat still banked behind his eyes when he met hers once more.

"What is it?" he asked, the avid interest fading from his expression.

"You don't think… Well, I suppose there's a chance it was…" She glanced up the stairs as if to see some supernatural manifestation taking shape at the very thought of it.

"The ghost?"

"Yes."

It was his turn to draw in a breath then exhale. "I think it was someone very mortal. I'm not discounting that there's a—a haunting, for lack of a better term. But if you're thinking poltergeist or something like that—"

She was already shaking her head. "No, I don't think it's a poltergeist. Just a plain old unsettled, unhappy ghost. The closest thing to a pubescent girl around here is Stephanie, and she's only been here that once for our interview. That's the way the poltergeists manifest, right? Through hormonal, pubescent—and troubled—young girls."

"That's what they say," he replied. Now it was his turn to glance up the stairs. Then he looked at her. "Whether or not there's really a ghost, I think this mess was made by a person who thinks there's something hidden here. That old legend about Red Eye Sal—I'm assuming you've heard about it."

"Yes, I have. I'm pretty sure those jewels in the paintings in the speakeasy are the ones of legend. There was a topaz necklace that definitely existed—it was stolen about thirty years ago from a high school girl after her prom."

Declan frowned. "I think I remember hearing about that. A friend of mine's brother use to tease us about going into the woods at night, telling us that was where a girl got strangled or something."

Leslie shivered, suddenly very cold. Her fingers felt like ice. All at once, everything felt so repressive here in this unsettled foyer, with the open speakeasy doorway leading down into darkness, and the place in shambles—a sign of ugliness and violation. It struck her so sharply that she felt a nauseating chill and eerie, hair-raising sensation.

She glanced toward the top of the stairs and stilled. Her breath caught, and she grabbed blindly for Declan. Was that a faint light? Something shimmering?

"Leslie?"

She exhaled. Nothing was there. Or…whatever had been there, ever so faint, was gone. "Let's sit down," she said, and abruptly turned. The kitchen, she hoped, would be more inviting. At least it was *her* place, her space: rebuilt, reconditioned, and stamped with her own intention and caring.

"You're going to call the police now, right?"

"Yes. Yes, I'll do that." She made good on her words, sitting at the sturdy kitchen table—thank God whoever broke in hadn't dared to inflict damage on her beautiful table.

Declan had gone to the fridge—the stainless steel side-by-side big enough to hold a horse—and opened it. "Beer? Or do you have wine—or even better, whiskey? Might be just what you need. A little toddy in your tea." He glanced around to give her a reassuring grin, but before she could respond, the police station answered her call and she had to give it her full attention.

To her shock and utter embarrassment, as Leslie began to form the words "My house was broken into," her voice stretched and broke, and she felt tears burn the back of her throat. It was as if by saying the words, it had become permanent. Real. Inescapable. *Someone had come into her home.*

But by the time she finished the call, her tones were firmly back to confident business mode. She felt a little foolish for showing such weakness at the beginning, but then again…she'd been violated. Her home, her space, her world had been violated.

"Try this." Declan set a cup in front of her. It was steaming, and it smelled really good—of cinnamon and cardamom, honey, and some very strong liquor. "I—uh—used one of those chai tea things for your coffee maker, and added a good dollop of whiskey and honey and lemon."

Leslie took a sip, and her eyes widened. It was good. Really good. And the whiskey…it burned delicately through her body, having the immediate effect of relaxing her. It was almost as warm and luscious as Declan's kisses. The thought of that added desperately needed warmth and pleasure to the moment.

"I took the liberty of calling your aunt," he said, leaning against the island. He had a longneck in his large, freckled hand, and Leslie felt a spark of affection that he'd made her a fancy drink and settled for his own twist-off beer. "She's coming over."

"I'll bet she is," Leslie said wryly, and took another fortifying sip.

"Listen, Leslie…I hate to bring this up, but…Brad's article about you and the bed and breakfast. That was published *before* we found the speakeasy."

She nodded slowly. "I know. Obviously whoever broke in here knew about it—where it was. How to find it. Which could be good or bad, I guess," she said, heaving a sigh. "Good in that it would limit the intruder to being someone in a defined group— someone who heard about the hidden room within the last day or two. Bad because…well…"

"Yeah." He drummed one set of fingers on the granite island. "So who knew about it? Besides me, of course." His grin was a little crooked, but his eyes were serious. "And I didn't mention it to anyone except Brad, just casually—and that was tonight, while we were up in the press box during the second half of the game."

So he'd been talking about her to Brad Beatty, had he? Leslie's whiskey-softened thoughts swam into a contented little cove and nestled there as she drank again from the spiked tea. Then she was dashed with cold water and brought abruptly back to the ugliness at hand.

"Who knew about it? Well, Aunt Cherry and Orbra, of course. And Iva Nath and presumably her husband Hollis—you don't know them, but they're friends of mine and of Cherry and Orbra's. Small world, running into them here," she added. "The Underwhites and Trib. They were all there when I was telling Cherry and Orbra about it—the day you and I found it. Later that night we were all at Trib's." She frowned. "I can't think of anyone—oh, wait, the man who's staying at Sunflower House. John Fischer. I guess he's really the author Jeremy Fischer, who writes—"

"The Bruno Tablenture books? Really? He's here in Sematauk?"

"That's what the rumor is. He and Iva came over today, to look at the speakeasy—so they actually saw how I opened up the door and went down." Leslie bit her lip. "A famous writer wouldn't jeopardize his career by breaking into a house, would he? Plus, why would he need the gems anyway—he's got to be doing pretty well with all those movie deals and a new release every year."

"Right," he said very casually. "Was there anyone else here at the time who might have seen the opening to the speakeasy? Any contractors? The UPS guy—did he deliver your light fixture? Anyone?"

She shook her head. "No. Even Iva's husband Hollis didn't come—not that I would suspect them for even a minute. Iva's all about the ghosts and Hollis only cares about his law firm—and her."

"You said you knew them from somewhere?" Declan glanced at his beer bottle, holding it up as if to read the label. Yet Leslie got the distinct impression he was more interested in her answer than where the IPA was brewed.

"From Philadelphia—I used to live there till I moved here."

Declan looked as if he were about to say something else, but just then they heard the sound of crunching gravel. Light scanned the parking area outside the kitchen window as the police car came around the driveway bend and turned to park next to Declan's car.

Leslie stood and went to meet the police. As she opened the door, something moved—streaking from the door to around the house. It took her a moment to realize it had been the butterscotch cat—but only after she swallowed her heart back into place.

Officer Morton introduced himself with a pleasant smile and handshake. As he preceded Leslie into the kitchen, he commented that he'd known Cherry for years because his wife took yoga classes from her. He was a big, lumbering man of about fifty whose figure went in a ruler-straight line from back of skull to heel, and curved out in a gentle arc in the front. His uniformed profile made the shape of a D.

"Anything missing?" he asked after he'd been shown around, settled at the kitchen table, and given a cup of coffee. Decaf.

"Not that I've noticed. I'll have to take a closer look... *Wait.*" Leslie's eyes widened. She shot to her feet. "Wait a second..."

She hurried out of the kitchen to the front entrance, frowning. When was the last time she'd seen the pink velvet wrap and glove she'd found inside the base of the stair rail? She'd folded them up, hadn't she? And put them on the table in the front hall...

But the table had been knocked over.

"There *is* something missing," she said, returning to the kitchen, still pondering. "Why would anyone take an old velvet stole?" She explained about what she'd found to Declan and the officer. "And if that's what they were after—well, it was easy to find. The stole and the glove were sitting right there in plain sight. But I have no idea why anyone would want an old, worn stole."

"Aren't vintage clothes worth a lot of money?" Declan asked. "Especially that crystal button on it—maybe it *was* a real diamond or gemstone of some type. Maybe the intruder—I guess we can call him a thief now—broke in for some other reason, but saw the wrap and decided to take it too."

"I don't think that wrap was worth anything. Besides, it was in bad shape—old and frayed. The button was probably just fake bling. And the fabric was stained with that same rust-like corrosion that's been discoloring the stair railing. At least it looked like it."

"When was the last time you remember seeing it? Are you sure it was still on the table?" asked Officer Morton. "Think back to the last time you know you saw it."

"I'll have to think about it…I'll be honest. My brain is a little fried right now. I put it on the table so I'd remember to take it into town—I wanted to show it to Gilda at the vintage clothes store to see if she could date it."

The sound of another car approaching—no, two of them—drew their attention to the kitchen door and the window next to it.

"That'll be Aunt Cherry, and if I'm not mistaken, Orbra too," Leslie said wearily. Quite frankly, if she couldn't be alone, the only person she really wanted to be with right now was Declan. At least she wouldn't have to answer a thousand questions. A thousand questions that were now going to include not only ones about the break-in, the speakeasy, and her mental health, but also about Declan.

Ugh.

"Do you think it's safe for me to stay here tonight?" Leslie asked, rising to open the door for the new arrivals.

"No."

"Yes."

The first answer was Declan, the second Officer Morton.

"Not alone, anyway," Declan said flatly.

The policeman glanced at him, pursed his lips, then said, "They're gone now. If they'd intended any harm, the intruder or intruders would either have stayed hidden—and not otherwise advertised their presence by creating such a disturbance—or have made their move by now. I'm not trying to trivialize the break-in, but I'm leaning toward it being a couple of teenagers messing around, since nothing of value seems to have been taken."

"Even though more than half the town and pretty much all of the school was just at the football game?" Declan asked coolly.

Morton shrugged. "All the more reason to take the opportunity, since no one would be home. Honestly, Ms. van Dorn, teenagers have been breaking into this house for as long as I can remember. Even I did it. There's something about the place that draws the interest."

Cherry and Orbra had entered the kitchen without speaking so as not to interrupt the conversation, though both of their faces held strains of worry. Leslie smiled up at her aunt as she patted her shoulder, then took a seat at the table.

Just then, the sounds of "Brown Eyed Girl" bubbled up into the room. Leslie looked over as Declan, whose cheeks were a little ruddier, snatched up his phone.

Leslie bid Officer Morton goodbye, and agreed to come to the station to fill out paperwork and make her official report the next day. "I hope you're right that it was just a couple of teenagers," she said, walking him to the door.

"Let me know if something else turns up missing. Other than that, we'll go with that assumption. Good night, Ms. van Dorn."

By the time Leslie returned to the table, Declan had hung up his phone. "That was Stephanie. She's spending the night at a friend's house tonight." His words were casual, so surely Leslie was the only one who noticed the disappointment in his tones.

Their eyes met briefly, then he eased his chair from the table and stood. "Well, I guess I'll hit the road—if you're sure you're all right here?"

"I've got my chaperones," Leslie replied brightly. But she'd chosen the word purposely to express her own chagrin at the situation—if Stephanie had only called thirty minutes earlier!—and he recognized it, rolling his eyes in agreement. "See you later. Thanks for the ride home. Oh, and watch for the butterscotch cat."

By the time she'd walked *him* to the door—chancing only a brief, subtle brush of fingers to express their mutual sentiment—Leslie turned to find Orbra and Cherry were fluttering around the kitchen—the former making tea (more tea? She'd be up all night!) and the latter digging through the fridge ("Don't you have anything in here for green smoothies? No kale? You could use a burst of energy, Les").

But as soon as the door was closed and locked and Leslie pushed none too gently into her chair, they were on her. And the first question out of Cherry's mouth, of course, was: "Are you having sex with that man? Because if you aren't, there is something *very* wrong with you, Leslie Annette!"

"But more importantly," Orbra said, fairly slamming a mug onto the table in front of her, "why the hell did you send him *home*?"

TWELVE

DECLAN WAS HOT, sweaty, and his eyeballs were dry and burning behind their protective guard. His bandanna was soaked, his leather gloves suffocating, his ears ringing with the metallic clank of metal on metal.

But he loved every minute of it: the rhythmic *clang-clang-clang* whenever he was hammering on a piece of iron, the way its fired end glowed like an asteroid, the way it made such a satisfactory zip-like sizzling sound whenever he plunged it into a tub of water.

He didn't mind that he tasted salt whenever he paused to think and plan the angle of the next blow, and how many more strikes until the curve would be just right. He didn't mind the smell of his sweat—the clean scent of good, hard work—for it was the sign of a job in process. Of creation.

And the heat…well, he didn't mind that either, because pretty much everywhere else on earth was cooler than his workshop, so the minute he stepped out of the place, it was a relief. Sure, the occasional sears he got when he wasn't paying attention, or the random sparks that flew and landed on, say, the side of his neck or chin—the only parts that were really exposed—were an annoyance. But all in all, blacksmithing was a great occupation.

He got to take out any aggressions he might have—and there were days when he had *many*—on whatever iron bar he was forcing into shape. And then there were days like today, Saturday, when he was in a great mood and the rhythm of his hammer striking the heated iron bar fell in blows that matched whatever song was in his head.

Literal heavy metal music.

He grinned to himself at the old blacksmith's joke and slid back into AC/DC's classic "You Shook Me All (strike!) Night (strike!) Long (strike, strike, strike!)."

For some reason, that tune brought to mind Leslie van Dorn: celebrity CEO, cat lover, wordsmith, and ghost hunter. And magnificent kisser. Oh, indeed.

He pretty much hadn't stopped thinking about those few moments of bliss, with her legs wrapped around his waist as she perched on the counter in her kitchen and gave it back as good as she got. Hoo boy. He was hoping to finish this piece of the railing so he could have a reason to stop by and show—

"*Dad!*"

Declan abruptly returned to the moment, his goofy grin fading when he realized Stephanie had been standing there, trying to get his attention, for quite some time. He'd warned her not to startle him when he was working, and had shown her where in the workshop was the safe area in which she could stand.

He lifted the hand holding his hammer in a "wait a sec" gesture, then gave one final *clang* and nodded with satisfaction at the nice curve that was taking shape. Then he shoved it back into the brick-oven forge for a few.

Turning back around, he stripped off his goggles and, stepping away from the work area, pulled off his heavy gloves and the heavy canvas work apron, hanging them in their places. Immediately, he was cooler—for beneath he was only wearing one of his old tees that had the sleeves torn off and most of the sides as well, for ventilation.

He snagged a towel and mopped off his face—and that was when he realized two of Stephanie's friends were with her. They (not his daughter, thank God) were staring at him with, he suspected, the same sort of goofy expression he'd just had thinking about Leslie van Dorn's sweet ass settling on the granite while he kissed the life out of her.

He paused from mopping the sweat off his face, and realized one of the girls was Emily Danube's daughter Brooklyn. She was ogling his sweaty biceps like she wanted to dry them off herself.

Good Lord. He sure as hell hoped he was mistaken about that.

"What's up?" He spun, walking over to turn down the volume of *Back in Black*, one of his favorite albums to crank up while he was working—and to put some space between him and the groupies.

"Here, Dad," Stephanie said, and shoved a button-down shirt at him. Christ, was she embarrassed too? But he could relate. It must be like the time she was walking toward him on the beach in one of those damn little bikinis the girls all seemed to wear now and he got to watch how all the young men noticed her as she strolled by.

Mortifying.

"Thanks. What's up?" he asked again, acutely aware of the blushes—yet avid looks—that had colored the faces of his daughter's friends. Awk-*ward*, as Steph would say. He began to struggle into the shirt—which was easier said than done, considering how damp and sweaty he was.

"We're leaving, Dad! I just came to let you know. You'll be at Paul Hammady's house by six, right?"

He realized for the first time that his daughter's hair was twisted up in a fancy style for which he'd paid an unreal amount of money, and that she was holding a garment bag and a pair of impossibly high-heeled shoes. *You're going to break your neck walking in those*, he wanted to say. *Forget about dancing.* But he didn't. He was still feeling his way around as the new dad, and wasn't completely certain what his boundaries were—both in general, and in front of her friends.

God help him if she ever got a boyfriend.

Which…would be over his dead body. At least until she was thirty.

Fortunately, she didn't have an official date for tonight's dance. It was just a group of friends—both guys and gals—eating dinner, then going together. He heartily approved.

"Right. I'll be there. Six o'clock at Hammadys' house. You left me the address?"

"I texted it to you *yesterday*, Dad."

"Right. Thanks. Okay, I'll see you then."

"I guess all the parents are going out for dinner after," Stephanie added with a sly look after her friends had stepped out of earshot. "I told Brooklyn's mom you'd definitely want to go."

"All right. Thanks," he said, then, despite the stinky sweatiness of himself, gave her a good smacking kiss on the cheek. "I'll see you there. You look great so far. I can't wait to see you in your dress."

"Thanks, Dad," she said, smiling. "And by the way," she said, leaning toward him with a furtive glance toward her friends' backs, her brow furrowing with disgust, "you should know they were creeping pics of you on their cell phones while you were working. I just hope they don't tag me when they post them online."

What? Holy crap—*post them online? What the hell?*

But Declan couldn't even get the words out—he didn't even know where to begin—before Stephanie was gone.

How did this happen to me? he wondered, turning around aimlessly. *How did I get to be the father of a teenager whose friends take pictures of me* on their cell phones?

His face was hot and flaming now, and it had nothing to do with the furnace or his work. Sonofabitch, if Brad ever heard about this, he was never going to live it down. If Emily Danube found out... Good God. Or Leslie...

Jesus. I need a damned beer.

But the forge was calling him, and if he got back to it, he could finish the main curve of that piece before he had to get in the shower and make himself presentable for the Homecoming Dance picture fest. As that might take some time, he mused, he figured he'd better get back to work.

—⚒—

By the time Declan emerged from his work, it was almost five. He swore when he saw the time—and the number of texts and voice mails that had come through while he was jamming to AC/DC and Coldplay.

At first, his heart leaped into his throat when he saw all of them from Stephanie, and a few calls and texts from a number that was familiar but he didn't recognize. What had happened?

But he calmed down after he realized if something was really wrong, someone would have come pounding on the door of the workshop…and then he smiled. The familiar number might be Leslie van Dorn's. It probably was, after all, checking in after last night…

Like a responsible father, though, he read the six texts from Stephanie first.

Mrs. Danube's car won't start. She really wants to be here for the pics. I told her you'd pick her up. Okay, Dad? Followed by winky face and laughing face.

The rest of the texts were along the same line: *Dad? Can you please get back to her? I told her you'd pick her up.*

Where are you????????? You get mad if I don't answer YOUR texts right away!

And so on.

And the semi-familiar number…not Leslie van Dorn, but Emily Danube.

With a sigh, Declan responded to Emily's text. *Sure. I'll be there at 5:50 to pick you up. Sorry for delay. Was working.*

Emily responded immediately with her thanks, and that she'd see him then.

Dec managed to put away his work, shower, shave, pick out something decent to wear, and get out the door just in time. It was only then he realized he hadn't eaten since the coffee and peanut-butter-slathered toast he'd had at eight that morning. A two-dollar granola bar would be pretty good about now—but he'd left without snagging one. If there were even any left.

And he was almost to Emily's when he remembered he hadn't brought the piece he'd been working on that he wanted to show Leslie.

"Thank you so much for picking me up!" Emily said breathlessly as she climbed into his truck in a waft of perfume. She smiled at him as she buckled the seatbelt around a trim waist below great tits showcased in a black V-neck tee. She wore a black leather jacket too—for, of course, Michigan had shifted her mood from bitterly cold to pleasantly cool since last night. "Britney would have been so disappointed if I wasn't there to take pictures. You know how they are about things like this."

Right. The girls who had cell phone cameras attached to their hands like another appendage and took photos of everything would have been traumatized if their parents missed the chance to take even more pictures of them…

But Declan didn't say a thing. He was *happy* to go and take pictures of Stephanie and her friends tonight—and even more happy that she'd *asked* him to. He just found it amusing that anyone would think the moment would be lost if one parent missed the photo-taking opportunity.

"What's wrong with your car?" he asked.

"I'm not really sure," she said. "It wouldn't start, and then it kind of did and then sounded really rough…I thought it might be better if I didn't try and drive it tonight. Just in case I couldn't get it started when it was time to go home after dinner. You don't mind driving me back after, do you?"

Uh. "Sure. No problem," he said before he realized what he'd just committed to. "We'll get you home," he added vaguely.

Hell, he hadn't even planned to go to dinner with the other parents after the picture taking…but then again, it would be a good idea to get to know the parents of the kids his daughter was hanging around with. And, of course, he was a small business owner, and you never knew where your next job was going to come from. And he hadn't eaten, so he'd be ravenous by then (how long did these picture-taking events take, anyway?).

Still…Declan had an uneasy sense that he'd just been neatly manipulated into a situation he didn't really want to be in.

He just hoped he'd have the chance to see Leslie as soon as he could escape from the clutches of teenager fatherhood.

Leslie clawed herself out of a deep sleep and looked groggily at the clock. Six.

She blinked, combing through the heavy shroud of sleep with effort. It took her more than a moment to assimilate that it was six *p.m.,* not six a.m.

No, she'd already seen six a.m. today, unfortunately. She'd been more wide awake then than now.

Leslie sagged back onto her pillow, trying to work the sleep from her eyes and clear her thoughts. That was what happened when you took a three-hour nap late in the day—it didn't want to let you go because it thought you wanted to sleep for a full seven or eight.

Nevertheless, five minutes later, she was in the shower and fully awake. And her mind was filled with thoughts of the events of yesterday and today.

She'd sent Orbra and Cherry home last night after one o'clock. "There's no need for you to stay here. Officer Morton said he didn't think there's anything to worry about."

"But the broken window!"

"You can help me tape it up and then go on home. I'm going to lock everything up, set the exterior lights to stay on, put in earplugs, and have a good shot of whiskey. I'll sleep like a baby."

The two older ladies grumbled and argued, and didn't agree to leave until Leslie faked them out by looking at her cell phone and pretending to have a text from Declan on it. She let them draw their own conclusions, but noticed it was a lot easier to get them to leave after that.

Then she did as she told them she would: fixed the lights to stay on, locked up tightly, installed earplugs, a sleep mask— and even turned on some white noise on her computer monitor. This was going to be her first night in the house since the ghost's appearance Wednesday, and Leslie was completely fine if she slept through any supernatural activity.

She really did agree with Morton that it had been a couple of teenagers who'd broken in, and was certain no one would be coming back. It was already after one thirty.

But the best laid plans…

Leslie had fallen asleep. She was certain she had, for all at once she was awake.

Damn, she thought, her heart pounding as she felt… *something*. She'd closed the door to her office/bedroom suite. But when she got out of bed, she saw a faint light glowing beneath it. Her heart lurched up into her throat, but Leslie pulled out her earplugs and opened the door.

The chill filling the kitchen felt sharp and abrupt as she stepped out of her suite, and the soft sounds of music drew her toward the greenish-yellow light down the hall to the foyer.

Heart thudding, hands cold and damp, cell phone in hand (she had no idea why), Leslie padded silently and slowly toward the illumination. This time, when she came around the corner, the *thing* was not at the top of the steps, hovering on the balcony. Instead, it shimmered halfway up the staircase.

It stood there, silent and still. Through the terror she couldn't quite control, Leslie discerned a shape. Tall, slender, willowy…it was a woman, in a long, slender gown that brushed her at mid-calf.

"What do you want?" Leslie asked, ruthlessly keeping her voice from shaking.

The image shimmered, shifted, and one hand lifted and pointed down the stairs…toward her. The face had eyes that glowed with anger, and the woman's ghostly mouth opened in a large, dark rictus as she suddenly swirled into a ball of light and glitter and *roared* down the stairs toward Leslie. The sound of a scream—high and shrill, and yet dark and deep—filled her ears, echoing in the high-ceilinged foyer, reverberating throughout the house as the ball of light and spirit came toward her.

Leslie gasped and stumbled backward, bumping her head against the wall behind her as an unimaginable cold embraced her, filling her with ice and paralyzing her as if she'd been encased in an iceberg.

She couldn't move, and all at once felt a rage and a fear rushing through her, squeezing and filling and heavy—

And then it was gone. Silent. The air was still. The world was no longer frigid. The room was dark.

And she could move.

Leslie staggered to her feet, panting, sweating, eyes wide, her phone forgotten on the floor.

"But you damn well didn't *answer* me!" she shouted. "I can't help you if you won't—tell—me—what you *need*!" Her voice was unsteady as violent tremors suddenly overtook her. Her knees gave way and she sank back to the floor. *Holy crap. Hohhhly* crap.

Her phone was there, and she picked it up, ready to dial…

Who?

No. She wasn't going to call anyone. She didn't need anyone to help her. It was only a ghost. It had done nothing but terrorize the hell out of her, but she'd met executive board members who did that.

Leslie grinned weakly in the darkness. Once more, she pulled herself to her feet. This time, she walked out into the foyer and stood in the center of the room, looking around. Her hands were still shaking. It was still dark, for she hadn't turned on the lights. The debris from the break-in had been cleared away, so she wouldn't step or trip on anything.

"Why the hell didn't you come out like that when they were breaking in tonight?" she demanded. "Maybe they wouldn't have made such a mess!"

Silence.

Stillness.

Not even a shift in the air.

Leslie heaved a great sigh. "I guess you're only a once-a-night trick, aren't you, whoever you are?" she said, still to the room at large. "And thanks to you, I don't think I'm going to be going back to sleep anytime soon."

She turned, making her way to the kitchen, still holding her phone. As she came into the room, warmly lit by one soft light under the counter, her attention flitted automatically over the windows and stopped short at the sight of a black shadow *right there*.

Leslie gathered up to shriek, then immediately deflated. "It's just the cat," she told herself out loud.

The cat?

The one that had run away every time she came outside? It was sitting on the flower box right outside the window, looking in at her as if it had every right to be there. She couldn't tell the color of its eyes, but they glinted as it looked arrogantly at her.

Leslie stared back at it for a moment, the trembling of her hands finally beginning to subside. "Well…all right, then. Fine. I could use some company."

And that was how she'd ended up with a cat in the house that night. Surprisingly enough, once she opened the door and set down an open can of tuna mixed with cat food, the feline deigned to enter the kitchen and sample the gourmet offering.

Leslie sat at the kitchen table and watched it eat, her bare toes cold and her body still wanting to shiver violently beneath the boxers and t-shirt she wore. She snagged a hoodie and pulled it on and made herself another cup of tea.

"I guess it's time for me to do some research," she said to the cat—who indicated its disinterest by remaining bluntly tail-side toward her and finishing its meal.

The poor thing's tail was half hacked off, with the top third hanging on by a thread. But the creature didn't let that imperfection, nor the matting of its long hair, affect its arrogance.

"I sure hope you don't have fleas," she said, realizing belatedly that maybe it hadn't been the best idea to let the thing inside. But there was something comforting about having another living thing here with her—as opposed to whatever *un*living thing had been screaming at her in the foyer a few minutes ago. Her palms went damp again at the thought.

And so she allowed the cat to stay while she pored over her laptop at the kitchen table—searching for information about anything that might explain a ghostly presence at Shenstone House—till the wee hours of the morning. When she finally stood, stretching her aching muscles and yawning, the cat padded softly to the door in an unmistakable command. Its flag-like tail twitched impatiently.

"Very well then," she said, and let him—she'd determined its gender when the beast had plopped onto the floor and yanked up a leg to wash itself with a complete lack of modesty—out. "See you…whenever. Thanks for keeping me company."

Dawn had broken and Leslie looked longingly at her bed, but she knew she wouldn't sleep—her mind was too keyed up, too awake. So she decided to clean up the speakeasy.

"Maybe I'll find something that gives me a clue down there." And now that it was daylight, she didn't expect any ghostly presences.

She worked down there all day, pausing only to check her phone a few times for texts or calls. There were several from Cherry and Orbra, to which she replied that, yes, she was still alive, and no, no one had broken in. There were no calls or texts from Declan, but she hadn't really expected any. Really. As far as he knew, her aunt had planned to spend the night and Leslie wouldn't be alone.

Stephanie wasn't coming over to work today either because it was the Homecoming Dance, and she needed all day to get ready—an opinion Leslie readily shared and supported. So she worked without interruption: cleaning, clearing out, organizing the place.

To her delight, she discovered more vintage clothing: a pair of shoes, two scarves, and something that looked like a woman's dinner jacket from the Roaring Twenties—a long, loose coat that a flapper might wear over one of the beaded shift dresses that were popular. The one she discovered was made of silk with incredible beading and embroidery. It looked like it could have belonged to the fictional detective Phryne Fisher.

There were other vintage objects, many of them recoverable: pillows, knickknacks, glassware, and even a jeweled hair comb. There were four unopened bottles of whiskey, and countless broken ones. She eyed the untapped bottles and wondered if any of them were any good. Maybe Trib would know.

What she didn't find was a safe or cache where Red Eye Sal might have hidden his jewels. And though she'd learned quite a bit about his history during her searches on the Internet, there was still a question as to what had happened to all of the jewels.

All the while she worked, Leslie blasted music. It helped to keep away stray thoughts of supernatural occurrences, and it kept her motivated and awake. But by two o'clock, her energy was lagging. She'd eaten a snack midmorning, but now she stopped and had a full meal, answered some email, put a new can of tuna outside for the cat, and then…took a blissful nap.

Now that she was showered and fully awake, Leslie decided to take the vintage clothing to Gilda's Goodies and see if the proprietor was interested in them—and whether they could even be salvaged enough to sell. She called Gilda Herring, using Aunt Cherry as a reference, and the proprietor was ecstatic at the thought of seeing some vintage twenties clothing.

"The shop closes at six on Saturdays during off-season," Gilda told her, "but I'll be here till at least eight. Come on over."

The cat—at some point, she'd begun to think of him as Rufus—eyed her speculatively as she climbed into her car, but made no move to gain entrance to either the house or vehicle, despite the fact that he should have been groveling in thanks for the tuna. The can had been licked clean.

"See you later," she said, then drove down the curving, tree-shrouded drive. It wasn't quite seven, but it was already nearly dark. Leslie had left the exterior lights on, and several more inside the house than she normally would have done. She knew she didn't want to return to a black-windowed building.

Gilda didn't look anything like Leslie had imagined. She was probably mid-forties, had sleek blond hair cut in a short, trendy style, and wore a dress that looked like it was from the forties. Showing off Gilda's goodies, of course.

"Let's see what you've got here," Gilda said, her eyes gleaming from behind lipstick-red cat's-eye glasses…and she moaned with pleasure when she saw the dinner jacket. "Where did you *find* this?"

Leslie explained, and all the while Gilda was humming and sighing over the detail stitching and beading and sequins. "This is just gorgeous. Needs a little recovery work," she muttered to herself, "but I can do that. I wouldn't trust it to anyone else."

She looked up suddenly. "I have to be honest, Leslie. Something like this probably belongs in a museum. Though I'd love to have it in my shop." She grinned and bit her lip as she looked back down at the jacket. "We could sell a piece like this for probably about a thousand dollars."

Leslie's eyes widened. "I figured it might be worth a couple hundred…but wow. Let me think about that. In the meantime, can I pay you to restore it and get it back to shape?"

"It would be a pleasure— Oh, Regina!" Gilda looked up as the mayor's wife poked her head into the office. "I wasn't expecting to see you tonight." She smiled.

"I know," said Regina. "But I was in the area and wanted to check up on that piece you're fixing for me. Hello, Leslie. Oooh, where did you get that?" She'd seen the dinner jacket spread out on the table. "That's incredible."

"I know." Gilda was gleeful as she explained where Leslie had found it. "I'm thinking late twenties. Maybe 1927. It could *possibly* be a Worth, you know. They weren't putting tags on everything at that time."

"If it's a Worth, it would definitely belong in a museum," Regina said. Her slender hand hovered over the silk, then dropped slightly—just enough to brush it with the tips of her fingers. "But I'd buy it in a heartbeat if it was available." She looked up at Leslie. "It would have gone perfectly with that vintage dress Kristen van Gerste wore to prom. But she didn't have anything like this." Sadness lingered in her eyes.

"Speaking of Kristen van Gerste," Gilda said, pulling out some tissue paper. "I heard Marcus Levin was back in town for the game last night. He did an interview with some of the alumni who played football."

"He is, and he did," Regina said, watching with interest as Gilda wrapped the dinner jacket in tissue paper. "We had dinner with him, Aaron and I—after the game, of course. It's always nice to see former residents—especially ones who are now celebrities." She laughed. "Aaron is very good about reminding them about where they came from, and how much we depend on tourism here in town."

"Marcus Levin? Why is that name familiar to me?" asked Leslie.

"He was the boy Kristen van Gerste had the big shouting match with at the prom," Gilda replied, smoothing the tissue paper over the jacket. "Is he still as much of an ass as he was back then?"

"If he is, he hid it quite well beneath a very polished exterior," Regina said.

Gilda burst out laughing. "Well, there's my politically correct mayor's wife!" She slid her hands beneath the tissue-wrapped jacket and folded the whole thing into thirds. Then she carried it with great reverence to a shelving unit and placed it there. "I should be able to get to it next week. Is that soon enough, Leslie?"

"Oh, sure. That's fine. I'm not in any hurry."

"So you didn't find any sign of Red Eye Sal's gems down in that speakeasy?" Regina said. She leaned against Gilda's desk, crossing her arms over her tailored suit.

"Nothing," Leslie said. "Not even a safe or cache where they could have been hidden. But I did find a pink velvet wrap. I wanted to bring it in for you to look at, Gilda, but it's gone missing."

"Gone missing?" Gilda frowned.

"Don't tell me it was stolen! Leslie had a break-in last night," Regina said to Gilda, then turned back to Leslie. "I'm sorry, maybe I shouldn't have mentioned it, but I heard about it. Small town, you know. I'm very glad you're all right, and that nothing else seems to have been taken."

"Thank you." Leslie smiled, but was a little put off by the fact that her business seemed to be so well known. "Well, the velvet wrap and a glove are missing, and I'm not sure whether they were taken then or not. But I was hoping you could date it for me. Not that it matters now anyway."

"Well, a couple rules of thumb, just in case you find something else," Gilda said. "First, look for machine serge stitching—see, like this. Although it can be found as early as the 1920s, it wasn't all that common until the latter part of last century. And the tag, of course—any care instructions would be after 1971, so that's an easy one. Any tags that are black and white would be before, say, 1930. That's a place to start. Rayon—that's popular from 1920s through World War II; nylon became popular after that. If there are undergarments, you aren't going to see plastic boning or hardware until much later. It'll be metal." She paused and looked up as if startled. "Maybe a little more than you wanted to know. But maybe that helped? Do you remember anything about the velvet wrap?"

Leslie and Regina exchanged amused glances. "I didn't see any tags on it, but I didn't look that closely. It had a large crystal button for a fastener on it—just one in the front, I remember that." Leslie shrugged. "I had put it aside to examine later, and then never got to it. I'll keep that information in mind if I find something else."

"Let me know if I can be of any help. But in the meantime—I'm starving," Gilda said. "Want to come grab a burger at The Owl's Roost with me, Leslie? It should be cleared out of Homecoming Dance students by now. I'd ask Regina, but burgers aren't quite her style."

"I'd love to. I haven't eaten much all day," Leslie replied. "You sure you don't want to come, Regina?"

"Reggie won't. She refuses to step foot in the Roost," Gilda said with a grin. "Says the wine isn't even a step up from Boone's. What a snob."

"I've got to meet Aaron anyway," Regina said. "I just wanted to check in to see if you needed me for a fitting on that dress."

"Probably not till Monday," replied Gilda.

"No problem. I'll see you then."

Leslie waited while the shopkeeper locked up, checking her cell phone to make sure she hadn't missed any calls. She had to admit she was a teeny bit disappointed Declan hadn't reached out even by text all day…but then she remembered it was Homecoming. He'd probably been busy schlepping Stephanie around and hadn't had a chance to even think of Leslie.

"I can't believe how much warmer it is tonight than last night," she said as they walked along the sidewalk. "I was in mittens and goose down and a big hat at the game."

"That's Michigan for you," Gilda said. "Tomorrow we could have eighty-degree weather. You never know."

"Wow. Trib's is hopping tonight," Leslie said as they approached and noticed people waiting outside to be seated.

"It's Saturday, and Homecoming. All of the kids would have eaten there, and then gone on to the dance—leaving the adults to have to wait till later. That's why I suggested the Roost."

And apparently, the adults were just getting seated, for as Leslie walked by, she glanced in the large front window just in time to see a smiling, laughing Declan pulling out a chair for an equally smiling and laughing Emily Danube…in a very tight, very low-cut black t-shirt.

Well. That explained why she hadn't heard a thing from him all day.

THIRTEEN

I N SPITE OF THE VERY UNPLEASANT shock of seeing Declan cozying up with Emily Danube (she *had* asked him if he was seeing her, hadn't she? and he *had* responded with a firm "No," hadn't he?), Leslie had an enjoyable time at The Owl's Roost.

The place was a dive—that was the only way to describe it. The floor was shiny from decades of spilled beer and countless shoes scuffing it, with peanut shells crushed into dust filling in many of the cracks. Every table had its own set of graffiti: carved or written with a variety of implements. Leslie was a little leery about even putting her hands on the sticky table, so she was relieved when the server brought over large paper placemats.

The wall was decorated with movie posters from the seventies through the nineties, each one stuck inside a cheap plastic poster frame that lined the room in a single row like a charm bracelet. Many of them were scratched or dull with age, and more than a few of the posters were completely crooked in their moorings.

No one seemed to care, for the place was packed and loud. An acoustic guitar player sat in the corner, but Leslie couldn't even tell what song he was playing it was so loud inside.

She'd just ordered one of B-Cubed's beers when her cell phone lit up with a text from Cherry, wondering what she was doing for dinner. Fifteen minutes later, her aunt, Orbra, and Iva Nath had joined Leslie and Gilda at the sticky, wobbly table in the quietest corner (which wasn't saying much) of the bar. Iva appeared less enthusiastic than the rest of them about sitting at the table, and she used a handkerchief to try and clean up a spot for her to rest her handbag. When the waitress brought her a placemat, she seemed only slightly mollified. "Everything go all right last night?" Cherry asked as soon as they'd ordered drinks. She looked at Gilda. "Did you hear Leslie had a break-in?"

This blithe statement launched the conversation into a long explanation, culminating with Leslie making a gross error.

"If the ghost had made an appearance earlier, maybe whoever broke in would have been scared away," she ended…then realized what she'd said.

Everyone froze, and Iva turned slowly to look at her. "An appearance *earlier?*"

So the cat was out of the bag, and Leslie had to field even more questions about the supernatural activity in her house. Fortunately, their waitress was on her game, and she brought a second beer just as soon as Leslie finished her first. She needed the lubrication.

"Mind if I join you?"

Leslie and her companions looked up to see John Fischer standing there. His dark hair was charmingly disheveled, and the design on his bronze and blue plaid shirt looked less lumberjacky and more trendy than previous ones he'd worn.

"Yes, of course," Cherry said, shoving Orbra's chair aside—or at least attempting to—in order to make room for a sixth person between herself and Leslie. "Have a seat. Les was just telling us about her ghost."

"So who do you think it is?" Iva asked. She was the one who kept bringing the conversation back to specifics, and Leslie felt a little like an insect being pinned to a board when the older woman fixed her with those bright blue eyes. "The ghost, I mean. Why is it haunting the place? What does it want? Did you find anything in your research?"

"Not really. Nothing obvious, anyway. From what I can tell, she—it—looks like she's wearing a flapper's dress: it's straight and ends well above the ankles. I mean, it's definitely not Victorian clothing, and it's too long to be forties or fifties." Leslie's cheeks warmed as she felt John Fischer's regard settle on her with interest. It felt ridiculous to be describing the clothing—or what appeared to be clothing—on a phantom. It might not be a dress at all—just a figment of her imagination, or the way the edges of the figure flowed.

Nevertheless, Leslie continued, sharing what she'd learned during her marathon research session in the early hours of the morning. "The only thing of interest I came across was there was a young woman who went missing in 1926 by the name of Dorothy Duchene. She was never found, dead or alive. She was a housemaid who'd worked for Red Eye Sal, so there's a connection there with Shenstone House. But the conclusion was drawn that she'd run off with her young man."

"Duchene?" John said, his brow furrowing. "Why do I know that name?" He sat back in his seat and frowned more deeply. His lips pursed behind the neat mustache and beard.

"So it's definitely a young woman," said Iva. Her eyes were sparkling as if she'd just won a million dollars. "Any other details?"

Leslie hesitated, then plunged on in. Why not? "Both times I've heard music—yes," she added, glaring at Cherry. "There was one time before."

"And you didn't tell me?" Iva cried, forgetting herself and slamming her hand on a naked part of the table. "I *knew* I felt something when we were there. Didn't I tell you, Mr. Fischer? I told you I felt some presence."

He nodded absently, for he was absorbed with tapping on his phone.

"The music sounds a little familiar to me, but I can't quite place it," Leslie went on. "And the first time, there was a noise—it sounded like something was falling down the stairs. Or someone. But it was sort of amplified. The sound filled the room—almost what you imagine that big rolling stone in *Raiders of the Lost Ark* would sound like if it were coming after you."

"It's the supernatural element," Iva said wisely. "Everything is bigger, louder, scarier—"

"Ah! I knew it!" John bolted upright in his seat, brandishing his phone. "I knew I knew that name. Duchene, Freddy Duchene, was an infamous gambler from Chicago in the late twenties. But more interestingly, he was accused of fleecing an elderly woman out of her fortune. Maybe," he said, his eyes sparkling in the same way Iva's had, "Dorothy was his sister…or his wife. And maybe they set up a heist to steal Red Eye Sal's jewels. And that's why she disappeared without a trace."

"So they somehow stole the jewels and escaped," Leslie said. "I don't remember reading anything about Freddy Duchene—but then again, if he was from Chicago, I wouldn't have found anything in my initial search."

"Or," Iva said, leaning forward on the table, heedless of her cashmere sweater brushing against the sticky wood, "what if… what if that was the *plan*, for her and Freddy to steal the jewels—but what if they got caught! Red Eye Sal caught them—no, he caught *her*—yes, that makes more sense. Freddy Duchene set up his wife or sister with references so she could get a job at Shenstone House, and the plan was for her to lift the jewels—or to let him in so he could steal them. Working there, she'd be able to learn where Sal hid them and how to find them.

"But something went wrong, and she was caught, and Sal—well, there aren't a lot of nice things to be said about him. He was a gangster. He might have murdered her right then and there, and then hid the body so she'd never be found." Iva was breathless, and everyone else around the table was listening with interest.

"That's a pretty good story," said John with a wry smile. "You ever thought about writing a book?"

"Well, I— No, not really." Iva settled back in her seat looking very pleased with herself.

"What if he didn't exactly murder her in cold blood?" Leslie said slowly. "What if…what if there was a struggle and she fell down the steps? And broke her neck, and that's why she's haunting the stairway?" Now she felt a rush of excitement. "That could explain that loud rolling sound—she made it both times I saw her.

And tonight, she was halfway down the stairs, and she pointed. I thought she was pointing at me, but now that I think about it—I was a little disoriented—maybe she was pointing down the stairs, as if to indicate what happened. I *asked* her what she wanted. Maybe she was answering me."

"You *asked* her?" Cherry said from the other side of John. "You mean you actually spoke to it?"

"Yes. Well, why not? Obviously the ghost wants something. I wanted her—it—to know I was willing to help." Leslie lifted up her beer and took a long drink, then set it back down, shaking her head. "I cannot believe I'm having this conversation."

Iva patted her hand. "It's all right. The first time is always strange. But after a while, you get used to it. Unless you're Hollis," she added with a roll of her eyes. "He doesn't quite get my interest in the metaphysical. It's a good thing he's at the football game in East Lansing tonight. He'd be bored silly listening to this."

Their food arrived at that moment, and conversation was suspended while the plates were distributed. Apparently Leslie wasn't the only one uncomfortable with the topic in front of anyone outside their group.

"Hi there, Brad," said Orbra, looking up suddenly.

It was Brad Beatty, and Leslie—who by now was nearly finished with her second beer and realized she wasn't going to be driving home tonight—lifted her longneck to show him that she was drinking one of his brews. "I really like it, and I'm not usually a fan of IPAs," she told him. "Want to join us?"

"Naw, that's all right. I'm meeting a friend. Just wanted to say hi and let you know the tea was a big hit at the game last night, Orbra. You might be giving me a run for my money when it comes to supplying locally brewed libation."

Everyone laughed, and he went on. "Did you all see the segment on Channel Four last night? With Marcus Levin? He was here for the game, and interviewed some of the players—and also some of the football alum who were in for Homecoming. Including Bill Gary, Declan Zyler—and yours truly."

"I missed it," Cherry said. "But I bet it's online."

"Yes—I'm going to ask him when he gets here. We're supposed to be meeting at eight. He's going to sample some of my beer, and I'm hoping for an endorsement." He glanced at the wall clock, which showed seven fifty-five. "He's coming from dinner with the Underwhites, and Aaron must be talking his ear off."

Leslie paused with her burger in hand, halfway to her mouth. "I just saw Regina Underwhite and she said they'd had dinner with Marcus Levin last night. After the game."

Brad frowned. "Huh. Well, maybe Trib got his info mixed up—that's what he told me. Or maybe he's being wined and dined two nights in a row. Levin might be an arrogant ass, but he's well known in Chicago as well as Grand Rapids. A good word from him could send a lot of tourists our way. And a lot of beer distributors." He grinned.

"Hmm. Maybe I ought to try and hook up with Marcus Levin, then," Orbra said, drawing another round of laughter.

"Have a seat till he comes in, anyway," Cherry said. "Leslie was just telling us about her ghost. And she's probably not going to eat all those fries."

"Oh yes I will," Leslie retorted, but smiled at Brad anyway. "But I'll share, since you did such a great article about Shenstone House."

He laughed. "That sounds like a great deal to me." He lifted his beer and they clinked bottles…then he dug in.

—◆—

Declan took a swig of beer—Brad's latest test brew. He was trying for something with cherries, since Traverse City, the Cherry Capital of the World, was only a couple hours north. Dec wasn't sold on it—a good beer didn't need frou-frou stuff like cherries or maple syrup (another of Brad's great ideas that, fortunately, didn't make it).

It was Sunday evening—soon to be too late for him to be out with it being a school night and having to get up at six a.m., but when a friend needed you to test out a new brew, you went.

"You met up with Marcus Levin again last night?"

"Yep. He wanted to try some of my stuff. I'm hoping if he likes it enough, I'll get an endorsement out of him." Brad took a sip of beer, swished it around in his mouth, closed his eyes, then swallowed. And sighed as if a woman was going down on him.

Declan shook his head, smiling. It was a blessing when a man loved his work that much. Fortunately, he could relate.

When Brad opened his eyes, he said, "Leslie van Dorn was there last night too—at the Roost. I sat down with her and Cherry and Orbra. Yeah, I was thinking I might see if Leslie wanted to have dinner some time or at least meet for a drink—she said she liked my IPA—but she was there with someone, so I guess it's a good thing I didn't step in that."

Declan almost choked on his beer. Leslie was there with someone? He blinked to make sure he'd heard that right. Well, damn. That pretty much sucked. He swallowed a large mouthful too fast and too hard, and barely managed to keep from choking on it.

"What, you don't like it?" Brad said, looking at him askance. "I thought it turned out pretty good."

"I don't think it needs the cherry flavor," Dec replied. His voice was rough from the beer. "Unless you're trying to attract more women to drink it, then maybe."

He frowned, still thinking about Leslie. Well, what the hell. That was not cool. Hadn't she been the one to grab him when they got inside her kitchen Friday night?

"Did you have a good time last night? Weren't you out with Emily Danube?" Brad pulled him out of his unpleasant thoughts.

"I wasn't *out* with her, per se...I was just sitting next to her. A bunch of us parents went out to eat after the kids left for the dance."

"Well, when I walked by and saw you two in the front window, you looked pretty cozy to me." Brad raised his glass in a toast. "Nice going. She's been running around as the most eligible single woman in town for about two years now, refusing to date anyone here. You move back, and two months later, *bam*! She's hooked."

"We're not going out," Declan told him firmly. "Our daughters are friends. So we do some carpooling and stuff."

"Well, she was practically in your lap the way I saw it, dude. Just saying. If you *aren't* seeing her, you sure could be."

Declan didn't want to hear any more. He was still mulling over the fact that Leslie had been out with a guy last night. Who the hell was it? That high-powered lawyer, Gideon Nath? Come in a few days early for whatever Wednesday-with-the-heart was? He realized he was gripping the beer glass tightly enough that his fingers were aching.

"So when do you think Levin will get back to you?" he said to change the subject back.

"He'll be back in town later this week, he said—for all the events around the big reunion. I'll corner him then," Brad said.

Declan's phone pinged with a text notification, and he dragged it out of his jeans pocket. It wasn't from Leslie.

Well, why *would* it be from her? Just because they'd done a little blow-your-mind tongue-tangling on Friday night didn't mean he expected to hear from her every day. She was a client, after all. He was only her hired hand.

Hell…

The thought struck him with an unpleasant, ugly force. What if she'd just been sort of going along with him because she didn't want to piss off one of her workers? Maybe she thought if she declined his advances he'd walk away from the job and leave her hanging.

After all, there were contractors who would do that. He'd known a few, as a matter of fact.

No, that was silly. Leslie van Dorn was a ball-buster. She wouldn't take that crap from anyone, and she sure as hell wouldn't do anything she didn't want to do.

Still…it was an unsettling feeling knowing that the woman he'd been really getting into seemed to be…not so much interested.

After all, he hadn't heard from her at all yesterday or today, and it was Sunday night.

He glanced at the text and actually read it this time. It was from Emily Danube. *Stephanie said tomorrow's good for lasagna. 6:00? I'll bring it over with a nice bottle of red so you don't have to stop work early.* She ended with a smiley.

He shoved the phone back in his pocket without replying.

Because apparently Emily Danube's car was now working just fine.

FOURTEEN

I REALLY APPRECIATE IT, Ms. van Dorn," said Stephanie as she buckled her seatbelt.

"Well, I wasn't going to have you bike home in this downpour," Leslie said as she started the car. "Besides, I've got a few errands to run in town, so I don't mind at all. Thanks for helping me get Rufus into the cat carrier. I'm hoping Dr. Vector will fix him up—at least his tail. And check if he has fleas."

"I'm sure he will. He takes good care of Genny's cat—that's why I thought he'd be a good person to call." She patted the cat carrier, which she'd insisted on holding on her lap, as if Rufus could feel it. "He's a sweetie, and I bet he'll be a really good pet."

Pet? Leslie's brows lifted. Well, she guessed that was the obvious next step—as long as the beast was de-flea-ed. She glanced over at Rufus, who was watching her with green eyes not unlike Declan's. Surprisingly, he didn't seem too unhappy about being in the carrier.

"Anyway, I really appreciate the ride," Stephanie chattered on, "because we're having some friends over for dinner tonight, and I'm sure Dad's busy getting ready. Otherwise I'd call him to pick me up. Though there's lots of times he doesn't hear the phone when he's working in his workshop."

"It's probably pretty loud in there," Leslie said, immediately shoving away the image of a shirtless Declan, sweaty and muscular, pounding away on an iron rod. Muscles bulging and sliding, smooth and slick and shiny. It made her mouth water just to think about it—which was not a good idea.

There'd been silence from him since he left Friday night, and in light of what she'd seen at Trib's Saturday evening, Leslie hadn't been moved to contact him. She didn't have the time or mental energy for drama or uncertainty or any sort of games right now. It was Monday, and Wednesday the 15th loomed like an ugly green ogre in the center of her week.

I'll be glad when I'm past that day.

It'll have to get easier then—a whole year would have gone by. All the "firsts" would be over with.

But even now, already, she was finding it difficult to keep from falling back into the memory of where she'd been a year ago as the leaves were falling and Halloween was on deck. She'd just been starting to wear maternity clothes. And thinking about and planning for a nursery. Pinterest had been her friend, and she'd toted around a copy of *What to Expect When You're Expecting* in her briefcase.

She'd been carrying a blessed burden of a baby, along with a less pleasant one: the truth about its parentage.

In a distorted way, perhaps one could consider it a blessing that she hadn't carried her infant, Gwendolyn, to full term. Looking back, Leslie wondered how she could have gone on with her life, holding the secret from Gideon that he was a father.

Had it been her punishment—that the baby had been taken from her? Was that why things had worked out that way? Her eyes stung and her throat burned.

"Ms. van Dorn? Are you all right?"

Leslie realized she'd been sitting at a four-way stop far longer than necessary, especially since there weren't any other cars in the vicinity. "Oh, yes, goodness. I was just distracted for a minute looking at—I thought I saw a hawk up there. I love hawks," she said lamely.

But Stephanie didn't seem to notice the oddness of her excuse, and once Leslie asked about it, she kept up a monologue about the Homecoming Dance for the rest of the short drive to her house.

"It looks like Dad's still working. I'd better let him know I'm home and the Danubes will be here soon. He's probably lost track of time by now, knowing him. You should check out his workshop. He's been working on your railing a lot lately. Come on." She muscled the cat carrier onto the passenger seat, then shut the door.

Leslie should have declined, but after all, she *was* paying for the ironwork and had a perfectly legitimate reason to check in and see how things were going. And there was that chance he might even be shirtless and sweaty.

The two of them dashed through the pelting rain, Leslie holding an umbrella and following Stephanie, who not only didn't have a jacket but ignored the umbrella.

The workshop was a separate outbuilding about the size of a garage. Even over the sounds of pelting rain, she could hear music blaring from inside—Ben Folds Five. She recognized "Song for the Dumped" and nodded to herself. *Yep. I can relate.*

Stephanie opened the door and they burst into a room smelling of burning coal and melting metal. Unusual smells, both, and the heat was pretty intense, but Leslie didn't really take much notice of either once she saw Declan.

Holy crap.

It was like her romantic fantasy come to life, but in a little more modern setting. No, he wasn't shirtless, but he didn't need to be for Leslie's mouth to go dry and her stomach to flutter. *To think I had that body all plastered up against me the other night.*

He had a pink bandanna tied around his forehead, and his face and throat were damp with sweat that ran in rivulets down into the opening of his shirt. His dark auburn hair, now wet, appeared almost black, and it stuck up and curled around the bandanna like wild little fingers. He wasn't actually hammering on anything at the moment; in fact, it looked as if he were cleaning up for the day, for he wasn't wearing any sort of smock or apron, and she saw a pair of long, heavy leather gloves resting on the counter next to him.

The shirt he wore was little more than a second skin, wet and clinging to every smooth muscle: from broad shoulder to round, bulging bicep to smooth, scarred, and freckled forearm. So he might just as well have had it off, really.

"My friends ogle him like that too," Stephanie said, laughing. "But he's my dad, so, well, you know, I don't really notice it."

Leslie's face rushed to hot, and she said, "Well, I don't want to disturb him, so—"

But Stephanie wasn't listening. "Hey, Dad, the Danubes are going to be here any minute now," she shouted over the blasting music.

He looked up in surprise, his eyes bypassing his daughter and going immediately to Leslie. He snatched up a towel and wiped off his face as he walked over to turn down the music.

"I didn't want Stephanie to bike home in the pouring rain," Leslie said, absolutely *refusing* to feel awkward. "Sorry to disturb you—I thought I'd just see how things were going while I was here. Not that I expected you'd be working on my project; I know you have other things on your schedule." *Okay, now shut up. You're on the verge of babbling, and Leslie van Dorn doesn't babble.*

"Right," he said. The expression on his face was inscrutable, and that made her edge toward the awkward end of the scale, despite her determination not to. "I actually was working on a piece of it today. Here, you can see what've been doing; it's had a chance to cool down."

He picked up an iron rod that had been about fifteen feet long until he started to force it into a spiral near the top. Now it was only about eleven feet long.

On a roomy worktable, Leslie saw a large piece of heavy paper with a drawing on it. When she and Declan moved closer—him on one side, she on the other—she saw that it was a life-sized drawing of the main design of her railing.

He laid the iron rod down over the drawing, matching it to one of the sketched rods that ended in a swirl near the top, and as she watched with interest, he eyed it, checking to be sure the curve was exactly right. "Needs a little more smoothing right there," he said, mostly to himself.

"It's looking really good," Leslie said, unable to keep her eyes from his strong, deft hands and forearms, freckled and solid with muscle and tendon. They were powerful arms, talented hands, marred with burns and fresh cuts. And they had been all over her butt.

It was really quite warm in the workshop, she realized suddenly. Uncomfortably warm. She glanced around and realized Stephanie was gone.

A large fire roared in a brick oven, and she saw a few rods sitting half inside. There was a massive machine that rose several feet above Declan's head, and had a steel cylinder the circumference of a salad plate that appeared to be a sort of piston.

"That's an air hammer," he said, noticing her looking at it. "It's an easier, more automated way to hammer on a larger piece that doesn't need as much finesse as something like this." He gestured with the curved rod. "I use it more for breaking up rods, or forging shorter ones together."

"Forging them together? How does that work?"

"You put two fired ends on top of each other, stacking them right where they're red and glowing, and the hammer sort of beats the shit out of them until they merge together. It can be done by hand, of course, but when I'm working with two rods at a time, I have to clamp one of them, and the other I can hold while the hammer does its work." He paused, glanced at her as if he were about to say something, then turned aside to shove the spiral rod into a long metal canister.

"You do amazing work," Leslie said, for she'd turned to see photos and other partial pieces of decorative iron all over one wall of the workshop. "It's hard to believe something as strong as iron can be forced into such delicate, smooth shapes."

"Thanks." There was a pause, and then he said, "So, no more break-ins?"

"No," she said. "I'm sure it was a couple of teenagers, like Officer Morton said."

"Right. Probably. Look, I—"

They both turned toward the door at the sound of voices. It was Stephanie, doing her job as tour guide and bringing her friend and Emily Danube out to see her father's workshop.

Skimming even further along the awkward scale, Leslie smiled at Declan and said, "Just let me know if you need anything else. It looks like it's coming along great."

"Right. All right, yes, I'll see you soon," he said vaguely.

Leslie wasn't certain who was more uncomfortable: herself or Declan. One thing was sure, she thought as she passed by the newcomers—Emily Danube wasn't uncomfortable at all. She was determined…and satisfied.

Like the cat who'd got into the cream.

—m—

If Declan hadn't been driving, he probably would have actually hesitated before turning up the driveway to Shenstone House. But that was a little more difficult to do when in a car on a street with other vehicles behind you.

After all, it was Wednesday, October 15. The day with the heart on Leslie's calendar. And the letter G next to it.

But as he was only a lowly contractor, a worker bee, a handyman, he wouldn't know any different—right? It was a weekday at four o'clock—still during business hours (not that contractors like him really had business hours), and he really did need to take a measurement of that railing before he went any further on the project.

It was a legitimate reason to be here. He knew that, and he sold himself on it really well as his truck rumbled up the drive.

If he happened to be aware that Leslie van Dorn had cancelled having Stephanie work that day, he could still discount that fact because he had a job to do, and he had no reason to think anything was strange because his daughter didn't have to work. Leslie had contractors coming in and out of the house all the time.

Still, when he pulled up into the parking area of the massive house, he got a sense of…something. Something quiet and sad and gloomy. There were only a few lights on; he recognized them as coming from Leslie's bedroom/office suite. There was also one in the kitchen.

And her dark blue Mercedes was the only car in the lot. So if the mysterious G was there, either they were out somewhere in his car, or she'd picked him up and they were there, in the house.

There *were* lights on in her private suite. He didn't really like what that implied.

Damn. Maybe he should just leave…

He put the truck in reverse, getting ready to do just that, when he realized he really kind of did need to get that measurement. Sure, he could have called first. Sure, he could have come over yesterday…or even Monday. But he was here now, and it would be a waste of time not to follow through.

She didn't have to answer the door if she was freaking busy.

Declan climbed out of the truck, his lips flattened grimly. Either way, he supposed they at least needed to have some sort of discussion about what had happened last Friday…and since. Sure, she'd come over to find Emily Danube at his house, but he'd already told her he wasn't seeing her. Wasn't that enough?

For his part, Declan wanted to know whether the guy she'd been with on Saturday was anyone important or not. He figured he'd find out one way or another tonight.

He approached the back door that led into the kitchen and looked through the window. No sign of life there. Just one light on over the granite island. A few dishes on the counter and in the sink…hmm. That was unusual. He'd never seen anything out of place in the room.

He knocked on the door and waited. Looked around to see if the butterscotch cat was lurking. No sign of him; no sign of a can of tuna left out.

Everything was eerily quiet. And being here, at the top of this small hill surrounded by woods, it felt as if he was miles away from civilization…even though just down the hill and over a few blocks were the lights from the town. In the distance was the hum of traffic. Less than a mile away was the downtown Sematauk business district.

He'd raised his hand to knock again when a figure appeared inside.

She pulled open the door. "What are you doing here?"

Her tone wasn't unfriendly or angry...just curious. Surprised. Confused.

"I—needed to get a measurement. Sorry to bother you. Am I bothering you?" He got a good look at her and saw, to his surprise, that she was in loose flannel pants and a hoodie. Her hair was in a ponytail that had seen better days, sagging, while random curls dusted her neck. Her toes were bare, and this time they had hot-pink polish on them. Her face was drawn and tight, with a sober expression that bordered on sad.

This was a completely different Leslie van Dorn than he'd ever seen.

Maybe she was sick?

She certainly didn't look like she was entertaining a man, that was certain.

"Come on in," she said, opening the door to give him entrance.

When he got inside, he saw a bowl of popcorn (it was obviously fresh, for it smelled heavenly) and a half-eaten pizza in a carryout box. All indicators were that she was alone, and not sick. People didn't generally eat pizza or popcorn when they were sick.

"Thanks," he said, still feeling his way—figuratively and literally. "It'll only take a second."

"No problem." She leaned against the island, idly eating popcorn instead of following him to the front hall, which seemed odd too.

"Leslie," he said when he came back after taking the measurement. "Is everything all right? You seem...well, not yourself."

She sighed and crossed her arms over her chest. "Did my aunt send you over?" She sounded a cross between annoyed and hopeful. "I told her not to worry about me. I'm fine."

"No, Cherry didn't send me. I told you, I needed a measurement."

She gave him a jaundiced look that was almost the old Leslie—one with wry disbelief. Yeah, it sounded lame to him too, but he wasn't about to admit it. "Well, I suppose we should probably talk anyway. About last Friday."

She shoved the bowl of popcorn toward him and he took a handful—partly because it smelled amazing, and partly because he figured it would give him time to figure out what to say next.

"Oh my God," he said when he tasted the popcorn. He'd forgotten lunch again. "This is really good."

A glimmer of a smile. "Old family recipe: lots of salt and more butter than you want to know. Popped in a hot air popper. The best cure for the blues."

"The blues?" he asked cautiously. Surely she wasn't *that* upset about their aborted whatever it was, and seeing Emily Danube at his house. That was just silly.

Though he kind of liked that idea, because he knew he could fix it.

Leslie drew in a deep breath, then exhaled. "Today's just a difficult day for me. It's an anniversary, an unpleasant one—and it's the first one. So I guess that makes it unusually difficult." She gestured around the room. "So I just holed up with some snack food and decided to pamper myself and binge-watch *Gilmore Girls*. In between shedding a few tears."

"An anniversary?" He couldn't seem to stop munching on the popcorn. It was like crack. "A breakup? Or…something else?" He forced himself to stop reaching into the bowl in order to give her his full attention.

"A miscarriage. I lost a baby one year ago today. Her name would have been Gwendolyn."

A number of thoughts and questions shot through his mind, but they could—possibly—be addressed later. The most important thing was: "Oh, Leslie. I'm so sorry." His words were heartfelt and honest, even though he couldn't really relate to the situation.

She nodded, reaching automatically for a handful of popcorn. "Thanks. I have my ups and downs. Today I expected would be a down day, so I just…cancelled everything. I figured I've been working so hard, I could use a day off. And I'd be—"

"Leslie, you don't need to justify yourself to me. Or to anyone. I mean, losing a baby…that's got to be one of the worst things in the world."

She looked at him with large, shocked eyes. And then all at once, she burst into tears.

FIFTEEN

LESLIE HARDLY REALIZED what she was doing—but the next thing she knew, she'd thrown herself into Declan's arms. It was as if she'd been waiting for it: waiting for someone to hold her, someone to listen, someone to comfort. And with that, the dam tumbled down.

His arms came around her immediately—protective, supportive, comforting. And every bit of grief she'd controlled for weeks and months in her iron-fisted CEO mind came pouring out in deep, wrenching sobs as he held her close.

"People…don't…under…stand," she bawled into his shoulder. "They think"—sniffle—"since the baby…was never born…it shouldn't"—*sob*—"affect me…so much…"

He patted her on the back, his fingers touching the ends of her messy hair, as he tucked her head beneath his chin. "Of course it would affect you," he said quietly. "You carried that baby *inside* you. You lost part of yourself, and another person as well. Someone *died*. A little defenseless creature *is gone*."

That made her bawl even harder. How could he understand so well when even Aunt Cherry couldn't get it? She knew Leslie had been grieving, and she was kind and supportive…but she didn't really seem to understand that a miscarriage was *losing a baby*… not just the hopes and dreams of a baby, but an actual child. Someone she'd spoken to, nurtured, planned for…*felt*. She'd felt Gwendolyn, held her deep inside, *connected* with her.

"Shh…shhh," he murmured, stroking her back in a long, easy slide. "I'm here, Leslie. I'm here."

"I was five months pregnant," she said. "Well past the danger zone. I started to wear maternity clothes. I—I ordered a c-crib…"

"I'm so sorry, darling. So, so sorry."

Leslie didn't know how long she sobbed messily into his shirt, but when she pulled away, there was a huge wet spot that went from shoulder to halfway down the soft, brushed cotton.

"I'm sorry," she said with a little hiccup and a short, pained laugh. She batted at the massive wet spot. "I ruined your sh-shirt. I hope you didn't have plans tonight."

Now that she'd emerged from the storm of grief and anger, she felt as if she were coming back to herself—back to reality. Here in her kitchen, with a soft, comforting glow, the smell of popcorn and old pizza—and, most of all, the smell of Declan: fresh, clean, male, delicious.

And in the very same position he'd been in the last time she was in his arms: up against the island, holding her close.

"Plans? Well, I was sort of in the mood to watch *Gilmore Girls*," he said, reaching casually for a big handful of popcorn.

Leslie burst out with a short, surprised laugh and looked up at him. Good grief, he looked *delicious*. Just…good enough to eat: all tall and sturdy, with his dark green eyes settled on her, a glint of humor and warmth in them. And a big wet spot on his dark blue and green diamond-patterned shirt.

"I'd have to make some more popcorn, at the rate you're going there," she said nonchalantly.

"Okay." He jumped on that immediately, a smile twitching his lips.

"But you have to promise you won't judge me when you see how much butter I put on it."

"Well, it's not like it's a whole stick, is it?" He was still munching away.

Leslie spun away neatly without answering, suddenly ridiculously, crazily lighthearted. Smiling.

"Is it?" he asked again, his tone lilting with laughter.

"What do you want to drink?" she asked. "Have you even ever watched *Gilmore Girls*?"

"Do I have a teenaged daughter and Netflix?" he replied. "And beer or iced tea works."

Leslie poured a scoop of popcorn into the hot air popper and turned to assess him closely. "Then tell me if you're a Jess or a Dean shipper, and a Luke or a Christopher shipper. Beer's in the fridge. So's iced tea."

"Shipper?"

"You said you had a teenaged daughter. Shipper—meaning, relation*ship*. Who are you rooting for in the relationships with the various Gilmore girls?" She shook her head, arms crossed over her middle. "See, I knew you were making that up—"

"Jess and Christopher," he said as he emerged from the fridge with one of the longnecks and the iced tea pitcher. "Jess because he's misunderstood, and Christopher because he should be with his daughter." He leaned back against the counter and crossed his arms, giving her a "*so there*" look.

"All right, then, you can stay," she told him, unable to hold back a delighted grin. Partly because he was here, partly because he was acting normally, and partly because…well, he hadn't asked any of the questions she knew he had. What a guy. "Even if I don't completely agree with you."

"Well, that's what makes things interesting, isn't it?" His voice dropped a little. Just enough to send a little frisson of awareness through her. He was watching her with those green eyes…very closely, very steadily, but without demand. Just…letting her know he was noticing her.

And she was certainly noticing him: all warm and bronzy and coppery, with his dark mahogany hair and the generous brush of freckles that made his skin look richer and duskier than a mere tan. The memory of the way his damp shirt clung to the muscles beneath had her mouth going dry. She wanted to touch that skin, feel the slide of those muscles and the warmth of him against her. And she wanted to taste him again. Taste, and lick, and nibble and more.

Leslie tucked away the delicate flutter in the base of her belly and savored it like a neat little secret as she made the rest of the popcorn. It was nice to have someone here—besides Rufus, anyway—even though she hadn't thought she wanted anyone around. And it was even nicer that it was someone like Declan, around whom she felt amazingly comfortable and relaxed.

And even more, it was a blessing that he not only listened and comforted her, but that he wasn't trying to move them back to where they'd been five days ago—plastered against each other, her butt on the island, hands everywhere.

Not that she wasn't interested in it, but she appreciated him taking it easy for the moment.

"I'm just starting season three," she said, drizzling an obscene amount of butter over the popcorn in a shallow twenty-four-inch-wide bowl. "It's my favorite."

"Ah. You must be a Jess shipper, then," he said, pouring two glasses of iced tea. He winked when she looked at him in surprise. "I told you I watched it! Between that and *Glee*, Stephanie and I have really done some father-daughter bonding."

She laughed, but said nothing as she led the way out of the kitchen into her bedroom/office/living room suite.

"This is really nice," he said, looking around. "Very cozy."

She smiled with delight. "I love this suite so much. It's really the first time I've ever had my own space, designed from top to bottom, if you will. Before, I just moved into an apartment or condo and…well, I didn't spend the time or energy to make it much of my own. I was too busy working. But since I plan to be here a long time…"

She looked around, seeing the well-lit space though his eyes. The main room was like a neat, compact library, with a desk and credenza at one end, shelves lining the walls wherever there wasn't a window, and a sitting area. The last had the most comfortable leather sectional she'd ever known in front of a television that raised and lowered on its own shelf from inside a cabinet.

The decor was eclectic, leaning toward spare and professional, with leather seating mixed with glass and mahogany tables and shelves, brightly colored throw pillows and area rug, and some eye-catching artwork. The lighting was fun: fancy and feminine with lots of crystals and unique textured shades, but also functional for work.

There were two doors leading further into the suite: one to a master bathroom, small but luxurious, and to a postage-stamp-sized bedroom that just fit her queen-sized bed with room to move around it. However, she had a large walk-in closet (the reason the bedroom was so small) that was lined with shelves and organizers. The closet was nearly the size of her bedroom.

"I see you've found a roommate."

Leslie laughed when she realized he was talking about Rufus, who'd made himself extremely comfortable in the exact center of the L of the sectional. "Yes, and you'll be glad to know he's been de-flea-ed, considering where he's chosen to ensconce himself."

"Wow. You two sure moved fast. A few dinners, and all of a sudden you're living together?"

Leslie gave a short laugh. "Well, why waste time? He's a great roommate—he sleeps a lot, doesn't drink my wine or eat my cupcakes, and he has yet to borrow any of my clothes. Of course, he does like to carouse and come in late at night. He had an extended visit at the vet Monday, and I only brought him home yesterday. He seems to like it here."

"I can see why." Declan's eyes slid around the room once more, then settled on her just long enough for her belly to flutter happily.

Leslie realized she was a little flustered—but in a good way. "Have a seat," she said, gesturing to the sofa. Sitting in it was like lowering oneself into the palm of a big hand: you were cupped comfortably in all the right places, and could lean back with neck support exactly where you needed it.

He hesitated perceptibly, then chose a spot just past the center of the L-shaped sectional. Close enough to touch Rufus if he liked, but far enough away that she'd have room to decide where to sit. Leslie smiled.

Touché, sir, she thought. *Now it's up to me to decide how close to sit to your handsome self.*

Then her smile faded. Something was bound to happen between them if she sat anywhere in his vicinity. Maybe it was best to clear the air first.

"So…" she said, picking up the remotes for the TV. "How was your dinner with the Danubes Monday night?"

His attention snapped to her; he even put the popcorn bowl on the table in order to look up at her. "To tell the truth…it was pretty awkward." He looked chagrined yet determined, and plowed on. "My daughter seems to think I need her help with my love life. So she's been doing her best to…ah…encourage Emily…ah…in my direction. Not that Emily has needed any encouragement anyway."

Leslie managed to smother a laugh. Well, that explained a lot. "I see. I guess Stephanie's a big fan of *The Parent Trap*?"

"Maybe…I don't know. Is that a movie? But I told you…I told you Friday night, there's nothing going on with me and Emily. Even if Stephanie has indicated otherwise."

"I have to admit, I wondered about that when I walked past Trib's Saturday night and you and she were sitting there in the front window, looking rather cozy." Leslie sank down on the couch, on the other limb of the L, and used the remote to wake up the video streaming device. Rufus apparently didn't like having his sleep disturbed, and he gave an abbreviated, irritated yowl before leaping lightly off the couch.

"Yeah. Well, I sort of didn't have much choice in the matter. Emily's car broke down and she needed a ride to the pre-Homecoming festivities, and then she needed a ride home, and she wanted to join the other parents for dinner at Trib's, and—"

"And you're too nice of a guy to say no, even when you know you're being—shall we say—managed." Leslie was grinning by now. Poor thing. It was amazing how powerful and strong and assertive men could be…and how completely and utterly clueless when it came to women and their machinations.

Females really were the stronger sex.

He laughed uncomfortably as Rufus slunk along between Leslie's legs and the coffee table. She bent to pet him, careful to avoid his tail—which had been carefully mended by Dr. V.

"Yeah, I guess," Declan said. "But I had a nice little talk with Stephanie and let her know she didn't need to interfere anymore. I didn't tell her the reason," he added hastily.

"*The* reason? What reason is that?" Leslie asked, her voice light and teasing.

His cheeks colored a little but his eyes narrowed with warning. "I think you know, Leslie van Dorn." A tiny bit of a smile teased his lips. Then he eased back, leaning against the couch. His expression lost the bit of levity and became closed off. "But I've been wondering whether you had a good time Saturday night yourself. I heard you were at the Roost."

"I was." Rufus settled on a puffy ottoman and turned around in four circles as Leslie replied. "With Aunt Cherry and Orbra and Iva. And that author—John Fischer? He stopped by too, and so did Brad Beatty. I'll be honest…I thought I might hear from you on Saturday sometime, but I didn't. And then I saw you with Emily and…well, I thought I'd *misread* things on Friday."

"You did not misread anything," he said in a sort of annoyed, growly voice. "Unless you don't know what it means when a guy can't keep his hands—or his thoughts—off you."

Oh. Well. Leslie subdued the sharp stab of lust that took her by surprise at his very honest, primitive words. She smiled a little. "It's been a while, but I'm pretty sure I have an idea about that." She turned toward the television and lifted the remote. "Now that we've got that settled…"

And she clicked play.

Declan gave a short laugh, relinquished the popcorn bowl to her, then settled back to watch *Gilmore Girls*.

And that was the moment Leslie fell hopelessly in love.

—⁊⁊—

Declan probably wouldn't have gone around telling Brad or his other guy friends how much he enjoyed the evening—

watching what amounted to a chick-flick television series with four feet of space between him and the woman he was *dying* to get with—but damned if he didn't have a good time.

Even if he did give up the rest of that sinful popcorn to her. It was more than worth it to see the expression on her face when he made such a sacrifice.

Even if he was completely and utterly aware of her the whole time. Her slender white feet were propped only a few inches away from his on the ottoman they shared with the cat. He swore he could feel the heat radiating from her toes.

Even if she looked pretty adorable, sort of bedraggled and frumpy after her long cry into the front of his shirt—which dried before the end of the second episode, by the way. Despite the fact that he thought Leslie looked delicious, he suspected if she saw herself in a mirror, she'd be horrified.

She'd pulled out the ponytail at some point, so her shiny black hair fell in loose, messy waves over her shoulders. Her nose was red from crying for quite a while afterward. Her eyes were still puffy from crying and lack of sleep. Bags under them too, and some dark circles. And her fingers were a little greasy from the popcorn, since she'd drowned it in butter.

Even so, he itched to pull her close, to slip an arm around her shoulders and have her scooch up next to him, especially now that he realized Brad Beatty had been totally wrong when he said Leslie had "been with" someone the other night. Clearly, she'd just been sitting at a table with this John Fischer person—which reminded him…

He'd been meaning to call his cousin Teddy about the guy. She'd know any scoop there was to know about the novelist Jeremy or John Fischer—whoever he was—being a big bestselling author herself. Whether the guy was a player, whether he was married. Anything important.

But for now, Declan just settled in quietly, enjoyed the show, and, even more, enjoyed the anticipation that sometime soon, he'd be doing exactly what he wanted to be doing. Sometime when the time was right. When she wasn't dealing with her grief so strongly.

Much as he wanted to move in, he didn't feel like it was right. Not tonight. Not when he was there just to comfort.

But man oh man…he really wanted to kiss her. To get closer…especially since he was pretty damn sure she wasn't wearing a bra.

The very thought of that…the temptation…the *knowledge* was just about enough to kill him.

—m—

When Leslie got up to use the toilet and caught a glimpse of herself in the mirror, she nearly shrieked.

Oh my God, I look like a hag!

She brushed her hair, brushed her teeth, put on some lip gloss, and snagged a bra from her bedroom—good thing her hoodie was loose; surely he hadn't noticed—and even shucked her sweats to pull on a pair of leggings. No wonder Declan was keeping his distance.

She checked her pits—thank God she didn't stink; she *had* showered early this morning before she decided to be schlumpy all day. Finally, she returned to the living area.

"I'm hungry. Are you? Do you want something to eat?"

He looked up at her and she felt rather than saw a flare of definite interest—and a very improper mental response to her question—and then he smiled. "You're hungry? After eating almost that whole bowl of popcorn?"

"Come on out to the kitchen. I feel like I could pull together the energy to make something to eat that doesn't have a whole stick of butter on it."

"Shit, really? A whole stick? I can feel my arteries clogging as we speak." He stood, giving Leslie the opportunity to admire the way his rugged jeans hung just perfectly: fitting closely in the right places, and relaxed in others. She'd been too busy sobbing earlier to notice.

"So I've been getting almost nightly visits from my ghostly friend," she said, opening the fridge to see what she could throw together.

"You *have*?"

She glanced over her shoulder. He looked utterly stunned. "Yes. And no, I haven't gone running away. I've slept here every night—well, almost every night in the last week. I spent Saturday at Cherry's because I had a couple too many beers at the Roost." She pulled out some queso fresco, cilantro, and fresh corn tortillas. "I hope you like Mexican."

"It goes great with beer," he said, eyeing her—or maybe it was the tortillas—with appreciation. No, it was her.

She smiled to herself. *Patience is a virtue, and anticipation is a gift.*

"Have you figured out anything about what it wants? The ghost?"

"I've asked her. She hasn't really answered me other than to point angrily at me—or down the stairs. I'm not sure which. And there's that sound of something rolling downstairs, so I think she fell down and that's how she died." Leslie found two ripe avocados and a couple of beefsteak tomatoes in her fruit bowl. Then she went back to the fridge to retrieve some cooked chicken she had left over from the other night.

"There was a woman named Dorothy Duchene who disappeared." She went on to tell him about the missing woman and the theory she and Cherry and the others had discussed at the Roost. "It could be her. The clothing is the right time period."

"But the ghost isn't being…destructive, is it? What happens during these—uh—visits?"

"They don't last very long. Ten minutes, maybe fifteen. Rufus has only experienced it once—last night—and he wasn't very keen on it. All that hair of his standing on end was quite a sight."

"So you don't believe you're…in danger. From the ghost, I mean?"

Leslie grimaced. "So far, she just seems to be sort of throwing her weight around. So to speak. Loud, windy, creepy—but so far her bark is worse than her bite. It's usually around two, two thirty. And there's this music that's always playing in the background…I feel like if I could place it, that might help."

"Can you sing it or hum it? Maybe I can help."

"I can do better than that—I actually recorded it on Monday night. It's not great sound quality, but you can hear it if you listen hard." She went over to stand next to him, maneuvering through her phone to find the voice memo. "Here, listen. Cherry and Orbra didn't recognize it, but maybe you will."

He did so, several times, as she mashed avocado, lemon, cumin, salt, and pepper into guacamole.

"It's definitely familiar. Right on the tip of my ear, so to speak," Declan finally said. "Maybe it will come to me later. By the way, did you ever find the pink velvet wrap that is missing?"

"No. It's definitely gone. I just don't understand why anyone would take that and leave a bunch of other vintage articles in the speakeasy. I found a ladies' dinner jacket from the 1920s that Gilda Herring said could be worth a thousand dollars."

"A *jacket* worth a grand?"

"That's what she said. So why would someone take the pink stole? And leave that?"

"Maybe they didn't have time to look through everything in the speakeasy? We might have interrupted them when we drove up."

"But if they were in the speakeasy, there's no way they would have heard or seen us arrive." Leslie shook her head. "No, I've done a lot of thinking about it, and I think whoever it was left on their own—either because they were finished with what they were doing, or because the ghost made an appearance." She grinned. "I'm kind of hoping for the latter, because then I doubt the intruders will ever come back. And so far—to my knowledge, anyway—they haven't."

She brought dishes of shredded chicken, guacamole, chopped tomatoes, queso fresco, and plain yogurt to the table. "*Et voila*— Soft Tacos a la Leslie," she said, returning to grab the cilantro and the warm corn tortillas.

"Wow. Will you marry me?" he said, looking at the array of food. "Neither Stephanie nor I are all that great in the kitchen."

"I'll consider it," she said, sliding into her chair as he began to heap filling into a folded tortilla.

"I sure hope so," he replied, glancing at her with an expression pointed enough to make her blush.

"So…anyway," she said, filling her own taco, "I've been searching in the speakeasy when I have some free time to see if there is any sort of hidden cache down there. If Red Eye Sal did have those jewels, it seems a likely place to hide them, right?"

"One would think. And you're sure they exist?"

"Yes. I've dug deep enough in old *Chicago Tribune* archives—online—to find a few articles about them, and even one photo of the rubies. They did exist. And no one seems to have seen them for almost a century. So the timing is right for them to have been hidden when Sal lived here."

"Maybe the ghost—if it's Dorothy Duchene—can help you find them."

Leslie laughed. "She's not been much help otherwise, but I guess I could ask her."

"So you really do talk to her?" He was already loading up a second taco. Good thing she'd made plenty of tortillas.

"Well…it's more like shouting at her." Leslie grinned. Then her smile faded. "You know…I was thinking. This is going to sound really weird, but…that sort of corrosion that's on the iron bars that's not rust? I think… I wonder if it might be some sort of physical manifestation of the haunting."

That caught his interest enough for him to pause, taco halfway to his mouth. "As if whatever happened to Dorothy Duchene—or whoever she is—is a sort of evil growth spreading inside the house? Inside the stairway?"

"Yes. I guess that's what I mean. Put that way it sounds strange—but what other explanation is there? It's not anywhere else in the house. And that makes me think that whatever happened to her has something to do with the stairs. Especially that section of the stairway." She scooped up the last bit of guacamole. "I sent away a sample of a piece of wood with the corrosion on it to friend of mine at a lab at Michigan State University. Just to see what it was. It's… Well, they're not sure what it is. They can't identify it."

"That is more than a little creepy."

"I know, right? So I really hope that whatever it is, it goes away once I figure out how to help the ghost settle back into her afterlife." She looked at Declan, then laughed, shaking her head. "If someone had told me I'd be a cat owner and also be having this very serious conversation about a ghost six months ago, I would have thought they were on drugs."

"Same here. And I've seen a lot of creepy things in my line of work." He stood and began to clear the empty dishes, sliding them into place in the dishwasher with the ease of a single parent. "So maybe we should take a closer look at that staircase, stair railing, and so on."

"I was so hoping you'd say that."

It wasn't long before they had the kitchen put back to rights and were standing in the foyer, looking at the majestic stairway. The temporary wooden poles Declan had put in while he was working on the railing looked horribly out of place.

"I really need to pull up that carpet. It's probably a hundred years old," Leslie said, looking at the swath of dark red Oriental rug that covered the stairs in a long, threadbare strip. It was held in place on most steps by a slender brass rod that fit flush to the back of each one. "I keep putting it off because of all those rods— they'd each have to be unscrewed, and there are twenty-six steps."

"Except for that one—the broken step," Declan reminded her. "Was that broken before or after your break-in?"

"If it was broken, I didn't notice it before. There are a few bars missing in the middle of the stairway, and the carpet is loose. I used a staple gun to punch the rug into place so no one tripped on it while going up and down—just a temporary fix." She paused suddenly, stilling as a thought struck her.

"What is it?"

"The second time I saw the ghost, and every time since then, she's no longer standing at the top, along the balcony, but on the stairs. About a third of the way down." Leslie's shoulders began to prickle violently. "She's pointing...and she could very well be pointing at *this step*. The broken one."

Just as she said those words, the house moved…groaned and creaked. And the air shifted. It wasn't a breeze so much as a… maybe an intake of breath. A subtle change. A shudder?

The prickling was strong, and her skin felt as if it were drawing tighter everywhere.

Leslie looked at Declan, her eyes feeling as if they were going to pop out of her head. He looked at her, shocked and aware. So he'd heard and felt it too.

"It sounds," he said just above a whisper as he reached for her hand, "as if you've hit on something very important, Leslie."

She squeezed his fingers, glad—so glad—someone was here with her. "That broken stair. Maybe…maybe the ghost somehow made it break or shift, so we'd find it."

Declan frowned. "Or more likely, the person or persons who broke in trod on it and it broke. Maybe the ghost chose that moment to make an appearance and caused it to happen?"

"I don't know. But let's take a look at that stair. Maybe that's how Dorothy Duchene died—she stepped on it and fell to her death."

"But then why haunt the place if it were just an accident?"

"True. It would have to have been something violent to make her haunt the place. Right?"

At those words, something brushed across Leslie's cheek…a whisper of wind, a cobweb…a ghostly hand. She stifled a gasp and said into the ether, "Is that it? You fell down the stairs? Or were you *pushed?*"

A loud roaring filled her ears, reverberating through the foyer: violent, angry, determined. The walls shook, the crystal lights tinkled, windows rattled. The entire house shuddered as if it were being buffeted by a gale…but the gale was inside the walls.

Declan grabbed her, wrapping his arms around her as if to shelter her from whatever it was…but after a moment, it calmed.

She calmed. The ghost.

"It's all right," Leslie said, slowly disengaging herself from his embrace. "But obviously we are on the right track."

Without another word, they climbed up to the broken step. It was one of the ones where Leslie had stapled the faded rug runner, and it was the only stair missing its brass bar.

Declan moved the loose step, but it was too difficult to pull out from behind the rug runner without cutting the carpet. The runner was tight and stretched almost the entire width of the step, leaving no room to maneuver it free. However, it tilted and slid down behind the carpet, pulling the runner taut from the top of the next stair down, revealing a hollow beneath the top of the step.

"Wait a minute." Leslie bumped against Declan as she moved shoulder to shoulder with him on the stairs. "You don't think there's anything down in that hollow, do you? After all…I did find that pink velvet stole tucked inside the base of the stair rail."

"You could be right. If Dorothy Duchene was pushed down the stairs, maybe the murderer needed to hide her—or her belongings." His voice was tense with excitement as they both peered beneath the raised carpet, trying to get a good view down inside the hollow.

"I can't see anything."

"We need a better light—and probably to remove the carpet." He eased back and so did she. "I'm assuming you have one in your toolkit? Something to cut the carpet with. Or I could grab my toolbox from the truck."

Leslie was already climbing back down the stairs. "Yes, of course." She headed toward the kitchen, and was somewhat relieved that he followed. Despite her excitement, she was still trembling from the massive supernatural response that had filled the foyer.

She retrieved a mega-flashlight, then set about looking for her box cutter. That would be perfect for slicing through the old rug. When she had them both in hand, she paused and looked at Declan.

"You don't think there's a *body* down there, do you?" she asked. "Like…in pieces?"

His face was sober. "I don't know. I'm beginning to wonder if it's possible. Something's not right."

"I'm so glad you're here," she said, biting her lip a little nervously as she leaned against the counter. "I haven't really told anyone much about all this, and…well, I'm just glad you not only believed me first, but also that you just experienced what I did. Just now. You did, didn't you?"

"I sure as hell did."

"Thank you." She started to walk past him, but he reached out and snagged her arm with a light but firm touch.

She stopped and looked up at him. His brilliant green eyes were steady and serious…and hot. Her heart started to pound a little harder as she allowed him to draw her closer. Their feet, both still bare, bumped against the other—his warm, hers cold.

Leslie was suddenly very, *very* glad she'd brushed her teeth.

"Something wrong?" she asked, her voice low and teasing. She had to resist the urge to reach up and touch a hank of hair that had fallen across his forehead. "Don't you want to go back out and investigate our ghost?"

"*Our* ghost?" He smiled, his lips curving into something halfway between a smirk and a pout. "I don't think so. I think she just belongs to you. And maybe Rufus too." His arm slid around her waist, easing her up against him without moving to kiss her. "You're a hell of a woman, Leslie van Dorn. Talking to ghosts. Demanding information from them. And just standing there when they nearly blow the damn house down around you. I just want you to know—*damn.*"

They both looked down, for the phone in his pocket had begun to tinkle with "Brown Eyed Girl."

He groaned and released her. "Hey, Steph," he said as soon as he'd worked the device out of his jeans pocket. "What's up?" He listened, and his cheeks turned a little darker. "I'm working… On a project—what else? I…" He listened for a sec. "What time? Can't you get a ri—" His face fell. "All right. I'll be there in about…ten minutes." He looked down at Leslie, who'd taken the opportunity to settle her hands right on his chest and ease in once more.

Because when it came to a choice between maybe finding a dead body or getting cozy with her blacksmith, Leslie was going to choose the latter. Every time.

She smoothed her hands up and over his shoulders, her hips settling against his. He was strong. And tall. And hard. And warm. She shivered deep inside. *Oh, yes.*

"Uh…closer to twenty minutes," Declan said, and to her ears, he sounded delightfully breathless. "I'll be there in twenty— definitely by thirty…minutes…"

His voice trailed off as Leslie pressed a light little kiss on his jaw. He tasted warm, a little salty; he smelled like popcorn and delicious man; and she immediately wanted a whole lot more.

A whole lot more than twenty minutes' worth.

SIXTEEN

DECLAN DROPPED HIS PHONE onto the counter with a clunk, causing Leslie to laugh and surge into him with great enthusiasm.

He started to say something, but she covered his mouth with hers, tasting his warm, full lips. She sighed and shivered from heart to belly to lower and dove deeper, pulling him closer.

He was an amazing kisser. She hadn't remembered that wrong. His mouth was so soft and sensual, nibbling and teasing and kissing her so delicately…and yet with passion and need. He *wanted* her. She gripped his shoulders, feeling the taut slide of muscle beneath her fingers, and the heat from his body leaching into hers.

Their feet touched and mingled, her toes sliding on top of his as she pushed him back against the counter, when all at once—

"Dad? *Dad?*"

Declan thrust Leslie away with shocking speed as they both looked down at his phone…which was somehow still squawking at him.

"Steph?" he said, fumbling as he picked it up. "Sorry. It didn't hang up—"

"What are you *doing?*"

Leslie could hear the girl's voice blaring through the speaker, and she could hardly contain her horrified laughter.

"I'm sorry about that. Butt dial," he said—which made no sense—but his face was flushed with irritation and frustration, even as his lips twitched with barely controlled laughter. "I'll see you in thirty minutes."

This time he made certain the phone call actually disconnected before looking at Leslie, who'd been laughing silently during the whole conversation. Her lips were still warm and throbbing—as were other parts of her.

"Thirty minutes, huh?" she teased, sliding back toward him. "You sound pretty certain about that."

"Believe me, the last thing I want to do is leave here in thirty minutes. Or even sixty." He glared down at the phone and shook his head. "I'm here for three hours, and I don't hear a word. Even through ghostly encounters. Even through tornadolike winds. But the minute things start to get…interesting…" His voice lowered to a delicious rumble, and his eyes scored her with bottle-green heat. "Damn," he muttered.

Then, just when she thought he was going to slide right in again, he surprised her and dropped a quick, loud kiss on her forehead. "It's just as well. I'd better go now before…well, before thirty minutes becomes a *hell* of a lot longer."

Leslie stepped back and watched with a smile. He was a good father. Her heart swelled at the thought. "I guess I'll be digging around in the hollow of the step by myself tonight."

"Be careful." He paused from locating his keys. "You don't know what might be down there. Old nails—are you up to date on your tetanus?"

Leslie rolled her eyes. "Right. I'm refurbishing an old house and I haven't had a tetanus shot. Me? The super organizer?"

"Right. I should have known, you little general. You probably bought the cat carrier the first day after you saw Rufus."

She laughed in surprise. "How did you know?"

His gaze turned soft. "Wear gloves. And *shoes*."

"I will."

"Hey, Les," he said, stopping sharply. "I just want you to know, I'm glad Stephanie called."

"You are?" She stilled and lifted a brow.

"Yes. Because I really didn't want this"—he spread a hand to indicate the evening—"to turn into…something else. Not that I don't want to carry you off into that bedroom you were teasing me with right behind the wall there," he said with a laugh, then sobered again. "What I mean is…you needed someone to listen. You know, someone to give you a hug—and it really should only have been that. Just me being here. A comfort. So…it's better this way. Do you know what I'm saying?" He frowned. "I wasn't going to take advantage of your sensitive emotional state. You know?"

"Yes. Thanks. I… Thanks," she said, a little breathless now. Her throat had started to burn with emotion. He was right. And she'd been the one to kiss him, to move into him. He'd been… restrained. She liked that a lot. A *lot*.

"See you soon. Very soon." He tugged her close, sliding his palm up around the back of her head, cupping her with his hand as he kissed her very slowly and thoroughly and sensually…and then stepped back.

Both of them were breathing hard. Both sighed with regret. Both looked at the clock on the microwave and sighed again.

"Text me. Or call me if you find anything out," he said. "I'll…I'll come by tomorrow? All right?"

"To take another measurement?"

"Oh, I'd like to be taking a measurement—that's for sure." He expelled a breath that sent the lock of hair on his forehead billowing. "Get going, Zyler. Get your ass out the door. Duty calls."

And with that, he swept from the house without another look back.

Leslie stood there in the kitchen for quite a while after he left, very nearly mooning over the guy. What a guy. What a great guy. A wonderful father. An anticipatory lover. A dude who liked chick-flick TV. And a man who didn't want to take advantage of her grief and emotional state to get her into bed.

No wonder Emily Danube was falling all over him.

—✺—

The next day while she was running a few errands, Leslie walked by the tea shop and saw Cherry and Orbra sitting at one of the tables near the front window. It was midmorning, and a slow time for the shop with the tourists gone, so she felt no guilt about slipping inside to join them.

"Guess what," she said, pulling up a chair without being invited.

"You got laid."

"You finally got that sexy-ass Declan into bed."

Leslie gave an exaggerated sigh. "Oy! Enough with the sex already!" But her lips were twitching with a grin.

"She's been watching *Gilmore Girls* again," Cherry said to Orbra, who looked unusually grumpy this morning. "And she sure looks satisfied!"

"Yes I have…and guess who I've been watching it *with*." Leslie allowed herself a full-blown grin as she swiped a miniature almond scone from her aunt's plate.

"Not Declan!"

"Yes, Declan. But there was no removal of any articles of clothing. At least…not yet." She sat back and enjoyed the reaction from the two older ladies. "Rufus chaperoned, and he frowns on jumping into bed on the first date."

"Praise God," Orbra said, her face lighting up with hope. "Please let us know when the rest happens so I can live vicariously through you. I want every minute detail."

"That's gross, Orbra," Leslie told her, laughing.

"Hey…when you get to be my age and your lady bits have all shrunk up because your husband can't find his way around down there anymore, you gotta have fun somehow. Even if it's just in your head."

"Okay, okay, TMI," said Leslie, holding up a hand while still laughing.

"And when you get to be *my* age and half the people in this town think you're a lesbian just because you have short hair— which I am not, not that there's anything wrong with that—"

"*Who* thinks you're a lesbian, Cherry?" Leslie hooted. She was laughing so hard that her sides were aching. It felt so good after yesterday's grief-filled day. "Have they been in your company for more than five minutes? You're the most hetero woman I've ever known."

"Oh, some woman who was staying at Sunflower House over the summer tried to back Cherry in a corner after one of her hot yoga classes last August. She was trying to get her to help her with some position—"

"It's called an *asana*."

"—that required some—*ahem*—major skin-on-skin contact." Orbra refilled the teacups on the table. "The way she talks, you'd think it happened every day. No one's hit on her since Gilda first came to town, and that was, what, ten years ago? Twelve? You don't give off a lesbian vibe at all, Cherry, dear."

"Fifteen, as a matter of fact. Soooo…Declan was over? When?" Cherry grabbed a teacup from a nearby table so Orbra could pour a cup for her niece.

"Yesterday," Leslie told them. Then she went on to tell them everything. Even the part about the ghost and the gale-force winds. She figured she might as well—they'd badger her until she did anyway. Plus, maybe that would get them off her case.

"And then after he left, look what I found inside the broken stair." She pulled a tissue-wrapped article out of her bag and unwrapped it.

"Is this the other glove? Matching the one you found before?" Cherry asked, taking it.

"Yes. It's the same length, and the buttons are the same— see, they're those little round brass ones with tiny floral designs stamped on them. I was taking it over for Gilda to look at, but her shop is closed."

"She's sick today—she called me this morning because it was her turn to bring the refreshments to the Chamber of Commerce meeting and wanted me to sub for her. Figured I could bring something from the tea shop, I suppose. Hate those damned meetings—at the butt-white crack of dawn they are. Six *thirty!*

'So we get the business out of the way so we don't miss our own business,' is what Regina always says." Orbra shook her head with disgust. "I was gonna skip myself, but then I had to go since Gilda asked me. Regina wasn't there either—she's in Chicago at an auction for one of her clients who wants some Frank Lloyd Wright piece she made sure to tell me about"—Orbra rolled her eyes—"and Trib left early to meet a produce truck. And Aaron never comes, and so that just left me, Emily Danube—who didn't look very happy, and now I know why—Jinny from KnickKnack Clothes, the ladies from the B&Bs on Fourth, and Mildred, and Cherry. Oh, and Brad. What's the reason for the damned meetings if no one comes, I want to know?"

"I was there. For the whole thing," Cherry said primly.

"That's because you get up at the crack of dawn every day anyway to do your meditations and star and planet salutations and green smoothies," Orbra grumbled. "And now I'm hurting for lemon tarts and blueberry scones because I had to bring a bunch to the meeting where no one showed up and I can't serve them to anyone else now."

"I'm *so* glad I mentioned it," Leslie said, suddenly glad Orbra didn't have a walking stick like Helen Galliday. That would be really frightening. She exchanged amused glances with her aunt, who grinned and shook her head.

"Incidentally, the scones were delicious," Cherry said brightly. "What are you going to do with the leftovers?"

Orbra huffed and grumbled. "Probably serve them to annoying people like you two. And maybe Declan, because he's smoking hot."

"So you wanted to see if Gilda could date that glove to see if it was from around the time of Dorothy Duchene, is that it?" Cherry asked Leslie, picking it up again.

"Yes. And at this point, I'm pretty sure the glove definitely belonged to our ghost. I guess the issue is whether we're right that it's Dorothy Duchene. She—it—was pretty—er—adamant when we started talking about whether she'd been pushed down the stairs, and focusing on that specific step. I just…have a feeling those gloves belonged to her. And so did the wrap. And both of them were stolen. *Why?*"

Cherry was examining the glove, turning it inside out, looking at the buttons and seams, then put it on the table. "There's no tag, though you can see where it was cut away. Probably scratched her skin so she got rid of it. The material's not nylon. It feels like a cotton blend, maybe with some rayon, and the stitching is definitely from a machine. It's long—past the elbow, so it would go with an evening gown or dress. Not day clothes."

"Right. All of which doesn't really help much—though it doesn't preclude it from being from the 1920s. They used some machine stitching then."

"But would Dorothy Duchene have been wearing long gloves if she was a servant? On what occasion would she have done so? Surely a servant wouldn't be invited to any sort of formal gathering," Orbra said, surprising aunt and niece.

"That's a very good point," Leslie replied, sitting up straight, her eyes wide and her mind working. "I hadn't thought of that."

"Guess I'm good for something. S'pose I better get ready for the lunch rush, such as it is." Orbra got up, grumbling under her breath.

"Geesh. What's up with her?"

"She *really* hates getting up in the morning. Simple as that. It'll put her off all day. And Bill's been on a long haul, so he's been gone for two weeks already," Cherry said. Orbra's husband was a truck driver, a fact that she alternately rejoiced over and grumbled about.

Just then, the bell over the door jingled and in swept Helen Galliday and her ever-present walking stick, along with Pauline Whitten. They were trailed by Iva Nath, whose blue eyes began to sparkle as soon as she saw Leslie.

But it was Helen's companion, whose arm had been commandeered by the old crone's talon-like grip, that surprised Leslie. John Fischer looked a little like a kitten who'd been captured by its five-year-old owner and was being toted around and shown off.

"Oh good, you're here! I was going to ask Orbra if she had any updates on the ghost, but here you are in person," said Iva, sweeping over to sit at the table with Leslie and Cherry. "And look who Helen and Pauline ran into on their way out of the inn this morning." She beamed at the writer.

John looked at Leslie with bald desperation. She took pity on him and sat back down at the table. Maybe she'd be able to help him extricate himself from the busybody ladies.

She could consider that her good deed for the day.

Leslie was immediately forced into retelling her story about the glove—though she didn't go into quite as much detail about the ghost as she'd done earlier—as Orbra brought out tea and scones for everyone. She seemed in a slightly better mood, and Leslie noticed with an inward smile that the small plates were filled with lemon and blueberry scones. *Way to go, Orbry.*

Helen was in the middle of interrogating Cherry about the difference between Pilates and tai chi (pretty much everything) when the bell over the door tinkled again.

Leslie looked over and a surge of pleasure—and warmth—rushed over her. Her cheeks got unaccountably warm.

"Well look who the cat dragged in," Orbra said with a very pleased smile. "Have a seat here, Declan. I've got some nice lemon and blueberry scones, just hot and fresh from the oven." She glanced at Leslie and Cherry as if to forestall any dissenting comments from them.

Declan pulled up a chair right next to Leslie, and she could feel her pulse kicking up as his jeans-clad leg brushed against hers. "Hi," he murmured under the guise of scooting his chair closer and sitting down, his breath warm against her cheek.

"Hi," she muttered back. "Nice to see you."

"What kind of tea do you want, Dec?" asked Orbra. Leslie couldn't help but notice she hadn't asked anyone else their preference, and she grinned to herself again. It seemed as if everyone liked the guy.

"I'll have some of your special autumn blend that you were serving at the football game," he said. "Though I've recently begun to enjoy chai tea as well." His leg bumped purposely against Leslie's. "And could I get it to go? I just had to stop in for a sec—I wanted to let you know," he said, turning to Leslie, "that I need you to take a look at one of the pieces for the stair railing. I can't go any further with the project until you give me the go-ahead on it. It's at my workshop."

"Oh, sure," she replied, managing not to sound too eager. "I'm pretty swamped today, but I could probably stop by sometime this afternoon." There was the definite sound of a snicker, and Leslie slammed the toe of her shoe into her beloved auntie's shin beneath the table. And if she caught Orbra's ankle on the way, that was nothing more than a two-for-one.

"It won't take long," Declan said, though the look in his eyes belied that statement. Fortunately, he wasn't looking at anyone but Leslie.

"All right. What time is good for you?"

"Say, two o'clock? Then I'll still have quite a bit of daylight to keep working after you give me the go-ahead."

Leslie was aware of Cherry shaking with suppressed laughter—apparently she could read a double entendre into anything—but she managed to keep her own expression impassive. "Sure. That sounds good. I'll be there around two."

"Great. See you then. Thanks a lot for the tea, Orbra," Declan said as he stood to accept the to-go cup. He brushed a kiss onto the sturdy Dutch lady's cheek, then gave a general wave to the group and said his goodbyes.

"Leslie's gonna get laid, Leslie's gonna get laid," Cherry chanted into her ear.

"I wouldn't be too sure of that," Orbra muttered, hands on her hips. She looked as disappointed as if it were *she* who wasn't going to get laid. "Don't the kids get out of school at two thirty, and get home before three?"

Cherry's face fell, and her brows knitted together in disappointment. "Damn. That's too chancy, anyway. We don't want him rushing things."

Leslie merely smiled to herself, for she knew something the other ladies didn't.

It was Thursday, and Stephanie Lillard had pom practice on Thursdays—right after school, until six p.m.

At least.

—m—

Leslie pulled up to Declan's house at two o'clock sharp. Her stomach was filled with butterflies in the same way they'd been the first time she'd had to do a press conference after the public offering was announced.

Only this time, the butterflies were much softer and more pleasant, and were accompanied by a soft pang of anticipation whenever she remembered the way Declan had looked at her this morning. As much of a planner and organizer as she was, Leslie couldn't ever remember having actually *planned* a sex date.

Especially the first time with a man.

It was a heady feeling.

She got out of the car and was heading toward the workshop when the door of the house opened. Declan stood there, looking… just incredibly delicious. So handsome, so solid and male and inviting.

Their eyes met across the way, and she felt a *zing* sizzle through her as she turned to walk toward him. He leaned against the doorway, wearing a heather-blue t-shirt that fit him just right and charcoal-gray jeans that rode low on his hips. No shoes. His hair was damp and he was clean-shaven.

"I thought you'd be in the workshop," she said, half to be sassy and half because she was afraid she'd say something else that would betray the nerves and anticipation she was feeling.

"I wanted to get cleaned up before you got here." His eyes didn't leave her; they were practically eating her up as he stepped back to allow her to walk through the door. "I was all sweaty and dirty."

"Well, that's a shame," she said, dropping her voice to something low and throaty as he closed the door behind her. She walked through the entryway mudroom and into a bright and cheery kitchen, utterly and jubilantly aware of how he watched her.

"And why is that?" Declan asked, sliding an arm around her from behind. With his other hand, he moved the hair off one side of her neck, combing it with his fingers so it fell over the opposite shoulder.

Leslie gave a delicious little shiver when his mouth slid delicately along the exposed side of her throat, nibbling lightly from ear to the curve of her shoulder. Pleasure and heat shuttled through her like sensual, feathery tickles, and she closed her eyes, leaning back against him. "Because," she murmured, "I have a feeling you're going to get all sweaty again. And I'm hoping for a little dirty too."

He gave a little laugh against her skin, warm and moist, then settled in to really taste and nibble, licking and sucking gently on the most sensitive, delicate spot beneath her ear.

Leslie sighed and shivered, her hands braced against the counter in front of her as liquid pleasure coursed through her, heading directly south. He was crowding her gently against the kitchen island, and she felt heat and muscle and the fact that he was *very* happy to see her. She smiled and moaned when he slipped his naughty, slick tongue around to trace the inside of her ear.

"Declan," she murmured.

"Yes?" he replied, moving his mouth away even as one hand slid around to cover her breast, pressing and molding it gently in his hand.

"Didn't you have something to show me?" she purred, half sighing, half smiling with pure, unadulterated pleasure as he found her taut nipple through several layers of fabric.

"I most definitely do," he replied, pressing himself more firmly into her backside. "How about I get right to showing you?"

"I think that's an excellent—"

Her words were cut off when he spun her around and pulled her close to cover her lips with his. But she hardly even had time to enjoy the full mouth-on-mouth kiss, for he swung her up in his arms—in those solid, muscular, bulging arms attached to those impossibly broad, square shoulders—and carried her out of the room.

She kicked off her shoes on the way, hearing the satisfactory *thumpity, thumpity* as they clunked to the floor in the hall. And then she wrapped her arms around his neck and buried her face in his throat—this time to taste and kiss and lick, instead of to sob and sniffle.

"Much better," she murmured as Declan eased her onto the bed in his room. The windows were covered with privacy blinds that let the afternoon sunshine filter in. It illuminated the man standing in front of her as she looked up at him from where she propped up on her elbows.

"Better than what?" he asked, joining her on the bed, sliding up to lie next to her, one hand bracing his head. The other hand took its time and skimmed along her belly to her hip and thigh, then moved back up—this time gliding under her sweater and the tank top beneath it.

"Better than me bawling into your shoulder," she said, arching a little as he found the lace of her bra, cupping the swell of her breast with a large, warm hand.

"I don't know about that," he said with a lascivious smile. "At least when you were doing that, you weren't wearing one of these contraptions." He tugged at the plastic clasp and let it recoil back against her.

Leslie laughed. "I didn't think you'd noticed."

"Oh, I noticed that you were out of uniform, my little general. I most definitely noticed." He eased up and over her, pushing the hair away from her face, one thigh sliding between hers and fitting very snugly against the crotch of her thin leggings. Leslie's eyes widened at the stab of pleasure from the pressure there, and he smiled back, slow and hot and filled with promise as he used both hands to ease up the two layers of clothing, baring her belly and then her dark blue bra. It was trimmed with white lace and barely covered her.

"Very nice," he murmured. "Very, very nice. I was hoping you'd stay away from red. It's so very…"

"Clichéd?" she muttered, tugging at his tee. It came loose from the waistband of his jeans, and she said, "You called me a general? Then I order you to take off this shirt."

He eased back and complied, and Leslie mentally swooned at the beauty of his bronze-gold torso. *Oh my God,* she thought. *Cherry's going to be so jealous.*

"What are you laughing about?" he demanded, trying and failing to sound offended.

"Nothing," she said, wriggling out of her sweater and tank top. "Nothing at all."

She tossed away her clothing and then they were skin to skin, there on the bed. He flipped open the front-clasp bra and sighed with pleasure when her breasts swelled open and free, with two hard, dark pink nipples that just begged to be kissed and touched.

He didn't disappoint, taking his time to taste and suck and tease. All the while, Leslie slid deeper into a hot realm of arousal. The center of her pleasure, the hot juncture of her thighs, swelled and throbbed against his knee, which he still pressed strategically against her. Declan nudged her a little and she moaned, and the next thing she knew, he was yanking the elastic waist leggings down over her hips with ease.

"I like these," he muttered. "A lot."

"Happy…to…oblige," she replied, then gasped and bit her lip when he slid his hand down inside the front of her panties.

"Holy shit," he whispered in a sort of groaning voice. "Leslie…you're *so* ready…" His voice trailed off as he stroked and explored, slow and easy, smiling as she puffed out desperate sighs, and moaned, and shivered and arched.

He found a sensual, insistent rhythm with her, his fingers playing her like delicious magic until she cried out and came beautifully against his hand.

"Declan," she sighed, her eyes having rolled gently back into her head. "Come here." She smiled as she heard the sounds of his belt clinking and the swish of jeans being shucked away.

"Your wish is my command, my sexy little general," he said, sliding his very naked, very sleek and warm body against hers. Her leggings and panties were somehow gone, and there they were, skin to skin, curves to muscle, toes bumping, mouths clashing, hands everywhere.

He paused to roll on a condom, which had materialized from somewhere during a frenzy of kissing, licking, stroking, and nibbling, and Leslie helped guide him into place. They both groaned loudly with delight when they fit together, and he slid in, deep and hard.

"Oh, God," he whispered. "Leslie." He moved a few times and she began to wind up again, tighter and hotter than before, full and slick and ready.

"Oh no," she muttered when he started to slow down. "No you don't."

"But—" He closed his eyes, and she felt his jaw move against her cheek. She shivered against him, arching and flexing against his hard, damp body, sliding back and forth so he pressed against her little sweet spot.

"Come on…show me what you've got, Declan," she whispered in his ear. "You promised to show me— *Oh!*"

They both cried out, one after the other, as he slid home with one last, violent thrust. He collapsed against her, holding himself away until she pulled him down on top of her, welcoming the heavy, solid, salty weight of him.

She throbbed delicately, happily around him, her heart thudding, her toes curled, her eyes closed. All of her was warm and sated and felt very cared for.

"That was…pretty amazing," she said when she felt like she could form coherent words. It was after a long while…after he'd eased away, disposed of the condom somewhere aside, and gathered her up against his magnificent body.

Legs tangled, toes mingled, breaths fenced, eyes closed. Limbs relaxed…pulses slowed.

Until the sound of a door slamming jolted them abruptly awake.

SEVENTEEN

DECLAN BOLTED UP and off the bed, nearly taking a header into the dresser because the sheets and blanket had somehow wrapped around his legs.

Holy shit. Holy frakking shit—what is Stephanie doing home?

He stumbled around like an elephant and yanked on his jeans—narrowly missing zipping up his very happy cock—and managed to find a shirt.

All the while, he was aware of the sounds of his daughter: "Dad? Are you home? Dad? Who's here?"

Leslie was goggling at him with wide eyes and a mouth open with horror and silent laughter as she too pulled her clothes back on. He had a moment of regret when she covered that lovely ass with drooping leggings, then pulled on her sweater, sans bra and tank.

"I'm here," he called when he heard the ominous sounds of Stephanie making her way down the hall. The last thing he needed was for her to bust into his bedroom. Not that she would…but one never knew with a fifteen-year-old.

Oh God, did he smell like sex? Could he even go out there? Would she know?

"Whose shoes are these?" Stephanie called just as Declan opened the door and came out into the hall. He closed it behind him in one last bid for privacy.

"Hey, Steph," he said, forcing himself to sound as casual as possible. "I was just—uh—"

"Who's here? Is that Leslie—I mean Ms. van Dorn's car out there?" Stephanie had an extremely suspicious look at her face. "Are you— Were you— *Oh my God!*" Her face turned pink then bright red, and she gawked from Declan to the closed bedroom door. "Oh my *God! Dad!*"

Declan had no idea what to say or how to react. He stood there, open-mouthed and confused as his daughter continued to repeat the same refrain as she turned in a circle in the hallway.

The bedroom door opened and Leslie came out, looking as cool and unruffled as she would have in the boardroom. "Hi, Stephanie. I guess you got done with pom practice early today, hm?"

"I— Yes, I— We did. Coach Sandra was sick, so she sent us home early." Stephanie was still looking back and forth between them, and her eyes were still wide, but she didn't seem quite as flabbergasted.

"I'm starving. Want something to eat? Let's see what we can find." Leslie started toward the kitchen—as if coming out of Declan's bedroom in the middle of the day, then deciding to raid his kitchen was the most natural thing in the world—and Stephanie turned to follow.

Declan looked after them for a moment, then went back in his room to...well, to pull himself together. He went into the adjoining bath and put himself to rights, splashed water on his face and brushed his teeth, washing up—all the while realizing he was shirking his parental duty by allowing Leslie to handle the moment.

But he was just simply so mortified. Yes, he was an adult. It wasn't so much a moral thing as the fact that *his teenaged daughter—whose friends ogled him, by the way—*knew *he had just had sex.*

Oh. My. God.

He looked up at himself in the mirror and suddenly grinned like a maniac.

Oh yes, indeed, he'd just had sex. He'd just had mind-blowing, intense, sweet, *amazing* sex with a gorgeous, smart, sassy woman. And he couldn't freaking wait to do it again.

And with that very happy thought as fuel, he grew a pair and went out to face the music.

"I wouldn't recommend it, frankly," Leslie was saying. She and Stephanie were sitting on stools at the small square kitchen island sharing a bag of nacho chips and salsa. "No matter how hot he is. I was young and very naive." She gestured with a chip. "It could have turned out to be a real career killer if people found out or it went on long term. Especially since the bastard was married and never told me. But he was *very* attractive and extremely charming. Difficult to resist."

Declan looked from one to the other. He didn't think he wanted to know what they were talking about. But apparently, what he wanted didn't matter…

"We're talking about the pitfalls of sleeping with your boss," Leslie informed him as she languidly dragged the chip through the salsa. "I told her I don't recommend it."

"But sleeping with your *daughter's* boss isn't really a problem," Stephanie added pertly, then crunched into a nacho as if to punctuate her statement—while giving him the stink eye. Her cheeks were still dull red, but apparently food had won out over awkwardness.

Declan didn't respond to her comment. Instead, he took refuge in the fridge, opening the door and peering inside to see if there was any sort of rescue therein. The only thing remotely close to an escape was a single bottle of a B-Cubed lager, and even that didn't look promising.

When the fridge began to ding its warning that the door had been open too long, he reluctantly emerged to find Stephanie and Leslie watching him.

"And he complains that I keep the door open too long," Stephanie said with an expert roll of her eyes.

"So," Declan said, getting out glasses to pour iced tea. Because he needed to be doing something. "How was school today? Any new projects or tests?"

"And just as important—any drama?" Leslie asked with a grin.

"Brooklyn Danube says her mom is really pissed at you," Stephanie announced, looking at Declan. "Just wait till she hears about *this*."

"Wait—*what?*" Declan nearly dropped the glass pitcher. "Now wait a second, Steph—you're not going to be going around telling people—"

He stopped when his daughter began to laugh uproariously. "Are you kidding? As if I'd be going around telling people I walked in on my *dad* having *sex*."

"You did *not* walk in on your dad having sex," he said from between clenched teeth, his thoughts exploding wildly. How did he ever think he could be the father of a teenaged girl—by himself? How did he ever think he could begin to understand them? Women were an exotic species, but teenaged girls…even more so.

"Well, practically. And with my *boss*."

Declan looked at Leslie, who seemed utterly unaffected by the whole situation. How was that even possible?

"I guess I should be going," she said, sliding off her stool. Her eyes lingered on him for a minute, then moved on to Stephanie. "I'll see you on Saturday, all right?"

"Right." But Steph seemed a little hesitant, and that made Declan feel even guiltier. He hoped she wouldn't quit her job because of this.

He walked Leslie to the door, then stepped out onto the porch where Steph couldn't see them and closed the door. "Sorry about all that," he said.

Leslie just smiled up at him, easing in so their bellies met. "It's all right, Dec. I'm sorry it put you in a difficult position."

"I'm not. It was worth every awkward moment." He bent to kiss her, with both thoroughness and regret. "This was not the way I hoped things would go—all rushing up and out of bed and scrambling into our clothes."

"Oh really? Does that mean you're interested in a second round?" she teased, her hands settled on the front of his shoulders, her smiling eyes only a few inches away.

"More like a fifth, sixth, tenth round," he said. "At least."

"Have a good night, Dec. I know *I'll* sleep well." She winked audaciously at him, then sauntered down the steps and to her car.

He turned and went back inside to face the music.

—⁂—

Leslie was still smiling and basking as she pulled up the driveway to Shenstone House. It was just about five o'clock, which meant she had plenty of workday left.

And she'd be doing it all with a grin of satisfaction and a gentle soreness from the excellent activity in which she'd been engaged that afternoon. Cherry might advocate yoga for physical release, but Leslie was partial to sex. Especially the toe-curling, explosive kind she'd had with Declan.

She let herself into the house and paused, calling for Rufus—whom she'd let out before leaving—to see if he was interested in coming in. No response, so she closed the door and dropped her keys, phone, and bag on the counter, then, smiling, walked into her suite to change into work clothes.

Ten minutes later, she was down in the speakeasy with two large work lights she'd bought that morning while out running errands. The extension cord had to be plugged in on the main floor, but at least she had full illumination for the first time.

"Now I can get down to business." She knew—just *knew*— that Red Eye Sal's jewelry cache was here somewhere. If it existed—which she'd already confirmed—and hadn't been seen or known of since 1926, it had to be here in the house. And since she'd found an old newspaper in the speakeasy with that year on it, Leslie was certain that was the last time the secret room had been used—for whatever reason. Prohibition hadn't ended for another five years, but there seemed to be no logical reason for a newspaper to be sitting on a table for that length of time in a room that was used regularly.

Leslie found the new lights both a blessing and a curse, for what they illuminated with their bright white bulbs was often something she'd have preferred not to see. A little mold here, the skeletal remains of more than one rodent, minor cracks in the foundation, and other details.

Still, she hummed and worked her way around the room, inch by inch, bringing one of the lights with her to blaze over the wall as she examined it for any sign of a hidden door or panel.

Someone had gone through a lot of trouble to make the room comfortable and elegant, for the walls were all paneled. Beneath the solid maple paneling was cinderblock—at least as far as she could tell without removing every wall. She pried off a few random pieces, taking care to keep them intact so they could be replaced. Beneath the carpet, the concrete floor was slightly damp, and though there was no sign of past water damage, Leslie was going to have the basement waterproofed anyway. Just in case.

She'd been working for a good long time; she had no idea how many hours had passed, but her arms were getting tired and her eyes irritated from the dust that continued to be disturbed. She spent an inordinate amount of energy on the built-in sideboard china cabinet on one wall.

"There has to be a secret panel here somewhere. This is where it would be!" she said, determined.

Suddenly, there was a loud noise from upstairs. Pounding and shouting and footsteps.

Leslie bolted to her feet, her legs protesting from being cramped in a squatting position for so long, and staggered to the bottom of the steps just in time to hear her name being bellowed.

"I'm down here!" she called back, recognizing Declan's voice.

Worried by the urgency in his tones, she began to run up the spiral stairs just as he appeared at the top of them.

"What's wrong?" she asked, as he demanded, "What the hell are you doing down there?"

Taken aback by his tone, she paused, collected herself—clearly he was upset about something—and replied very calmly, "Working."

He was out of breath and came bounding down the stairs. "You scared the hell out of me, Leslie."

"What? How? What are you talking about?"

"I've been trying to reach you for the last hour and a half! Why don't you have your phone with you? *And why isn't the door to your house locked?*" His eyes, which had been a little wild when she first saw him, were narrowed in anger. "You've already had one break-in. You should take more care! Anyone could just walk in!"

"Apparently they did," she said quite frostily with a nod in his direction.

"Aw, damn." He took her by the arms, glared down at her, then hugged her close, dropping his chin onto the top of her head. "I'm sorry, Leslie. I'm sorry for yelling, but I was really worried about you. Considering…everything."

"Everything?" Leslie pulled away to look at him. He was—good grief, he was trembling. "Is there something else wrong, Declan?"

"Besides the fact that your house has been broken into *and* that you have an active ghost that tends to be a little…violent and loud sometimes? Isn't that enough? Besides the fact that…well, hell, today was—it was—damn near perfect."

She couldn't hold back a smile, and her cheek moved against his warm shirt. "It really was. I'm still humming along very nicely."

He pulled away to look down at her. "I am sorry for yelling, but you really should lock your door. And…try and keep your phone with you. What if something happened down here and you were injured…you'd have no way to call for help and no one would find you." He shook his head.

She smiled up at him. "Want to go upstairs and make up?"

"Sure." His grin was wide and his eyes lost their frustration and glinted with pleasure. "If you're done down here."

"I'm done for now, but I'd like to show you something later, when you have time. In that cabinet over there. If it's the hiding place for Red Eye Sal's jewels, that seems to be the best option. Maybe you'll see something I don't."

"Of course."

She led the way up the spiral steps. "I take it Stephanie is otherwise occupied?"

"Oh, right, yes. That was why I was texting you in the first place. She apparently was so traumatized by what happened today, she needed to go hang out with her friends. I told her she had to be home by nine thirty, but fortunately for me…I don't have a curfew." He snagged her by the arm at the top of the stairs and maneuvered her close for a kiss. "Lock your door from now on, okay?" he said when he pulled back.

"I will," she replied. "I normally do, you know."

He sighed as she took him by the hand and they walked back toward the kitchen and her private suite. "I guess it's just as well you didn't lock it tonight, because otherwise I wouldn't have been able to get in—and you wouldn't have heard me pounding on the door."

"What would you have done?"

"Broken in, of course."

She raised her brows. "Really."

"Your car was here and you weren't answering the phone. It was seven thirty at night, your lights were on, and your house had been broken into *and* you have a very vehement ghost. *Yes,* I would have broken in."

"Well, when you put it that way…" They'd reached the L-shaped sectional, and though he paused as they went by, she tugged him along with her. "Thought you'd want to see my bedroom, scout."

"Scout?"

"Well, if I'm a general, you're going to be a scout."

"So I clear the way, huh? Make sure everything's safe and ready," he said, easing her back against the bed, then sliding her leggings down as he knelt in front of her. The skin of her abdomen trembled lightly as his thumbs made soft little circles on her sensitive flesh.

"Yes," she said on a sigh, "but more importantly, you take orders from the general."

His head snapped up to look at her from below, as he was still kneeling, and she smiled archly. "Hey, you're the one who called me…a…general," she breathed as he bent close to kiss the swell of her belly, his lips curved in a dangerous smile.

"We'll see who takes orders from who," he said in a dusky voice, his breath warm against her navel. He hooked his thumbs inside the edges of her lace panties and yanked them down sharply.

And then he looked up, still kneeling in front of her. His eyes were hot and wicked. "Sit down and spread your legs, general. I'm going in."

—ɯ—

Some time later, Declan opened his eyes. He lay there for a moment, basking in the deliciousness of waking slowly next to a warm, soft, curvy bundle of woman he'd recently made thorough love to.

A glance at the clock told him he still had more than an hour before Stephanie was due home, and thus more than an hour before he had to even *think* about taking leave from his sexy little general.

His lips curved in the low lamplight as he stared at the ceiling, one arm settled comfortably around her shoulders, her face nestled against his chest. Her sweet-smelling hair mingled with his on the pillow, and her breath puffed lightly over the hair on his chest, ruffling it and heating his skin in a soft rhythm.

This was good. *So* good. He didn't remember feeling this good—well, ever. There was something about this unbent former celebrity CEO, this metaphysically curious and brave and sensible woman that drew him.

And it didn't really have anything to do with her perfect ass. Though that sure helped—that and the fascinating personality combination of sexy and sassy with organized and thoughtful: all of which made her the most interesting and satisfying partner he'd ever had.

It's awful soon to be thinking in absolutes, Zyler.

I've never thought in absolutes before. Maybe there's a reason why I am now.

Plus, she smelled so damn good. He could bury his face in her hair all day long and it would never get old.

She stirred next to him and sat up, propping on one bent arm. "Much better this time."

His brows lifted. "I don't know—you were yelling pretty loud both times."

She shoved him lightly in the shoulder, laughing. "I meant waking up—instead of being yanked from bliss into teenaged chaos." She slid from the bed with a bounce of breast and a flash of heart-shaped ass. "Are you hungry? I'm starving."

"Oh, I could eat." His eyes traveled over her slowly and he waited, unmoving, until she caught his meaning.

"Could you?" She grinned back just as slowly. "Well, come and get it, scout." She ducked just out of his reach and bounded into the bathroom, where she quickly flipped on the shower.

He was right behind her, and moments later, they were plastered against each other, hot and wet and slick, sliding and stroking and moaning in the midst of steam from dual showerheads.

"I was hoping those two showerheads would make up for their extra cost someday," she panted happily a few moments later, when they sagged into each other's arms as the hot water pounded in tandem on both their backs.

"I think you've damn near killed me," Declan said, gathering her close. "But what a way to die."

She laughed and pulled reluctantly away from nibbling on his wet shoulder. "Now I really am hungry."

She dug some food out of the fridge as he sat at the island and watched, feeling awfully homey and comfortable. Then his eyes fell on the calendar with yesterday's date marked with a G and a heart, and he remembered all the questions he'd wanted to ask but hadn't.

"So," he said, trying to figure out how to broach the subject tactfully. "Yesterday was a hard day for you."

Leslie glanced at him as she slid onto a chair at the big slab table. "Have a seat. It's more comfortable here."

She had put out cold pizza (from yesterday?), some lemon and blueberry scones from Orbra's, cut-up apples, some white cheese, and a small bowl of cashews. It looked delicious to him.

"Of course you'd want to know about that." Her eyes were serious. "It's normal, given…well…" Her lips moved in a gentle smile and the corners of her eyes crinkled.

"I'm mostly curious about the father—for obvious reasons," Declan said. "I mean, is he in the picture at all? Because—well, I'm getting pretty attached to you, Leslie, and I'm not the type of guy who plays around. Or who is played around *on*. You know?" He reached for her hand and covered it with his. "It's been a long time since I've been with someone long term, and I'm pretty sure I'm moving in that direction with you." More quickly than he thought he should admit.

She squeezed his hand and then released him. "The father was Gideon Nath—you met his step-grandmother Iva, I think, at the tea shop this morning. The one with rosy red cheeks and snow-white hair? Not the obnoxious one with the cane."

"Oh, good." He picked up a piece of apple and examined it. "So, Gideon Nath. Is that what the G is for on the calendar hanging in your kitchen?"

"The G— Oh, no. No, no. The G is for Gwendolyn, the name I had picked out for the baby."

"And so Gideon Nath is no longer in the picture…? Even though you…um…" He lifted his brows and waited.

"Even though he was the father of the baby, no, he's not in the picture at all. He never really was. We were friends from college, dated a few times, but nothing serious. We stayed in touch afterward—his grandfather's firm did estate planning for me—and Gideon and I… Well, we were each too busy to date. But we often needed an escort to business functions." She shrugged. "So we were each other's plus-one when we needed to be. It was all a very casual friends-with-benefits arrangement with no attachments…

and then I ended up pregnant. Completely unplanned for both of us, and pretty much a devastating blow for him too."

"A devastating blow? That he was going to be a father?" A few months ago, Declan might have felt the same way, but he'd come to look at things a lot more differently since Stephanie had come into his life. He sneered mentally at Gideon Nath's idiocy. The man was probably a real tool.

"He was devastated not so much because he was going to become a father, but because it was with me. What I mean is," Leslie said quickly, for she must have sensed Declan's growing dislike of the knobhead H. Gideon Nath III, "he'd met someone. Someone he really fell for—and they belonged together. He wanted to be with her and not me."

"And you were okay with that? You didn't feel…" He wasn't sure how to say it without making her sound weak—and his Leslie wasn't weak. But he wanted to know if he was competing with the memory of a failed relationship. Or if Leslie held a torch for the guy who'd gotten her knocked up, or if she'd been hurt beyond the miscarriage, by the man who'd got her pregnant in the first place.

"No, I didn't feel sad or betrayed or even hurt. I really didn't. Gideon is a great guy—when he removes the stick from up his butt, which Fiona—that's her name—does very well. And I'll admit, I was lost and shocked and confused when I found out I was expecting a baby. It was in the middle of the prep leading up to the public offering, and my life was—well, it was insane. I could hardly keep my head above water; I was working seventy hours a week, and I was pregnant. Fortunately," she said, looking at him with dark blue eyes limned with worry and grief, "at least I knew I would have the resources to raise the baby as a single parent. Maybe not as much time as I might have wanted, but the resources to make sure she was raised with everything she needed."

"And so what happened when you told Gideon? Was he already married to Fiona?"

"No. They weren't married or even engaged—but it was obvious the way things were headed. They were so perfect together—he would unbend and smile and even joke. And if you knew Gideon, you'd know what a big deal that was. Fiona was kind of goofy and all about New Age things—she and Iva get along really well." Leslie's eyes seemed far away, and Declan took the opportunity to snag a few cashews to build up his energy again.

Shagging a woman three times in one day—in, oh, less than six hours—took a lot out of a guy.

"So when I told Gideon," Leslie said, reaching for a piece of apple, "he immediately insisted we get married. Even though we weren't at all committed to each other, or in a relationship, he insisted the right thing to do was to get married."

"Oh boy." Declan paused as those words sank in and he realized… *That could have been me.*

So true. He would have insisted he and Cara get married— because what else did you do at eighteen with an unexpected pregnancy? Or, apparently, even at thirty-something.

He felt a little queasy thinking about it.

"Right. Even though he was in love with Fiona. So he immediately dropped her and decided he should marry me. Just like the man I always knew: the almost priggish, always-do-the-correct-and-perfect-thing Gideon."

"And you told him…?" Declan's appetite was failing all of a sudden. It was like *déjà vu* for him…but not exactly.

"I told him no. At first. But then…well, he was insistent, and honestly—I was a hot mess. I held it together at work, I really did—no one knew, and I mean *no one*—but otherwise…hell, they probably would have put me on medication if I hadn't been pregnant. No, not suicidal or clinically depressed or anything like that…just…confused, messed up, overtaxed, and being faced with two of the most important, life-altering things anyone could ever have happen to them—plus I was not only responsible for leading the entire company through the offering, and taking care of all of them, but I was also going to have a *child*. And so I said yes."

Declan realized he was holding himself tensely, and that his belly was tight and starting to churn, so he forced himself to relax. Whatever had happened with Gideon and Leslie was over—and obviously, there was a happy ending for the Gideon and Fiona shippers. So why was he feeling all knotted up over this?

"So you got married."

"We actually didn't." Leslie was playing with her napkin instead of looking at him…which made the warning bells begin to jangle deep in the back of his mind. "So this is where things get a little…murky."

"Murky?"

Leslie was silent for a moment, making those jangling bells even louder inside his head. "I didn't want to be the cause of breaking him and Fiona up—they belonged together. And I realized I didn't want to marry a man I only really liked, but didn't love. And I knew he'd be miserable. So I made a…let's call it an executive decision."

"An executive decision?" Declan was aware that he seemed to only be able to parrot her words, but there was nothing he could do about it.

"I told Gideon the baby wasn't his. That way he was off the hook and could marry Fiona."

"So…you lied to him?" Something red had begun to creep into the edge of his vision, but he managed to keep his voice calm and steady.

Leslie seemed to sense his unrest. "Not technically. I didn't know for certain. I never did genetic testing before—before I miscarried. But the only other possible father was a—a one-night fling I had on a business trip." To Declan's surprise, she wasn't avoiding his eyes. Nor, though she was subdued, did she seem ashamed or repentant for her decisions. Calm, deliberate, intense…but not apologetic.

"So you let Gideon off the hook, as you say, and planned to raise a child on your own that was his."

"I didn't really have a choice," she said. "I didn't want to marry him—"

"So don't marry the guy. What's he going to do, drag you to the church? If you said no, what was he going to do?" Declan was aware how tight and hard his voice had become, but he couldn't help it.

This was…this was not what he'd wanted to hear. Not what he'd expected from Leslie. This sort of deceit. This high-handed chief executive officer ploy.

"Right. I know." Her laugh was now—but too late—ashamed and abashed. "It wasn't the best decision—"

"It definitely wasn't."

She looked at him quickly. The initial shock blazing there faded, and her eyes became remote and her expression turned reserved. "Well, I've apparently hit one of your hot buttons."

"Uh…I'd say that's probably a hot button for most men. Not being given the chance to raise or even know about their child? Being lied to so they can be manipulated into marrying someone else?" Declan was so angry, so upset, he was nearly blind with rage. He stood, his fingers curling into fists on top of the table. "I think it's best if I leave now."

"If that's what you want." Leslie stood, still the calm and cool executive. "I'm sorry to have upset you—"

"Yeah, well, so am I." He let himself out without a backward glance, his body shaking with both sorrow and fury.

EIGHTEEN

LESLIE DIDN'T SLEEP WELL that night, despite her earlier prediction that she would.

In fact, she and Rufus stayed up far too late, idly viewing some random *Glee* episodes, simply because Declan had mentioned he'd watched it with Stephanie and she'd never seen it before.

For some reason, the in-your-face high school show peppered with pop songs from the last four decades made Leslie feel like her life was slightly less messy. After all, she was no longer in high school and didn't have to try and deal with figuring out who she was. She'd done that long ago, and let the chips fall where they may.

Apparently, Declan didn't like the way the chips had fallen. That hurt Leslie far more than it had when she realized Gideon and she didn't belong together; that even though he loved Fiona, he had to make a sacrifice and do the right thing—which was to marry Leslie and create a home for their child.

What a clusterfrak that would have been: the two strait-laced, driven, unbending and arrogant executives married to each other when neither of them wanted to be.

Too bad Declan couldn't understand.

And too bad Gideon had been so bloody damned rigid and unbending that she'd *had* to make that executive decision.

Would she have made the same decision now?

Probably…not. Who knew?

What did it matter? It was done with—completely a non-issue.

Except where Declan was concerned. And the status of Leslie's heart. Damn, she'd really started to fall for him—way early on, in fact, when he came practically barging into her house on a mission to protect his daughter from the child labor law violator.

Leslie laughed, but it hurt. Oh, her heart hurt.

Damn, I really screwed this up. And now she'd ruined everything—over something that happened more than a year ago, before Declan even came into her life.

It was late, and she was drowsing in front of the television on the sumptuous leather sectional, half watching, half sleeping.

Suddenly, her eyes bolted fully open.

The music. *The ghost's music.*

It was here, in this room, for the first time ever. Much louder than ever before, encroaching on her private space, moving deeper into the house. What did this mean? Was Dorothy getting impatient? Had something happened?

Leslie was wide awake now, looking around the room wildly for the ghostly image. This was new. It had never come in here before. It was always—

She stopped and looked at the TV. And then she looked at Rufus, who hadn't even stirred.

The music wasn't filtering in from the front of the hall, or even from the ghost…it was coming from the TV, from the crew-cut character named Puck, who was playing a guitar and singing a ballad.

The hair on Leslie's arms prickled, and her hands turned clammy. But it was the *same music.* She recognized it as the music that always filtered through the night whenever Dorothy's ghost appeared.

But that music…it wasn't from the 1920s.

No, this song was much more recent than that.

—∽∾—

"I can't believe I didn't recognize the song right away. I mean, who doesn't know 'Waiting for a Girl Like You'?" Leslie said, uncaring that her voice carried.

She and Cherry were sitting at Trib's for lunch. They were the only ones there, as he opened at eleven and they'd shown up minutes before.

"Seeing as I only have thirty-five minutes till my vinyasa class," Cherry said when Trib opened the door to them at ten fifty-five, "I figured you wouldn't mind letting us in a smidge early."

"Whatever," he said. Today his bow tie was carnation pink and he wore a charcoal-on-black striped shirt, charcoal suspenders, and excellently tailored black slacks. He looked like a million bucks—at least, as far as his attire went. His mood, however, seemed distracted instead of its normal cheery one. "Have a seat. Wherever you want. I assume you want your regular, Cherry?"

No sooner had he minced off to the kitchen in his Italian loafers with their order than Leslie launched into her news. "So that means," she said at the end of the story, "the ghost can't be Dorothy Duchene. I've been looking at it all wrong."

She and Cherry glanced up as Trib brought them water (no ice for Cherry—"it's better for the digestion") and a plate containing three small puddles of…something.

"This is my blueberry pâté, my homemade pear marmalade, and cherry-mint preserves. I'm sampling them today," he said, placing a tiny basket of rustic-looking crackers next to them. "Enjoy, ladies. I'll be tied up for a few minutes in back with Aaron finalizing the catering numbers for the mega-reunion on Sunday—that'll be the pâté's official debut, in fact. I'm *so* excited. Incidentally, Luddy's working on your order, and it should be out in *plenty* of time for you to get to your vinyasa class." He gave them a slightly harried smile and rushed off to the back.

"I forgot he was doing the catering on Sunday," Cherry said. "Maybe I *will* make an appearance at the reunion. At least the food'll be good."

"Who knows—maybe one of your old flames will show up and you'll be able to forget about stalking the blacksmith in town." Leslie managed to say the words lightly, but inside she felt the unpleasant lurch of her heart.

She didn't really know what to do—if anything—to mend the rift with Declan. Maybe there wasn't even enough there to try. After all, they really didn't know each other that well. And she couldn't change the past, as much as she might like to.

"The blacksmith is taken," Cherry said, then looked at her sharply. "Isn't he?"

Leslie frowned and, to her embarrassment, realized her eyes were burning as tears gathered there. "Not so much."

"Oh dear." Cherry reached across and patted her hand. "I'm sorry, Les. What happened? Want to talk about it? I promise not to make any jokes about too many irons in the fire or anything like that."

Leslie laughed reluctantly, then told her briefly what happened. "And that's how I ended up watching *Glee*—which, I'm not sure what all the fuss was about over that show anyway—at one in the morning. And I sort of woke up hearing that song, and that's when I realized what it was."

"So the ghost must be someone who died in the eighties—or after, I guess. I'm not sure when the song came out. Early eighties, I think."

"I was thinking…I wonder if it could be Kristen van Gerste," Leslie said. "She was wearing a flapper dress that night, remember?"

"What about Kristen van Gerste?" Trib said as he set two plates on the table. One was a salad, heaped high with roasted fall veggies, sun-dried Traverse City cherries, and kale for Cherry. The other was Leslie's sandwich, made from a crusty whole-grain loaf with house-made chicken salad, artichoke hearts, and roasted red pepper tapenade.

Leslie's mouth watered, for she hadn't felt much like eating since her aborted dinner with Declan last evening. But she responded before taking a bite of her sandwich. "Whether it's possible the ghost at Shenstone House is Kristen, not Dorothy Duchene, as I'd thought."

"But don't ghosts only haunt where they die?" Trib asked with a frown. "She was found in the woods, you know." Then he stilled, his eyes widening hugely behind his glasses. "Unless she was killed *at Shenstone House*. Oh my God." He clapped a hand over his mouth and goggled at them. "What if she was killed there and moved to the woods…" He looked white as a ghost himself.

"Poor sweet, darling Kristen. She didn't deserve any of that." He blinked rapidly, then removed a pale blue handkerchief from his trouser pocket. "Damned Marcus Levin. If he hadn't been such a prick, she'd probably still be alive today. Oh," he wailed softly, removing his glasses to dab at his eyes. "It just brings it all back, doesn't it? This, and the reunion, and just…all of it. It brings it all back like it was yesterday."

Since neither Cherry nor Leslie had actually been around at the time, neither could respond appropriately. Still, Leslie didn't disagree with any of his sentiments—including the suggestion that Kristen could easily have been killed inside Shenstone House, and then, for some unknown reason, had her body moved and left in the woods. And the topazes stolen.

"I was going to see if I could find a picture of Kristen that night at the prom—to see if she looks like the ghost," Leslie said as Trib was called back to the kitchen.

"That'll be easy—she'd have been in the paper, not only as Homecoming queen but also, unfortunately, because of the disappearance, of course," Cherry said. "Let's see…the *Enterprise* would have been the main paper in town at the time. You can look online, but the library probably has archives." She glanced at her watch and grimaced. "If only I had time, I'd come and help you look."

"No problem, auntie," Leslie said. "The guys are coming to sand the upstairs hallway and bedroom floors, so I was planning on clearing out of the house for most of the day anyway. I have to pick up a special order in Grand Rapids—the antique pulls for the guest bathrooms came in—and I'll probably stop at the mall there, so I won't get to the library till later this afternoon."

Plus, I don't feel like doing much else of anything. Might as well go to the library. Bury my nose in a book—or some archives—there.

—⁂—

There was something about a library that comforted Leslie, even though she hadn't been in one for ages—nor had she had much time to read for pleasure over the last ten years, due to her all-consuming career.

The smell of old books—especially in an older building like the one she visited in the larger city of Holland, the nearest library to Sematauk—the tall ceilings, the shelves upon shelves of goodies… She wondered what would happen if the apocalypse came and people had to rebuild civilization. Wouldn't everyone want to live in an old library?

She decided that if something like *I Am Legend* ever happened, she'd definitely take up residence in a library.

In hopes of ensuring the sanding guys would be gone by the time she got home, Leslie wandered through the children's books section and found many of her childhood favorites. And then, because she was really feeling down and more than a little sadistic, she searched out the old historical romance novel about the blacksmith she'd read to pieces over the years.

Whether it was fate or just good luck, she didn't know—but not only did the library have that book, it was for sale in the used book section. The paperback was just waiting for her, with its aged taupe pages, bent cover in lurid pinks, golds, and oranges, and creased binding. She snatched it up and paid a dollar for it with enthusiasm.

That would be one way to mourn the loss of her true-life blacksmith tonight.

Then, finally, she went to the newspaper archives to do some real work.

Everything was on microfilm, so it was easy to ask for May through June of 1985—the year Kristen van Gerste had been killed. Then it just took a little time skimming through the daily papers until she found the right one. Prom would have been on a Friday or Saturday, she reasoned, so the photos would have been on Saturday or Sunday.

She was just getting into the hang of loading the microfilm into the viewing machine and skimming through it with a smooth, satisfactory whir when she found it.

The headline leaped out at her: *Prom Queen Found Dead.* She shuddered; that sounded like something out of a Stephen King novel.

A large photo of Kristen van Gerste was there on the front page, and the moment she saw it, Leslie gasped audibly. There was no doubt. It had to be Kristen who was haunting Shenstone House—for in the photo, which was in color, the lovely young woman was wearing the legendary topazes, long white gloves... and a thick pink wrap that looked like velvet.

She'd found her ghost.

And, quite possibly, had uncovered a lot more questions about the murder from thirty years ago.

And now—

"Well, hello, Leslie."

She jolted, looking up to find John Fischer standing there. He was holding a box of microfilm rolls as well.

"Doing some research?" he asked, glancing toward the screen.

"Yes. You too?"

"As a matter of fact I am." He smiled and gestured with the small cardboard box. The rolls shuffled inside. "Just finishing up, actually. And I'm so happy to have run into you. Because I happened to be doing some research about old houses—for my project, you know—and I came across some interesting information about houses built in the same era as Shenstone. They built expertly hidden cabinets to hide liquor from the fuzz— as they called them," he added with a grin, "and this article had some mention of the ways they'd mask them from the authorities, who were pretty good about finding hidden caches. I noticed something at Shenstone when you were showing me and Iva Nath around the other day that could possibly be one of those well-hidden cabinets...I was wondering if you'd let me come by and show you sometime."

Leslie had turned off the microfilm reader and removed the roll. She'd found what she needed; now she just had to figure out what to do next to put Kristen's ghost to rest—a necessity before the inn could be opened for business.

But John's idea sounded just as intriguing. She'd pretty much exhausted all of her own ideas for where the gems might be hidden; she was open to hearing others. "Sure. I was just getting ready to head back home now, and I don't have any other plans tonight."

Unfortunately.

"As a matter of fact, neither do I—other than taking all my research back to the inn and typing it up. Which is just as boring as it sounds." He smiled behind his beard.

Just then, a well-modulated female voice came over the loudspeaker. "Attention, library patrons: the library will be closing in fifteen minutes. Please bring your selections to the circulation desk as soon as possible. Please return any checked-out reference materials to the appropriate desk."

"Oh, wow," Leslie said, shoving the roll of microfilm into its box. "I had no idea it was almost six o'clock." She stood. "I guess I'd better return these to the desk… So, anyway, John—I should be home and have all my stuff put away by seven thirty or so. I was in Grand Rapids most of the day while they were sanding my floors, and the workers should be gone by now. Is sometime around eight tonight a good time for you to come by?"

John smiled with delight. "Absolutely. I'll be there at eight. How about I bring a bottle of wine?"

—m—

"Thanks for coming over, Dec," Brad said as he opened the door to what he called his "tasting room." Really, it was just an excuse for a tricked-out man cave that he could write off as a business expense, for the walkout basement part of his house was licensed as a commercial kitchen. This brewing and bottling area was set off from the "tasting area" by a half-wall and chrome counter.

"No problem, bud. You sounded pretty upset."

And besides, what else would Declan be doing on a Friday night? Stephanie was at an away football game and was spending the night at a friend's house after. Which should have been a boon for Declan—except that things had gone to shit last night at Leslie's house, and now he didn't have anything else to do but sit around and brood. Hanging out with Brad was far better than that, and marginally better than working at his forge on a project for the woman with whom he *should* have been hanging out.

Somehow he'd lost his mojo when it came to wanting to work on those sexy spiral iron bars. The thought of making them just right, of coaxing those babies into the perfect curve, wasn't as much of a pleasure anymore.

Declan *was* glad Steph's game was away, for otherwise he might have found himself face to face with—or, even more awkward, sitting next to—Emily Danube.

He sank down in one of the dark brown club chairs in front of a wall-sized TV that weighed about two hundred pounds. He knew this for a fact because he'd helped to move the mother down the hill and into the walkout basement a few months ago. He told Brad the only way the damned thing was going back out was in pieces.

Strangely enough, Brad looked about as tense and unhappy as Declan himself felt. He handed him a dark brown bottle. "You got here in good time. I just got home from the police station."

"The police station?" Declan froze from reaching for a bottle opener. "What the hell's going on?"

"You know I was supposed to meet Marcus Levin the other night—last night, it was. He'd agreed to give me an endorsement for the Sematauk Straw Lager, and I was going to get it on video, and buy him dinner, and all that."

"Right. And congrats, by the way. That's really going to help the stuff sell even better than before."

"Yeah, well…it's not quite going to work out that way." Brad looked at the beer he'd opened but hadn't touched, as if he'd never seen it before, then put it aside. Declan thought he was looking a little green around the gills.

"So what happened? He stand you up? Change his mind?"

"No. I found him. With his head bashed in."

Declan gaped, setting his bottle on the table next to him without even looking. "Are you telling me you *found* Marcus Levin's dead body and *he was murdered?*"

"Yep. With a five iron. His five iron, I suppose."

"*Where?* Where did you find him?" And Declan thought *he* was having a bad day. "When?"

"At the high school, up by the football stadium. We were going to meet there so I could do the video in the press box, you know, with the football field down below—for atmosphere. Like he was casting a game, but instead he was talking about Sematauk Straw. Man, you gotta wonder if it coulda been me too if I'd been with him." Brad shuddered.

"You mean he was killed at the high school?" Declan went cold and still. Stephanie had been there just a few hours earlier. "Where? When? Weren't there people around?"

Stephanie had been on the same grounds as a murderer. That realization was sinking in like a heavy lead ball melting into his consciousness. He stood, his fingers shaking a little, and pulled the phone out of his pocket. He'd text her to make sure she was all right.

"It was in the back behind the bleachers—in the coaches' parking lot up near the locker room. Not a well-traveled area on a night when there's no football game. I doubt anyone was around, and one of the floodlights was out too."

Declan had calmed down slightly by now. After all, Stephanie had been with the entire pom team, plus the football team, the cheerleaders and the marching band, boarding buses for the away game by four thirty…and surely if something had happened to *anyone*, he'd know by now. It was after ten o'clock, so the game they were at was probably in the fourth quarter, if not already over.

"When did you find him?" he asked again, still watching the phone for a text from his daughter. Or anyone else who might care to contact him. Not that he was expecting or wanting anyone to.

Declan went a little colder. Leslie's house wasn't that far from the high school. Just through the woods and up the hill… He swallowed hard. *Good God, I hope she remembered to lock the door like I told her.*

He looked at his phone. Maybe he should text and see if she was all right. Let her know. He hesitated, and realized Brad was still speaking.

"Eight thirty. A little before eight thirty I found him. Looked like he hadn't been there all that long, either. I mean…I went over to him and touched his hand—you know, just to make sure—and it was warm. And…and the blood was still—" Brad's expression changed and he gave a weird swallow—like he'd thrown up a little in his mouth.

"Christ," Declan said, shaking his head. "Who'd have wanted to do something like that? I mean, was it random or was it because he was Marcus Levin? Did the police say anything? Did it look like he'd been robbed or carjacked?"

"No. His car was there, and so were the golf clubs in the back seat. And you know Ken Morton—always pretty solid and keeping it close to the vest. He wasn't going to tell me much, though he asked a lot of questions. As for whether it was random or not…I dunno. Levin's kind of—or *was* kind of—a celebrity, being a news anchor and all, but he's—*was*—pretty much a real prick. Real full of himself because he played for the NFL till he torqued up his knee. Now he's on TV. Could be anyone who got tired of his bullshit, you know?"

"Right. Wow. I can't believe we were just sitting in the press box with him at the game the other night, and now he's murdered." Declan sobered even more. He'd never known anyone, even distantly, who'd been killed. It kind of put life into perspective with a large, sharp jolt.

"I know." Brad looked at his untouched beer and let it be. He clearly wasn't in the mood to taste it. "I called the editor of the paper and told him I'd get him the story by midnight. Talk about an eyewitness. It sure as hell won't take me long to write it—I don't have to interview anyone about the crime scene." He laughed hollowly. "Lucky me. I think that image's gonna be haunting my nightmares for a while."

Declan grimaced, then sipped his beer. It didn't taste very good to him either, so he set it down. Just then, his phone lit up and began to ring.

Not who he was expecting, or even hoping for. "Sorry, bud, but I'm going to take this—it's my cousin Teddy finally calling me back." He answered, "Geez, nice of you to find the time for the little people, Teddy."

Teddy Mack, a.k.a. *New York Times* and international mega-bestselling author T. J. Mack, laughed over the line. "Sorry, Dec—I was in Frankfurt and London, and it's ridiculous to call back home on my cell. I tried to text you but I don't think it went through. But I'm back Stateside now."

"London, huh? What were you doing there? Book tour?"

"Meeting with my UK publisher, and before that I was in Frankfurt for the big book fair."

"What a life," Declan said, sinking back into his club chair and not feeling one iota of envy. Not even a twinge, except... "How's it going with that guy you were seeing? What was his name? Oscar something? He sounded like a Brit—did you take him with you?" Last he'd heard, things had been very hot and heavy—and very happy—for his cousin.

"Oscar London, and...well, things aren't going much at all with him anymore." She sighed. "He's a nice guy—a *really* nice guy—but...well, it's a long story. Maybe someday I'll tell you about it. The next time you come visit me in New York...?" she said suggestively. "You could write it off—I've got some iron scrollwork that needs to be done for my new brownstone. You've been putting me off for months now, Dec."

"That would be great." Maybe he'd even do that sooner rather than later—get out of town for a while and clear his head. Of course, now that he had Stephanie...he couldn't just up and go.

Damn.

"Any time between now and February—that's when I start my next book. So, what were you calling about? What's up?" Teddy asked.

"Besides wanting to catch up with my favorite cousin," he said, smiling and imagining Teddy rolling her eyes, "I wanted to ask you about Jeremy Fischer. Do you know him? Have you met him?"

"Yes, I've met Jeremy Fischer a number of times. We happen to have the same agent, as a matter of fact."

"Oh, great, because…he's here in Sematauk. And I just wanted to get any dirt—uh, I mean—any information on him you might have. He's—uh—getting kind of friendly with one of the local women here, and, well…I wouldn't want her to get hurt or anything."

Lie, lie, lie…and maybe it didn't matter anymore, now that he and Leslie were…whatever they were. But there was something about the Fischer guy that'd bothered him when they met at Orbra's yesterday morning. Something about him didn't sit right. Something was off.

"You said Jeremy Fischer. You're saying the author Jeremy Fischer is in Sematauk?"

"Yes, that's right. He's staying at an inn, supposedly working on his new project, but he's not really telling anyone it's him—"

"That's because it's *not* him."

Declan sat up straight. "What do you mean? How do you know? Was he at the book fair with you?"

"No, no, Jeremy Fischer is utterly reclusive and never goes to anything like that. That's because it's a closely guarded secret that Jeremy Fischer—the author of the Bruno Tablenture books—is a little old lady of about sixty years old. Never held a gun in her life."

NINETEEN

I HOPE I'M DOING *the right thing*, Declan thought as he once more drove up the driveway to Shenstone House, uninvited.

Of course he was doing the right thing.

Even if he and Leslie were…whatever they were—or weren't—anymore, it was the right thing to do. The safest, smartest, most caring thing to do—and he'd be doing it for any person he knew.

Especially since someone had just had their head bashed in less than a mile away from Leslie's house.

He gripped the steering wheel tightly and took slow, deep breaths. There was no reason to think that John Fischer—if that was even his real name—intended Leslie any harm.

What reason would he have to hurt her?

What reason would he have to lie about who he was?

Declan looked at his phone. He really should call Ken Morton and tell him what was going on. Just in case.

Instead of barreling up the driveway and showing up, with figurative guns blasting like a hero, maybe he should at least let the cops know. After all, they were in the middle of a murder investigation.

He stopped the car halfway up the drive, out of sight from the house, and called Ken Morton's personal cell phone number.

"It's Declan—I know you're busy. But I think you should know something."

"You talked to Beatty, then?"

"Yes, I just left his house. He told me everything. Listen," he said, "I just found out that the man who everyone thinks is Jeremy Fischer—"

"The big celebrity author?"

"Yeah, him. Well, I just found out from my cousin, who knows Jeremy Fischer, that the man who is here in town calling himself John Fischer and pretending to be the author *isn't* Jeremy Fischer. I thought under the circumstances, with a murder investigation, you'd want to know."

"Are you certain about this?" Declan could tell he had Morton's full attention now.

"Absolutely. My cousin knows Jeremy Fischer personally." That was all he needed to say. "It can't be him. And here's the other thing…the reason I'm calling right now. I just found this out, and I tried to contact Leslie van Dorn to let her know, because she and Fischer were somewhat friendly and I found out through Cherry that Fischer was coming over to her house tonight. I never heard back from Leslie, I mean, so I contacted Cherry. So that worries me a lot."

Morton swore, short and loud. "Probably worth checking out, I'd say. I'll get over there—"

"I'm already here. At Shenstone House. But since I don't know what he's up to—if anything, and I'm not packing—I thought you should know. There could be a perfectly innocent reason, and, hell, I could be interrupting a romantic dinner," Declan said very lightly and humorously, "but something about it doesn't sit right. I'm afraid Leslie might be in danger. And I'm already here."

"Wait for us to get there," Morton said. "Damn, I'm going to have to call in a trooper. This is getting…pretty intense."

"I'm pulling up the driveway now. I won't knock or do anything until you get here." Maybe.

"All right. Sending two men over now."

"No sirens or lights," Declan added quickly. "In case—"

"I'll make that call. Don't do anything stupid, Zyler. This isn't like the movies."

Declan hung up and continued up the driveway with his headlights turned off. He thought it might be best if he arrived unnoticed, for several reasons—one of which being, if he was terribly wrong and interrupting something innocent, that he didn't want to announce his mistake. He could just slink off home. In light of this decision, he parked as far away from the house as possible, out of easy sight from the windows.

What a creeper you are.

It's for a good reason.

The motion-activated lights came on, however, illuminating two cars: Leslie's and, presumably, Fischer's.

Lights were on in the kitchen, but Declan couldn't see any movement inside. There didn't seem to be any lamps on in her suite. He wasn't certain whether that was good or bad.

Unable to wait, his nerves jumping and thoughts popping, he climbed out of the car and closed the door quietly. Then he slunk up to the house, feeling like nothing more than a burglar himself.

If Leslie sees me, it's over.

But when he got to the kitchen door and saw the scene inside, his heart dropped to his feet and he no longer cared about being circumspect.

For there, slumped over the table and unmoving, was Leslie. There was a dark puddle of blood on the table…and John Fischer was nowhere to be seen.

TWENTY

LESLIE HEARD A VOICE from far away. It dug into her mind and pulled, dragging her from the depths of darkness.

"Leslie! *Leslie*, wake up! Are you all right?" Something pulled at her, touched her, *bothered* her.

She fought it for as long as she could, but finally she opened her eyes. She had no choice. She opened them, blinked, focused—all with great effort.

"Declan?" she whispered.

"Oh, thank God," he said. His face was tight and white. His hands were on her shoulders, turning her to look up at him.

"What—what are you doing here?" She blinked, sifting through the tangle of her mind. "What happened?"

"I don't know." Declan was speaking to her, but he was looking around the room with an arrested expression, as if he was expecting to see something dangerous.

She looked around too, and pieces of her memory began to clunk into place when she saw the two wine glasses and the half-empty bottle on the table. "The last thing I remember…I was sitting here with—John! John Fischer—he's here. Or he was here—"

"His car is outside. He's still here," Declan said grimly. She realized with a start that he was holding one of the iron bars he used in his trade, and that her kitchen door was open. The window—smashed, and glass all over.

"Sorry about that," he said in a low voice, still looking around, still brandishing the iron bar. "I saw you on the table like that, lying in a pool of blood, and I didn't…" His voice stretched tight and he let it cease.

"Blood? Not from me…I don't think." Leslie touched the back of her head, which was pounding as if she had a migraine—not as if she'd been hit in the back of the skull.

"It's red wine. But I thought it was blood."

"That's right—he drugged the wine. We were sitting here chatting, drinking the wine, and then I started to feel very strange…I think I realized what he'd done just before I lost consciousness." She stood, gripping the edge of the table when her knees wobbled. "But why? What would he— *Oh*. I know."

"Leslie," Declan said, grabbing her arm when she took two unsteady steps toward the hall. "Where are you going? What if he has a gun or some other weapon? The police are on their way—"

"They are? But surely he doesn't have a gun. If he did, wouldn't he have used it instead of drugging me?" Her head was still muzzy, but she grabbed on to coherent thoughts and forced out the words. She thought they made sense.

"Probably." Declan's expression changed from intense to pleased, and he hefted the iron bar in his hand.

Leslie took his arm. "He's down in the speakeasy, I think. He's looking for the gems. He wanted to come over because he thinks he knows where—"

"So he can't hear us, can he? Down there? Good." Declan suddenly looked very determined. His jaw set, shifting slightly. "Let's go have a chat with Mr. John Fischer, who, by the way, *isn't* the author Jeremy Fischer at all."

"I think I figured that out by now," Leslie said wryly. Her head was pounding as if she'd had too many margaritas the night before, but she went over to her purse and pulled out her pepper spray.

Declan gave her a brief grin when she showed it to him, then sobered. "Maybe you should stay here. You don't look too steady on your feet—"

"Hell no," she said, and started off without waiting for him. But, fortunately, Declan was right behind her, and his strong hand steadied her as they made their way quietly to the speakeasy entrance.

They found John Fischer—or whoever he was—kneeling on the floor in the speakeasy with tools and measuring equipment all around him. He barely had time to scramble to his feet before Declan swung himself down the center of the spiral staircase, ignoring the actual steps. He landed in front of Fischer and brandished the iron bar.

"I'm not going to be shy about using this," Declan said. "And I suspect Leslie won't hesitate to blast you with pepper spray. So I suggest you take a seat right there on that sofa until the police get here."

"The police?" Fischer's face fell behind its beard as he moved to follow Declan's orders. "What do we need the police for? I'll leave, I swear. I just wanted… I was *sure* I knew where the gems were. I just needed more time. I didn't hurt anyone. I wouldn't hurt anyone."

"You call drugging me not hurting anyone?" Leslie had managed to make her way down the stairs on her still-unsteady knees, and now she stood in front of the sofa, aiming her pepper pray at Fischer.

"It was just a little sleep aid mixed in with your drink," he whined. "Just to knock you out for a bit so I could— Aw, *damn.*"

He looked up at the ceiling, for the sounds of footsteps above, and shouts of "Police! Show yourselves!" echoed through the house.

"Did you really have to call the police?"

"Considering the fact that someone's head was bashed in less than a mile away from here earlier tonight, *yes*," Declan said as Leslie spun toward him in shock.

"What?" Now her head was pounding even harder.

"I'll tell you about it in a while—as soon as *this* is taken care of," he said, gesturing at Fischer with the iron bar. "What's your real name, anyway? And how do you get off on pretending to be Jeremy Fischer?"

"My name really is John Fischer. And I never *said* I was Jeremy Fischer," the man sneered. "You all just thought I was. Especially once I dropped a few hints to that old bat with the damned cane. What a loon."

"So you admit you led everyone to believe you were Jeremy Fischer?" said a new voice.

Leslie turned to see Officer Morton easing his way down the spiral stairs.

"Hey, there's no crime in people misunderstanding things I said. I never claimed to be anyone I wasn't."

"Which is…who? Or what? Wait a minute…John Fischer? I know that name." Morton's eyes narrowed and he looked at Fischer more closely. "You're that treasure hunter, aren't you? I remember—was it two years ago?—you were sniffing around trying to get inside the house here under the guise of wanting to buy it. You didn't have a beard then."

"No crime in growing a beard," Fischer retorted.

"Well, I can't argue with that. So let's go down to the station and talk about what crimes there *are* at stake here. I'm going to take Ms. van Dorn's statement, and then we'll see what sort of excuses you can dredge up to try and wiggle out of a jail cell."

—m—

"I'm feeling much better," Leslie said from her position on the sectional. Rufus was in her lap, and she was petting him as if *he'd* been the one who'd been drugged. "There's no need for me to go to the hospital. I'm fine."

She looked from Declan's stubborn expression to Cherry's exasperated one, to Orbra's steely blue eyes.

"Damned lucky I wasn't here," said Orbra. "I'd have taken a frying pan to that man! Why, you could have died if he'd given you too much of that sleeping pill! And mixed with alcohol?"

"That's why she should be checked out," Declan said. For about the tenth time.

"I'm fine. My head's not even pounding anymore. I've got my spiced warm milk—thanks, auntie—and he's gone and I feel fine.

No residuals. So what's this about a murder?" she said, abruptly steering the conversation away from herself.

"A murder?" Cherry looked from one to the other. "What are you talking about?"

Declan had no choice but to acquiesce—on all counts. "Marcus Levin's body was found with his head bashed in at the high school."

"At the high school? That's only—that's only a short way away from here!" Cherry exclaimed. Her platinum-blond hair was spiked up all over the place, as if to punctuate her shock.

"Which is why I was a little concerned when Leslie wasn't answering her cell phone," Declan said. She felt a little shiver of warmth at the concern in his voice. Maybe all was not lost. "I was trying to let her know John Fischer wasn't who he'd led everyone to believe, and when she didn't answer and I learned he was coming here, and that there'd been a murder—well—"

"Well, obviously you came over here." Cherry was looking at him like he was a hero, and Leslie—though she felt a little awkward, considering how they'd left things last night—was growing some very soft, very fuzzy feelings herself.

"Thank you," she said, and reached for his hand. To her relief—for she saw Cherry's and Orbra's eyes follow her movement—he curled his big fingers around hers and squeezed.

We need to talk, was the message in the squeeze.

Yes, she squeezed back.

"That's very…coincidental," Leslie said, casually releasing his hand.

"What do you mean?" Declan asked.

"That Marcus Levin should be murdered. Because, well, Cherry and I just figured out earlier today—or, I guess, yesterday," she added, realizing it was well past midnight now, "that the ghost isn't Dorothy Duchene. It's Kristen van Gerste."

As she said those words aloud, Leslie waited and listened… and yes, there was the faintest—oh, the very faintest—movement in the air. A shifting. A *sigh* from the depths of the house. Rufus's eyes bolted open, and he lifted his head warily.

"Kristen van Gerste? She's the prom queen who was murdered on prom night—what, thirty years ago? Her body was found in the…woods…" Declan's voice trailed off as he put the same two and two together.

"She was wearing a pink velvet stole and long white gloves that night," Leslie said, stroking Rufus gently. He relaxed back into her lap. "Kristen was only found wearing her dress. The topazes were stolen and her wrap and gloves were missing—though that wasn't ever made a big deal about. It was the missing gems that were all over the news."

"And how is Marcus Levin involved?"

"He was her date to the prom. They had a big row in the middle of—wait for it—'Waiting for a Girl Like You'—"

Declan's eyes widened. "Wait. The music! I knew I recognized that song…I just couldn't place it. That's the music that's been playing while the ghost appears."

His comment had both Cherry and Orbra looking at him sharply. "So you've seen the ghost yourself?" Orbra asked.

"Not really seen…but *felt* her," Declan admitted. "Really felt her."

Leslie explained about the gale-force winds inside the foyer, and their conclusion about the hollow beneath one of the stairs being related to the murder. "I think Kristen was killed here, and the murderer hid her stole and gloves here in the house, and then took her body and left it in the woods to make it look like it was a robbery over the topazes."

"That makes perfect sense," Declan said. "Although…why not leave the stole and gloves with her body? That doesn't really make sense to keep them separate."

"Unless there is or was something on them that would identify the murderer—blood, maybe? DNA?" Leslie said. She tried to remember whether she'd seen anything like that on the clothing.

"Right, true. But either way, the prime suspect would have been Marcus Levin—the guy she fought with."

"But now he's dead," Cherry said. "And is that a coincidence or conspiracy?"

"If he did kill her, we'll probably never know."

"But if he *wasn't* the one who killed her—maybe he knows something about what happened. And that's why he was killed. You know, everyone's coming back to town for that reunion on Sunday. Maybe that's dredging up a lot of this…stuff."

Everyone looked at Orbra in surprise, and she shrugged. "Hey, I read a lot of murder mysteries—and you know I've just been bingeing on *Agatha Christie's Poirot*. I love me some of those old-fashioned murder mysteries."

"You mean where the butler did it?" Cherry teased.

Orbra huffed. "There's never been one where the butler did it, I'll have you know. Though there was one time when the housekeeper did it, but it was really the mistress of the house *pretending* to be the temporary housekeep—"

"All right, Miss Marple," Cherry said with a laugh. Her expression turned sober. "Either way, we know two things for sure: One, there's a murderer on the loose, and it's not John Fischer. Two, the ghost is Kristen van Gerste, and until we figure out who killed her and why, she's going to be haunting this place and throwing all sorts of tantrums and—"

The lights flickered violently…and then went out with a sharp pop. Rufus bolted off Leslie's lap, heedless of where his claws dug in the process. Ungrateful beast.

"Great, Cherry," Orbra grumbled in the pitch dark after a moment of stunned silence. "Now look at what you've done."

"Now wait a second, you don't really think—" Cherry stopped as a definite chill invaded the room, as sudden as the lights had gone black.

"I'm pretty sure you've offended someone," Leslie said, choking on a laugh. Her thighs were stinging from Rufus's hasty exit.

"All right, all right—they're not tantrums," Cherry said, raising her voice to the level of the supernatural. "I didn't mean it was a tantrum. Kristen has the perfect right to have her killer brought to justice. And I want to do whatever I can to help."

Leslie held her breath as the lights flickered, then slowly came back on. The room went back to a normal temperature just as quickly. "Now you're just showing off, aren't you, Kristen?" she said on a relieved chuckle.

Orbra laughed nervously when the lights flickered again, but this time they stayed on.

Leslie looked around at everyone. "Now...I think it's time for me to get some rest. Anyone who wants to stay is welcome—but I'm going to bed."

She got up, surprised at how wobbly she felt, and went into her bedroom. With a last glance at Declan, who was studiously not looking at her, she closed the door and sought her bed.

*

Declan opened his eyes to something that smelled heavenly.

Not as heavenly as Leslie's hair, but delicious enough that he was wide awake in an instant.

Coffee. And something cooking...bacon, maybe. Whatever it was, he had to investigate.

He slid off the sectional in Leslie's living room/office, where he'd remained even after Cherry and Orbra left for the night, and padded out to the kitchen in his bare feet.

"You must be feeling much better," he said, taking in the sight of her in those very flattering yoga pants and a hot-pink t-shirt. She'd clipped up her inky hair into some sort of twist, and one thick lock fell in an S-curve down the back of her neck. His mouth watered at the sight of that slender, elegant neck. It sure had tasted sweet and warm, and smelled oh so good when he'd kissed her there the other day...

Damn. Regret pinged in him, then simply ebbed away. Maybe things didn't have to be so...black and white.

"I am feeling better," Leslie said from the stove. "Thank you so much for staying last night—I'm sure it wasn't convenient for you having to figure out what to do with Stephanie, but I really appreciate it. Are you hungry?"

He cautiously took a seat at the table, aware of the achingly formal tone of her voice and the nonchalant words—while he, on the other hand, was thinking about anything but formalities and the distance such implied. "Yes, thank you, I'm starving. Whatever it is, it smells good. Uh—can I do anything to help?" He made to push his chair back from the table to do so, but she was already walking toward him with a plate.

"No, it's all done. Thanks, though. How do you want your coffee?"

"Black is fine. Thanks."

Hoo boy. Could their conversation be any more stilted? How did he even begin to talk to her?

He'd thought he couldn't handle being with a woman who'd made the sort of decision she'd done, but here he was—and there he'd been last night, about to go to pieces at the thought of something happening to Leslie.

He definitely didn't want anything to happen to her…and, black or white or gray, that was the simple truth.

"I have something to show you," she said as she took her seat at the table with him. Her plate was laden with the same food—albeit a smaller portion—as his: eggs scrambled with green onions, bacon, tomatoes, and feta cheese. And…were those avocado chunks in there too?

Damn, she was a great cook. How had someone like her— who'd worked seventy hours a week—learned to cook like this?

Will you marry me? The memory came back to him in a nostalgic flash from the last meal they'd had at this table.

He wasn't quite ready to mean those words…but he was a damn sight closer than he'd ever been. Even with this rift between them.

Which he really had to address. But first… "What do you have to show me?" he asked, then took the first bite. It was even better than he'd imagined—she must have put something spicy in it, because it had a little bit of a kick. The bacon was super crunchy—and there was a lot of it.

"This." Leslie put a small yellow stone on the table.

Declan looked at it for a moment before comprehension dawned. "Is that a topaz? Where did you find it?"

"Inside the side of the stair railing—where I found the velvet stole. I'd seen something glinting way down inside there, and I was trying to get it up a few days ago—remember, you were going to help me?—but then I got distracted, and I forgot about it. Until last night. I woke up at five—you were snoring on the sofa with Rufus," she said with a bashful smile, "and I was thinking about everything—about Kristen and Marcus Levin and the prom night and the topazes, and I remembered that glinting thing. I was wide awake, so I just got up and worked on it for about an hour till I got the damned thing out from down in there. Rufus was not amused, by the way. He sat there and yowled at me the whole time."

"So it's just one topaz, but you think it might be from Kristen's necklace? From Red Eye Sal's gems?"

"Here's my theory," Leslie said, and her eyes began to sparkle so brilliantly his heart squeezed. "Somehow, she ended up here after prom that night. Someone else was here too. She died—maybe it was murder, maybe it was an accident, I don't know—but whoever was with her—and I'm guessing it was a schoolmate, because that makes the most sense to me—panicked and decided to make it look like a robbery. So he put the body in the woods without the necklace and stole and gloves, and hid them here in the house so everyone would think that's what happened."

"I like it," Declan said with a smile. "Both the breakfast and your theory."

She smiled back and his heart warmed even more. *Gray area. Got to find the gray area.*

"And so everything was fine until I came along and began renovating the house. And even that probably wouldn't have worried the killer, except that I was restoring the *stair rail*. Which meant the hiding place would likely be exposed. Remember that photo of me in the paper? You can see that the stairway has been partially dismantled."

"So anyone could have seen that picture and realized his secret was about to come to light."

"Exactly. And if people started asking questions about what happened that night—if it became obvious that someone local was involved, probably one of her schoolmates—then everything could come to light and the murderer could be exposed."

"And that's why he—or she, I suppose—let's be fair," he said with a gesture of his fork, "broke into the house. Did anyone know that you'd found the velvet stole before the break-in?"

"I'm not sure whether I'd mentioned it to Cherry or Orbra— and if I had, then anyone could have known. You know how they are. But it probably didn't matter because maybe he—or she— broke in so they could remove the incriminating evidence from the stair rail base and beneath the step before it was found. But it had already been found—I'd left it sitting on the table in the foyer—and so they considered themselves very lucky to be able to steal it. And I suspect the rest of the topazes were down inside the stair rail base. I just didn't see them before—there was a lot of debris and insulation in there. And one gem, unfortunately, fell out of its setting and was left in there as a final clue."

"Wow. You're a regular Nancy Drew. But the big question is… who's the culprit? And did Marcus Levin's death have anything to do with it? I'm thinking yes. What Orbra said last night makes sense: if Levin knew something about the murder, for whatever reason—maybe he saw someone leaving Shenstone House that night—someone who shouldn't have been there. He might have thought nothing of it at the time, but now…if all the questions start being asked…"

"Exactly. So that means…probably…that whoever murdered Marcus Levin also killed Kristen van Gerste thirty years ago."

"And whoever they are…they're still running around here in town."

Leslie nodded, her face sober. "The good news is…whoever it is doesn't have any reason to break into Shenstone House anymore—or any reason to bother me. I mean, I wasn't around thirty years ago—"

"That's bullshit."

"What? That I wasn't around thirty years ago—"

"I know what you're trying to say—that you don't have any reason to be nervous or to take precautions—and you might be right. But maybe you don't want to stay here for a while. Until everything gets taken care of and Levin's murderer is caught."

Leslie's mouth flattened. "If this is your way of making up with me by insisting I come and stay at your house, you've—"

"Whoa." He held up two hands. "Just, whoa."

She stopped all right, but the glare she gave him was sharp enough to cut glass.

"Okay, look…aside from the fact that we have to talk, and that I really damn well missed you last night, what I said was true: I don't think it's safe for you to stay here—by yourself—until things get taken care of. And to be honest, much as I might like to, I wouldn't ask you to stay with me because of Stephanie. So, no, there was no ulterior motive in my suggestion. Only concern. Even fear. Jesus, Leslie…I don't want anything to happen to you. And last night when I saw you lying here on this very table, well… my heart pretty much stopped."

"I'm pretty sure anyone's heart would stop if they thought someone they knew was dead," she said, but her lips twitched in a wry smile. "All right, I'll talk to Cherry and Officer Morton and see what they think. I'm not about to take any unnecessary risks—I'd like to live to see my next birthday. And now that he's infiltrated my life, I'm guessing Rufus feels the same way."

"That makes three of us, then." He drew in a deep breath. "I should probably explain my…reaction the other day. When you told me about Gideon and Gwendolyn."

Her eyes suddenly turned misty. "Gwendolyn?"

His heart nearly stopped. Had he screwed that up too? "I thought you said her name was Gwendolyn…I'm sorry if—"

"No, no, don't apologize."

Geez—he looked closely at her. Was she really tearing up there? Her voice was all rusty and she was blinking. The tip of her nose was even turning pink.

"You're right—her name was Gwendolyn. It's just that…no one ever refers to her by her name. Usually as 'the baby' or 'your baby.' You…startled me, is all. In a good way." Her voice was soft and low. "Thank you."

"Well, okay." He was a little confused, but he guessed he'd done something very right. Instead of resting on those laurels, though, he continued on to the more difficult portion of the conversation. "I'm not sure if Stephanie—or anyone—has told you anything about why I'm here in Sematauk with my daughter, and her mother is in New Hampshire."

"Not really. From what I understand, you didn't really get to know Stephanie until recently." To her credit, there wasn't a trace of judgment in her voice.

"That's true. But what no one knows—except for Stephanie, me, her mother Cara, and Cara's husband—is that I didn't even know I had a daughter until this past year. Just about nine months or so ago."

Leslie's eyes went wide with shock, then immediately softened with comprehension. "Oh my God, no wonder you…had such a strong reaction to my—my decision."

"Well, yeah. The baggage certainly helps when it comes to forming one's opinions." Declan gave her a wry smile, then went on and explained how his life had been turned upside down—but in the end, in a good way—by Cara's phone call.

"I can only imagine the hurt and anger and shock you must have felt when you found out," she said. Her eyes were filled with pain and sorrow—he wasn't sure why; was it just for him?—and she settled back in her seat, putting a little distance between them. "Partly because I spent quite a lot of time thinking about what that would be like for—for Gideon, you know, if he ever found out."

"Cara kept the secret for sixteen years," Declan said. "I had no clue it was even a possibility that I had a daughter out there. So, yes, it pushed a very sensitive button for me, and I'm not going to lie—it's definitely a bump in the road of…this. Us. But," he said with a forceful exhale of breath, "I don't want it to be a dead end, Leslie." He spread his hands. "I don't know how else to explain it. I really…I really feel a lot for you. A deep connection that I haven't felt with anyone else…ever. But…it's hard for me to ignore the fact that you made the decision to lie about something like that—something so personal to me."

Tears glistened in her eyes and she leaned forward again. "I understand, Declan. I really do. I am not proud of that decision at all. It's not something I would expect you to forgive and forget, especially since it's something so close to your heart."

They looked at each other from across the table, sorrow and confusion mingling with hope and affection.

"I'd like to say a few more things about what happened with Gideon. Not to excuse myself, but to give you more information."

"Go on." He was more than ready to let her talk. Truth be told, he was hoping she'd say something that would…well, help him accept and forgive. Even though the lie hadn't been told to him, even though he hadn't been in her life during that time, Declan couldn't help but feel as if it were a personal betrayal—not only to him, but to any man who found himself in the same situation as he and Gideon Nath had.

Huh. Who'd have thought he and the knobhead lawyer would've had so much in common?

"I didn't plan to lie. I—we—were at a big fundraiser function together, Gideon and I. And Fiona was there too. I came upon the two of them together, and I overheard their conversation. Gideon was just madly in love with her, but he was doing what he believed was the right thing—in his old-school, conservative, Main Line Philadelphia way, he didn't believe he had any other choice but to marry me. I could see how miserable he was, how awful she felt. I could *feel* the tension and the love between them.

"It was terrible to witness this—not only because it was such an intimate moment, but because they were both so much in love. I just couldn't do it. So when I confronted Gideon right afterward—"

Declan couldn't help but wince. "Ouch. Poor guy—being caught by his fiancée telling another woman he loved her."

Leslie's lips wavered and almost slid into a smile, but she continued. "When I confronted him, I told him I wasn't going to marry him, I didn't love him and he sure as hell didn't love me… and then the words just tumbled out. 'And the baby isn't even yours.' Just like that."

She bit her lip, curling her fingers around the bowl-sized coffee cup in front of her. "If you could have seen the unadulterated joy and relief in his face…well, it was impossible for me to take the words back at that point. And so I embellished a little to make certain he believed me…and that was that. I sent him off after Fiona—and by the way, he ended up saving her life that night too."

Declan's brows raised at that last bit, but he'd get that story later. "So it was sort of like second-degree lying instead of first-degree lying," he said slowly. There might be a light at the end of this tunnel yet…

"Maybe even self-defense?" she said. "For him, I mean. That doesn't really make sense, but—"

He was laughing. Despite everything, he couldn't hold back a little chuckle. "All right, counselor. Maybe. I guess I can see how you might have acted under duress. That does make it easier for me to understand."

"I'm not telling you this to excuse my actions, really, Declan. I just was hoping to help you understand that I wasn't really… in my right mind. And I did regret it…and to be honest, I did think I would probably tell him the truth. Someday. After he and Fiona were safely married and he couldn't get too mad at me—or, at least, make me marry him." Her grin was crooked and her eyes were sad. "But that doesn't change the fact that I did completely mislead him."

"No. But…I guess I understand better now."

"Thank you for coming over last night, and for helping me," she said, and abruptly rose. She was blinking, and he thought she might have been tearing up a little. "Oh, by the way," she said, with her back to him as she began to clean up some of the mess in the kitchen. "I might actually have learned something from John Fischer last night."

"What's that?"

"He was telling me that a lot of times, the bootleggers—or even normal people who wanted to keep whiskey or beer or wine during Prohibition—would build special hidden cabinets. Lots of times, it would be behind a false window."

"Interesting." He glanced automatically toward the windows in the kitchen. "So he thought he could find the gems."

"He was very certain they were in the house. He told me all about the research he'd done—I had no idea at that point he was a professional treasure seeker. But he was obviously certain enough of what he'd find to risk breaking the law."

Declan shook his head, then all at once he noticed the time on the clock. "Holy shit." He erupted from the table and banged his knee. "I have to pick up Stephanie...like, right *now*."

Leslie looked at him with faint amusement. "All right, then—off you go. I hope...I hope I'll see you again soon, Declan. And not just when you've got to take a measurement, or fit an iron rod into pl—" She stopped short, her eyes wide with mirth as he let out a short guffaw.

At that moment, he would have been very happy to be fitting a rod—of iron or otherwise—into place. His laugh faded into a mere smile and he came up to her at the sink and slid an arm around her waist. "I'd stay to help you clean up, but I'm already late. But...what do you think about dinner tonight? Just you and me—at Trib's, if you don't mind eating there again. We can...talk. If you still want to...talk...to me. I have been maybe a little bit of an ass."

"I'd love that, Declan." There was relief and pure pleasure in her voice. "I really would. What time?"

"I'll pick you up at seven. Does that work?"

"How about I meet you at Trib's instead—I have to go into town and drop off something for Cherry after her last class ends, then I'm going to see if Gilda has finished repairing that thousand-dollar dinner jacket for me. How does that sound?"

He didn't say anything. He just slipped a hand around the back of her neck and brought her to him for a sweet kiss filled with promise.

"I'll see you at Trib's," he said, then took off before he could change his mind and go back for more.

# TWENTY-ONE

"So...Declan and I are meeting for dinner tonight at Trib's," Leslie told Cherry. "I think things might work out after all."

They were in her aunt's upper-level yoga studio and the last class had just ended. Cherry was straightening foam blocks, arranging rolled-up yoga mats, and closing the blinds. The place smelled faintly of lavender, and a soft breeze scuttled the wind chimes that hung just inside an open window. The strains of flute-heavy music filtered through the air at just the right volume.

"Thank God. I just don't think we need *another* sexually frustrated woman in this town," Cherry said. "On a happier note, I just found out that William Reckless—yes, that's his real name—is going to be at the reunion tomorrow."

"You mean the guy who went to Tibet for a year to live with the monks? And this is good news...how?"

"He was there for five years—I think he even climbed one of the big mountains there—then he spent four years in the Amazon jungle working for the Peace Corps. And some other places. He's back in the States to stay...believe it or not, he just bought a house in Grand Rapids." Her eyes were gleaming with delight, and maybe even a little bit of lust. "He's not married. Did I mention that? And he's definitely straight...so...Grand Rapids is just far enough away that he won't be all up in my business every day. But close enough for a booty call whenever I need one."

Leslie laughed. "Go for it, auntie. I don't think William Reckless will know what hit him."

"Oh, I think he will. Didn't I mention…he was the guy who popped my cherry—no pun intended—way back in the day."

"Are your cheeks *pink*, Aunt Cherry?" Leslie hooted. "You're really excited about this guy, aren't you?"

"Well…let's just say…I wouldn't mind if things went full circle. He was the one who got away—and spoiled me for everyone who came after him."

Leslie softened. "I hope it works out for you, Aunt Cherry. You deserve to find someone who's just right for you."

"And so do you, Les. Ever since I found out Declan was a blacksmith, I just knew you two were meant for each other too. So…keep the peace. He's a wonderful man, a great father, and an honest, hardworking businessman. You couldn't ask for anything more."

Leslie nodded, but she had a lump in her throat. Despite their conversation this morning, she wasn't certain what sort of future they had. After all, she hadn't been a completely honest person herself. And there'd been times when she was ruthless and cutthroat in her own business dealings in the past. What would a man like Declan want with someone like her?

Well. The only way to find out was to have dinner and see what happened.

When she left Cherry's studio, it was only quarter past six, so Leslie had plenty of time to walk the four blocks to Gilda's Goodies to check on the dinner jacket. As she'd feared, the shop wasn't open—only belatedly did she remember that Gilda told her she closed at six on Saturdays during the off-season.

However, Gilda mentioned she often stayed late to work in the back, so Leslie walked to the end of the block then into the alley that led to the backside of the shops. It was nearly dark by now, but she was able to figure out which was the back door to Gilda's. A light was on inside, so she knocked—and the door opened under the gentle force.

"Hello? Gilda? It's Leslie van Dorn," she called, stepping inside. Everything was quiet and still. The hallway was lit with a dim light, and there was a more vibrant stripe of illumination under the door at the end of the hall.

But no one seemed to be around.

For some reason, Leslie's palms became damp and her pulse kicked up a bit. Maybe it was because of all the talk of murder, and the fact that a man had drugged her last night.

For whatever reason, Leslie felt that strange eeriness settle over her as she poked her head around the corner, looking down the short hall leading toward Gilda's storage room. No lights down there. The silence was heavy, which made her skin prickle. But the light was on, the door had been open—maybe Gilda was expecting someone and she'd just stepped into the restroom, or out front in the shop, or—

"Leslie?"

She nearly jumped out of her skin and spun around. "Good grief, Regina, you scared the heck out of me. I was looking for Gilda."

"She should be back there. I was coming to see her myself." Regina looked mildly concerned. She was also dressed more casually than Leslie had ever seen her: in jeans and a simple twin sweater set. "Gilda?"

Just then, a door closed somewhere and there was the sound of rushing footsteps. "Oh, thank God you're here, Reggie. I've got it all figured— *Leslie?* What are— I mean, hello. Sorry, I—I'm a little distracted."

"I think we all are," Leslie said, suddenly feeling very awkward for a reason she couldn't quite identify. Her instincts were pinging wildly. "Especially after what happened to Marcus Levin."

"I know," Regina said in a low voice. "It was just awful, wasn't it? And at the high school too, with his head bashed in." She shuddered.

"Well, what can I do for you, Leslie?" asked Gilda in a businesslike tone as she gestured them into her office. "Come on in."

"I'm sorry I didn't call. I was just in the area and I thought I'd stop by and see if you had any news on the dinner jacket."

Leslie wanted nothing more than to leave, for she got the distinct impression that she was interrupting something between Gilda and Regina.

And then, all of a sudden it hit her.

Could they be lovers? It was… It made sense really, when you looked at all the signs. Gilda had hit on Cherry, so clearly she was a lesbian. And hadn't Regina said something the other day? No, it was Cherry who'd said it: "You'd have to be a straight man or a gay woman not to be interested in Declan Zyler."

She'd been joking, of course, but later…Regina once made a comment about how Declan didn't "do" anything for her. Not that those facts were conclusive, but once Leslie thought about them and noticed the way Regina and Gilda looked and acted around each other…everything sort of clicked into place.

Gilda had even called Regina "my politically correct mayor's wife" last week…but most importantly, it was the sort of awareness or sizzle that flowed between them that sold Leslie on the idea. Their connection was very evident if you were paying attention.

She started, realizing Gilda had been answering her question and she hadn't heard a word she said. Something about needing another week—that's right, because she'd been sick. Agitated and still feeling awkward, Leslie turned sharply, ready to leave, and the roomy handbag over her shoulder knocked over a small pencil cup.

"Ugh, I'm sorry," she said, feeling even more foolish now. She scrabbled on the floor as Regina and Gilda spoke in low voices—probably wishing their unwanted visitor would get the hell out of there—and picked up all the pencils to put them back in the jar.

But just as she reached for the last one, Leslie saw something on the floor, right by the corner of the desk leg.

It was round and made from brass, about the size of a pea. Confused and shocked, she picked it up and stood slowly, looking at it in the full office light as the dawn of realization rushed over her.

It was a button…from the long white glove that had belonged to Kristen van Gerste.

Leslie looked up just in time to realize Regina and Gilda were staring at her…no, they were staring at the button she was holding.

"Well, dammit," said Regina, moving swiftly toward Leslie before she could move. "That's going to really fuck things up now."

TWENTY-TWO

W HAT THE HELL are we going to do with her?" Gilda said. She didn't sound very nice at all. In fact, the tone of her voice was a lot more threatening than Regina's.

Leslie had lunged for the door as soon as she realized what finding the button meant—but the tall, wiry Regina stopped her, giving her a shove that sent her reeling into the side of a tall metal filing cabinet.

She cut her temple on the sharp edge of the cabinet as she stumbled into the credenza, sending boxes of thread, beads, and other finishings tumbling to the floor. "Jesus Christ, sit down before you destroy the whole damned place," Gilda said, turning back from her desk. She had a gun in her hand.

Leslie sat down, her heart pounding hard enough to make her ill, and her temple screeching with pain. She could feel the blood pulsing from the cut, dripping down the side of her face.

"For God's sake," Gilda snapped, and handed her a scrap of cloth. "We don't need blood all over everything." She pursed her lips and paced the room, then stopped and looked at Regina. "She knows. We're going to have to take care of this."

"But Gilda…" Regina's voice was taut. "We can't— I don't want another—" She shook her head and sank down onto a chair. "But we have no choice, do we?"

"Not if you don't want to go to jail, love. And I don't want that—and Aaron certainly doesn't either. It'll just ruin everything you both have worked so hard on."

"He'd be more worried about what it would do to his reputation than me anyway," Regina said in a hard voice. "But you're right, Gildy." She looked at Leslie, who suddenly felt very lightheaded—and not from blood loss. "We can't afford you telling anyone about this."

"But wait," Leslie said desperately. "You don't want a *third* murder on your hands, do you?"

"Another murder?" Gilda said. Her eyes glittered behind the trendy red glasses. "My, you have grasped the situation quite readily, haven't you, Ms. van Dorn?" She looked at Regina. "I have an idea. I know exactly what to do—and no one will be the wiser. It worked before—why recreate the wheel?"

She held the gun closely on Leslie and said, "You're going to walk with me like we're old chums—you get that, right? The three of us—and we're going to walk to your car, Regina—you're parked where you usually are, right?"

"Yes. All right. Of course." Regina actually smiled. "I think I know what you have in mind. It's perfect, Gilda. Just perfect."

Leslie had no choice but to walk side by side with Gilda, who had the gun pressing directly into the skin of her abdomen beneath the blue cashmere sweater she'd chosen for her dinner with Declan.

Declan. He'd wonder when she didn't meet him at Trib's. But how would he know where to look for her? She didn't know where these two women were taking her...though, unfortunately, she had a good idea of their ultimate goal. Her knees wobbled at the thought, and she bumped against Gilda, whose arm was around her shoulders in order to keep her flush against her. Regina walked on the opposite side, carrying her car keys.

I'll figure something out.

Gilda climbed into the back seat of Regina's car, which was, unfortunately, parked in the dark alley just around the corner. No one was around to see Leslie get shoved into the back and the gun flash ominously in the dim light.

Regina climbed in the front and started the engine. "Where to?" she asked, turning her head to look around.

"You know," Gilda replied.

Regina smiled, and Leslie saw the way the two women's gazes connected in the rearview mirror. She was definitely the crowd in this two's company.

"Look straight ahead and don't wave to anyone if you happen to see someone you know," Gilda said, pressing the gun barrel into Leslie's side as the car pulled out onto the main street.

Leslie complied, but as they drove down Main, past Cherry's yoga center and Trib's, she prayed someone she knew would see her. Maybe even Declan, walking to Trib's... *That would be a really nice thing to happen, God,* she thought as the car turned off the main drag and headed out of town.

And that was when she realized where they were taking her: to Shenstone House.

Where it all began.

—⁂—

As they drove up the dark, winding driveway, Leslie gathered her thoughts. For the first time, she felt somewhat optimistic. If she didn't show up for dinner, this was the first place Declan would look for her.

And with a murderer on the loose—and currently in the same vehicle as she—he would be right to do so...

But... Oh God. Nausea surged violently in her belly as she realized that if he showed up here, he would walk right into a situation for which he was ill prepared—unlike last night. A gun against an iron rod was not good odds.

He can't come here. That was clear. She couldn't risk it—risk him, risk Stephanie's father, risk *anyone.* Or Cherry or Orbra... The nausea swished like a storm and she beat it back. *I have to remain clearheaded and calm.*

"I'm supposed to meet people for dinner at Trib's at seven," she said as the car came to a stop in the parking area of Shenstone House. "If I don't show, Declan's going to be looking for me. He'll probably come here."

The two women exchanged glances, and Leslie could tell they were trying to figure out whether to believe her or not—or whether there was a trick involved.

"Believe me, I don't want him in the middle of this," she said, using her best CEO voice.

"It's only six forty-five right now," said Regina. "We've got time. This won't take long." Her smile was cold and calculating. "By the time he figures it out—or any of them—it'll be too late. So don't dawdle, or maybe we *will* wait until your boyfriend shows up—and then he can join you in your fate."

Leslie couldn't argue with that, and she also realized she'd set her bag down in Gilda's shop when she was cleaning up the spilled pencils…so she couldn't even contact Declan if she wanted to.

That wasn't good.

However…she had one last possible way out. One little trick up her sleeve, so to speak. She looked up at the looming house. Her house. It glowed softly with light—though, strangely, one of the windows near the front seemed to be dimmer than the others. But the building seemed to welcome her, comfort her, by its very stability, familiarity, and age.

"I told you to stop dawdling." Gilda rammed the gun barrel into the soft skin above Leslie's hip, causing her to grunt with pain. "No one will hear a gunshot up here."

"But leaving a body with a bullet in it…not really part of your plan, is it?" Leslie said coolly. "And since my purse—and my blood—is all over the back of your office, it won't be hard for the authorities to put the pieces together. Will it? I'm going to go inside, don't you worry, but you don't have to be rough about it. I've already told you I have no desire to stall and get anyone else involved."

"Smart woman," said Regina, following Leslie as she led them around to the front door. "No wonder you were so damned successful." Her voice contained an envious sneer. "I would have been a celebrity CEO myself if all of this hadn't happened."

Exactly the segue Leslie was hoping for. She shoved the door open and walked into the front hall. The dismantled staircase swept in its elegant curve in front of her. The room was lit by two small table lamps. As she stepped in, Leslie swore she felt the house gird itself…sort of take a deep breath, and straighten.

"So you killed Kristen van Gerste," Leslie said. "Regina. It was you. Because you"—she looked at Gilda—"didn't move here until years later. Right?"

"That's right." Gilda was looking around, gun still in hand. The gun was what worried Leslie the most, but at least neither of her captors were physically holding on to her at the moment.

"But why did you kill Kristen?" she asked Regina. "Wasn't she your friend?"

"Yes. But—" Regina's voice tightened. "Marcus Levin was an asshole, and I couldn't stand to see her with him. He was such a prick, and so arrogant."

Comprehension dawned for a second time that evening. "You were in love with her. With Kristen, weren't you?"

Regina's eyes suddenly filled with tears, and she glanced at Gilda. Her lover nodded, strange compassion etching her face—even as she held a gun in her hand.

"I never told her," Regina confessed. "I never let on. But that night…after she left the prom, I ditched my date right after he dropped me off at home. I slipped back out and found Kristen—she was still walking home, and like a good friend, I was there to comfort her. We—we decided to come here, so we could drink some of my dad's whiskey in peace.

"It was just the two of us…just how I'd always imagined it. I brought my boombox for music. We went upstairs—she was just curious about what was up there, but I was…I was hopeful. Maybe tonight would be the night. Maybe now would be the time…to tell her. How I really felt."

Leslie was entranced by the story, by the raw emotion in Regina's face and words…but even so, she felt the house responding. The air shifting, a slight movement…almost sad.

Sad. Sorrowful.

A chill filtered delicately through the room, hardly enough to notice.

"We were upstairs and went into one of the bedrooms. There was still furniture here. I was playing 'Waiting for a Girl Like You' on the boombox. I was a little drunk, and we were sitting there on the bed, just talking, and I…well, I did it. I grabbed her and—and I kissed her."

The air kicked up in the room a little more sharply, causing Gilda to look around, startled. "What's going on? Who's there?"

But neither Regina nor Leslie responded.

"Kristen rejected you?"

"It wasn't just a rejection," Regina said, her voice tightening. "It was…it was horrible. She pulled away, and started calling me the most filthy, horrible, ugly names you can imagine. It was like she turned into a harpy, a monster. She was going to tell everyone. She would ruin me, tell everyone what a disgusting creature I was." Her voice was thready with tears. "She turned and stormed out of the bedroom, and I—I went after her. I couldn't let her tell them. I couldn't let her leave me. I loved her, and I wanted her to understand that there was nothing wrong with that sort of love."

The room was ice cold now. The draperies were fluttering. Gilda was staring with wide eyes, spinning in a slow circle, still with her gun. "What is going on here?" she whispered. "Who's there?"

But Leslie paid her no attention, and neither did Regina, who clearly had to finish her story. "I caught her by the arm, but she pulled away and then started hitting me, calling me those terrible names again…all the while that song was playing in the background…'Waiting for a Girl Like You'…and then I shoved her. Hard. I was so—so filled with anger and shame and revulsion—for myself, for what I felt. I lashed out. I pushed her. And she fell."

The air whipped up into a sudden, biting frenzy. It roared, the sound filling Leslie's ears. Her hair was being buffeted about, and she felt the icy breeze scoring her face. Gilda was stumbling along the wall, trying to get away from the melee of wind, dust, and noise. She was making quiet, panting cries as she edged toward the front door.

"Is that you, Kristen?" shouted Regina over the blast. Tears were streaming down her cheeks. "Is that you?"

Then she stilled and looked up. Leslie didn't have to turn to know what caught her attention, but she did anyway.

It was Kristen, glowing more sharply and in more detail than ever before. Her eyes were angry pits of fire, and as she lifted her arm to point at Regina, the wind screamed through the room and the sounds of the old song filled the air. This time, it was so loud and violent that Leslie had to cover her ears and duck.

But she could see Regina—who hadn't moved. Who just stood there, staring up at the furious spirit. Tears poured down her cheeks as her hair whipped and danced in the midst of the storm. "I'm sorry," she cried. "I'm sorry, Kristen. I never…meant…to…hurt…you…"

"The door's locked!" screamed Gilda. "I can't get out!" Leslie spared a glance at the terrified woman, but turned her attention back to the scene happening before her.

Kristen spiraled up into a tall, glowing image of herself—slender and beautiful and furious. The now-familiar music was ear-splitting, dark and ugly and low.

Then, as Leslie watched with terrified eyes of her own, the ghost roared down the stairs, bringing more icy, biting winds with her, shuffling the half-moored carpet, shaking the old sconces on the walls, the crystal of the unlit chandelier. Debris flew, the walls shook, and Gilda screamed as the glowing specter swept down into the room and shot right through Regina.

The woman cried out, shuddered…and then suddenly, Regina softened. Collapsed. Slid slowly to the ground, landing in an unmoving heap there.

And then…everything went utterly silent and still.

"Reggie!" cried Gilda, moving from the safety of the door for the first time.

Leslie noticed she'd dropped her gun, but it didn't even matter—she knew she was safe.

It was done.

TWENTY-THREE

By the time Declan arrived at Shenstone House—as Leslie knew he would—the police and EMTs had arrived. She'd used Regina's cell phone to contact both, for Regina appeared to be dead, and of course Leslie's own phone was at Gilda's Goodies.

Gilda herself was a wreck and hadn't even realized she'd dropped her gun. She sat in a corner, her trendy red glasses long gone and her hair in a waxed-up mess, sobbing and shaking as if she'd seen a ghost.

Which…

Leslie signed. She wasn't sure how she was going to get Officer Morton to actually believe her, so when she saw Declan rush into the foyer from the kitchen, panic on his face, the first thing she did was launch herself into his arms—rift or no rift.

"Oh my God, Leslie, two nights in a row—you can't keep *doing* this to me!" He was shaking as he crushed her against him—and he didn't even know what happened. "I've been trying to call you, and text you, and—you absolutely *can't* keep doing this or I'm going to have to break up with you. And I'll take Rufus with me."

"Does that mean we aren't broken up anymore?" she said with a small laugh. She kissed him. "Oh, Declan, I knew you'd come—and though I'm glad you were late, you really missed a hell of a show." She glanced at Officer Morton, who was trying to get a coherent story from Gilda, who still sat, white-faced and trembling, in the corner.

"So what happened?" Declan asked, looking at the disaster in the foyer. "Oh, hell, you can't imagine what I thought—driving up the driveway to find police cars, EMTs, the house ablaze…I never want to go through those minutes again." He shivered and hugged her tightly. "Good God—is that a body under the sheet there?"

"Regina Underwhite is dead," she told him. "They're saying a heart attack, but…" She glanced up toward the top of the stairs, and Declan followed her gaze.

"Do you mean she was killed by—" He stopped when she pressed a finger to his lips. But his eyes looked like they were about to pop out of his head.

"Shhh. Let's just go with heart attack, shall we?" Before Leslie could tell him more, Cherry and Orbra clattered in—bringing with them the expected exclamations, stunned shock, and remonstrations.

"Let's let the police do their job in here…I've already given them my statement, such as it is. I'll tell you all what happened," Leslie said. She was beginning to get a little tired of giving statements and telling stories…but hopefully this would be the last time. For a long time. "It's quieter in my suite."

Once her friends were settled, Leslie gave them all the details of what happened. "And what Regina didn't tell me, but I managed to get from Gilda before the police got here, was that after Kristen fell down the stairs, Regina panicked. She didn't know what to do. So she called Aaron Underwhite—who'd been in love with her for years—and asked him to come and help her figure out what to do.

"In exchange for that, she agreed to marry him and dote on him like a perfect and devoted wife for the rest of their lives. They'd build their own empire together, using his money and both of their brains and drive. If she didn't hold up her end of the bargain, he'd show everyone what was hidden in the stairs here at Shenstone House. The velvet stole did have Regina's blood on it—from a scratch when she and Kristen were struggling, and so they couldn't leave it with the body. Making it look like a robbery was the perfect solution. Apparently, Aaron knew about her and

Gilda—and as long as they were discreet and Regina remained his wife, he didn't care."

"And Marcus Levin was involved how?" Cherry asked.

"He saw Regina and Aaron when they were going back to Shenstone House after they left Kristen's body in the woods. They made it look like they were just having a lovers' tryst, so he wouldn't have thought anything of it…unless people started looking at Kristen's death in a different way and asking questions. Which is what I unintentionally did when I came here and started renovating the house."

"So Aaron is complicit too. Looks like we'll be needing a new mayor. And who bashed in Marcus's head?" Declan asked. He'd slid his arm around Leslie and hadn't let her move more than an inch from his side since.

"Gilda. She was trying to protect Regina, whom she loved very deeply."

"And who broke into the house here?"

"That was Gilda too. While Regina and Aaron were presenting the Homecoming court, she sneaked out over here—knowing I wasn't home and no one would suspect her. I'm not sure whether Kristen made an appearance or if Gilda just got spooked or what…but obviously she got what she came for: the velvet stole, one glove, and the topazes."

"What a story. And you're saying that Kristen actually…killed her own murderer?" Orbra said. "That's a great story."

"Well, I don't know if she actually killed her, but when that energy—that spirit—rushed through her, it seemed like Regina's heart just stopped. And that was it."

Just then, a tentative knock sounded at the edge of the door to the suite.

"Come on it," Leslie called.

To her surprise, it was Stephanie Lillard whose face poked around the corner.

"Steph?" Declan yanked away from Leslie and bolted to his feet. "Is everything all right?"

His daughter was looking around with a curious expression. "Well, it is for me…but what's going on here? I heard there were all these sirens here, and then Trib said you took off for Leslie's—I mean, Ms. van Dorn's house, and the sirens were here…and I just wanted to make sure everything was okay."

"It is now," Leslie said. "But surely you didn't walk here from town?"

"No. This nice man gave me a ride— Don't worry, Dad, *geez*. I'm not *dumb*. Trib knows him, and he just got back from the Amazon jungle. He even climbed a mountain in *Tibet*. He says he knows you too," she added, looking at Cherry, whose cheeks were suddenly turning becomingly pink. "And that your niece lives here, and he thought maybe you might all need some help."

"I hope that's all right," said a deep voice as a tall, lanky figure stepped around into the doorway. He was wiry and tanned, with short-cropped white hair—and Leslie was pretty sure her aunt just about had an orgasm right there.

"Well, if it isn't William Reckless," Cherry said, rising casually from her seat. Her voice was low and throaty, but Leslie could hear the depths of emotion in it. "It's been a long time."

"It certainly has," he said, his eyes never leaving her as she stood there staring at him.

As if they were the only two in the room, perhaps even the world, Cherry moved toward him. He took her hand and, without a word, led her from the room.

Everyone stared after them for a moment, partly in shock and partly in pure enjoyment. A moment later, they heard the sound of a car engine starting and a vehicle driving away.

Stephanie was the one to break the ice. "Well. That was… interesting."

"It sure was. Anyway, everything is fine here, Steph. I guess I'd better get you home—since it appears your ride just left." The regret in Declan's voice was noticeable to Leslie, and she privately agreed with both the regret and the sentiment. They wouldn't have any quality time alone until Morton and his team were gone, so he and Stephanie might as well leave.

"Well, aren't you coming?" Stephanie asked, pausing at the door. She was looking at Leslie.

She shook her head regretfully. "I should probably stay here until they're finished—in case they need anything. Your dad can fill you in on what happened."

"Well, all right, then. Maybe Dad can come back later…and check on you," she said, looking back and forth between them.

"Well, it's almost nine o'clock—it's getting pretty late," he said, looking sadly at Leslie.

"If you let me have a sleepover at Katie's, then you can have a sleepover here," Stephanie said cheekily.

Declan's face turned red. "I don't think—"

Leslie jumped in. "I think that's a great idea—especially since my car, my purse, and my keys are still in town. Maybe you could come back later, Declan. And bring them to me."

He smiled, the color receding from his face. "Sounds good to me." He turned to Steph. "Ready?"

Once Stephanie and Declan were out of earshot, Orbra stood. "Well, I guess that leaves me and my old, dried-up parts to go home by myself and wait for my old man to get home. Should be sometime tonight. Maybe we'll *all* get lucky before tomorrow."

EPILOGUE

LESLIE WOKE to the most delicious smell ever. Cinnamon, cardamom, honey…and man.

She opened her eyes to find Declan sliding onto the bed next to her, holding a small tray with a cup of what could only be a chai latte. Also on the tray was a small bouquet of the last few mums that decorated her porch in pots, and a piece of thick toast with a pot of jam.

"What a wonderful breakfast," she murmured, sitting up back against her pillow. "And the serving boy as well," she added, her eyes skimming over his bare muscular chest and ridged abs.

"So now I've been demoted from scout to serving boy?" he asked, leaning forward to kiss her gently before releasing the cup of tea into her hands.

"Apparently so. Maybe you better get back to work and try to get reinstated," she joked. His eyes darkened with lustful speculation, and she laughed. "Maybe after breakfast, so I can get my energy back up. It's been a rough few days."

"Ain't that the truth." He was still looking at her with heat in his eyes, but he eased back and reached for his own drink, which he'd set on the table next to her.

"So, I've been thinking about something John Fischer told me—about the fake windows they often put on the houses that were really there to hide liquor cabinets during Prohibition."

"Right," Declan said.

"You know I never use the front door of the house, but last night when I brought Regina and Gilda in here, I took them through the front door. They didn't know any better, of course, but I knew that was where Kristen might be…and I was definitely hoping for her help in resolving this haunted status. Anyway, since I never come in that way at night, I never noticed before how one of the windows isn't lit up when the lights are on. Strange things you notice sometimes, you know, even in the midst of all that stress? But even though things were tense, I was starting to relax. Because I was pretty certain Kristen would be more than happy to make an appearance. So anyway, I noticed that one of the windows was dark…and it shouldn't have been."

Declan straightened. "Do you mean you think there might be a secret liquor cabinet in the foyer?"

"Yes. See, they would put two windows next to each other—on the outside, anyway. But inside, there'd be only one actual window. The other window would be the backside of the liquor cabinet. There was probably a light that was on inside the cupboard, so from the outside it looked like both windows were lit up…but inside, there's only one. No one would really notice that, especially if it were two windows together—inside you probably wouldn't notice if it was more narrow than what you saw from the outside."

"Holy crap," he whispered. "Do you think Sal's gems might be hidden there?"

They looked at each other, and she felt a sparkle of excitement.

"Let's take a look," he said.

She bounded out of bed—which was almost a mistake, because she was buck naked and he definitely noticed. But Leslie neatly evaded his grabby hands and slipped into her robe. "I'm on the trail of some missing gems, scout. We'll celebrate if I'm right," she promised, dancing away from him with a sassy grin.

"And if you're not?"

"We'll celebrate me being wrong."

"Let's *go*," he said, leading the way to the foyer.

First they went outside so she could show him the window she meant. He had to drag on his jeans, but she wouldn't let him take the time to put on a shirt. "It's not that cold out. Besides, I like looking at all those blacksmithy muscles."

He complied, his unshaven face slightly pink with pleasure. "If you insist." They stood on the porch.

"This is the window. See how it looks like there are two next to each other? But only one is lit up."

"I think you might have something there, general."

Excitement coursed through her as they started back inside to examine the interior wall. "Let me get some tools from my truck," he said as she went back in.

"Hurry! I'm dying here!" she said, fairly dancing around the foyer in front of the wall in question. "Look—you can *see* the seam in the paneling if you look carefully enough."

"Patience, woman," he growled, but he went immediately to the wall and began to examine it. Then he laughed. "The molding around the real window. Look." He shifted the old, carved piece of wood that framed the window and a door slid open—easy as pie.

"Oh my God," Leslie squealed, not caring that she sounded like a girl. A girl could get very excited over secret panels and hidden stairways…and maybe even jewels. "Is anything in there?" she demanded.

But he'd stepped back, smiling at her with affection. "It's your house, Leslie. You look."

The space was small—just big enough for four bottles of liquor to stand in a tight square. There was one bottle still in there…and something else. Leslie's heart leaped when she saw the lump in the back of the space, and she locked eyes with Declan as she reached in—only belatedly realizing it could be a dead rodent.

But it wasn't. It was a velvet pouch, and it had a mass of hard objects in it; she could tell that as soon as she touched it. Her hands shook.

"Oh my God, Declan," she breathed as she pulled it out. It clinked softly.

"Careful there, sweetheart," he said, practically breathing down her neck.

With trembling fingers, she pulled the pouch's cord loose and tipped it so the contents spilled out onto his cupped hands.

Sparkles: rubies, garnets, sapphires, emeralds…a cascade of jewels, still in their elaborate settings, tumbled into his hands in a rainbow pool.

"Oh…my…" she breathed, hardly able to believe her eyes. "Oh…wow… They're beautiful."

"Whoa," he said, looking down at the treasure he held. He shifted his fingers so the gems moved and sparkled. Then he took the pouch from her and slid the jewelry back inside.

"All right," he said with a lascivious grin, "let's celebrate!"

—∞—

A long while later—thank goodness it was Sunday and neither Leslie nor Declan had to be anywhere today, and Stephanie was more than happy to be hanging out with the girlfriend with whom she'd spent the night—Leslie slipped lazily from her well-used bed.

She looked down at the delicious man lying there, tumbled among the sheets with his dark hair glinting faintly red from the shaft of sunlight shining through the window. The broad, muscular shoulder, dusted with bronze freckles. The thick-lashed eyes, closed in repose. The slack jaw, unshaven and glinting red and gold and brown. The powerful, gentle, skilled hand curled on the sheet next to him.

Her heart swelled, and she drew in a soft little hope that this would only be the first of many days like this.

I'm totally falling for you, my blacksmith scout.

She toddled off to shower, her legs still a little unsteady from all of the delightful "celebrating" they'd done…some of which had included her modeling the different necklaces.

Whether the gems were real or not, it didn't matter…for she'd found her own personal treasure in Declan Zyler.

Leslie hummed and smiled the whole time she was in the shower, half expecting him to join her.

Instead, when she came out of the bathroom, hair wrapped in a towel and body swathed in a fluffy pink robe, she found Declan sitting up in her bed. He was reading.

It wasn't until she got closer that she realized just which book he was looking at, and she dove for it in an attempt to snatch it away.

"Oh no you don't," he said, laughing as he held it out of her reach. The towel holding her hair slumped to the side and her robe gapped. "I found this on your bedside table. *Love's Forbidden Caress*? I couldn't help but look at it. And what should I discover, but the guy is a *blacksmith*." He was laughing as he wiggled his eyebrows suggestively while she tried to grab the old book from him.

She gave up—his arms were too long—and collapsed on the bed next to him. "So, yeah. It's one of my favorite books, okay?"

"And it's about a hot blacksmith?"

She shoved at him because he sounded much too satisfied. "I found it one summer when I was in college. And I read it. A few times. So, yeah." She glowered at him, challenging him to tease her about it.

"Well, it looks pretty good so far. I mean, I've only gotten to the part when he takes her against the wall of the smithy—not very realistic, I'll say, and really dangerous—but I can kind of see the attraction."

"That's halfway through the book!" she exclaimed, trying once more to grab it from him. Her cheeks were burning.

This time he acquiesced and let her have the book. "I was flipping through, looking for the good parts. I mean, with a cover like that, I knew there had to be good parts."

He smiled down at her, and there was deep warmth in his emerald eyes. "I've been waiting for a woman—notice I didn't say *girl*—like you for a long time, Leslie…and apparently, you've been waiting for a blacksmith like me. So what do you say we really try and work this thing out?"

She laughed, blossoming with happiness and warmth. "I think that's the best idea I've heard in forever."

"Same here." His eyes narrowed and settled on her thoughtfully. "And since I'm sure you know where all the good parts are, what say you read some of them to me…and then we can act them out?"

—◆—

H. Gideon Nath, III, is the stiff and oh-so-proper attorney who helps settle Fiona's inheritance, and despite her flightiness and fascination with all things New Age, he finds himself attracted to her against his better judgment.

After she finds an unpleasant surprise in one of the shop's closets, scares off an intruder in the store, and uses her skill at palmistry to read Gideon's future--of which she seems to be a part--Fiona begins to realize that her free and easy life is about to change...whether she wants it to or not.

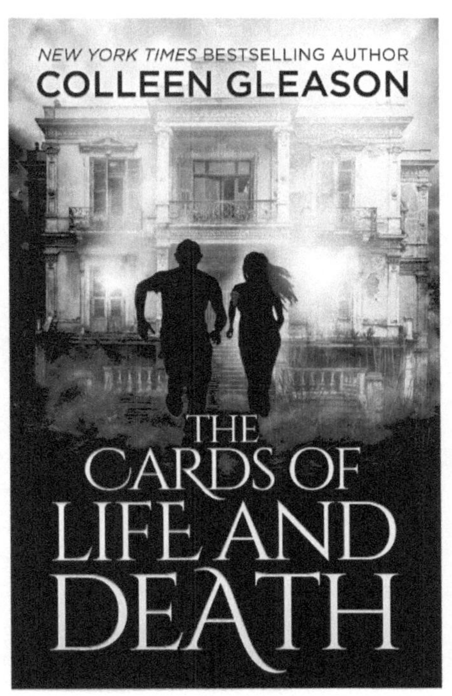

The Cards of Life and Death
featuring Fiona's brother Ethan Tannock

A small-town summer romance spiced up with moonlit boat rides, handsome neighbors, and a haunted deck of Tarot cards....

Diana Iverson is a sharp, up and coming malpractice attorney with a logical, scientific mind and a handsome fiancé—until the rug is pulled out from under her feet and her life is upended.

When her crazy Aunt Belinda dies, leaving her a big old house in Maine along with a box of Tarot cards, Diana takes the opportunity for a summer get-away away from the rat-race of Boston and the painful memories there.

She doesn't expect to meet up with Ethan Tannock, the handsome neighbor next door who seems to be some sort of eccentric ghost-buster—along with his big, black Labrador Retriever.

But when the old house becomes the scene of vandalism and a number of break-ins, and it begins to appear as if Aunt Belinda's death was not as it seemed, Diana finds that life isn't always black and white and filled with logic.

And then there are Aunt Belinda's Tarot cards...which seem to be trying to tell her something from beyond the grave.